THE SENTIMENTAL BLONDE
By Elle Croxford

Table of Contents

The Sentimental Blonde 1

Prologue 8

PART 1 – QUIET ON SET 13

Chapter 1 14

Chapter 2 23

Chapter 3 29

Chapter 4 31

Chapter 5 34

Chapter 6 40

Chapter 7 43

Chapter 8 49

Chapter 9 57

Chapter 10 63

Chapter 11 69

PART 2 – CAMERAS ROLLING 73

Chapter 12 74

Chapter 13 83

Chapter 14 95

Chapter 15 101

Chapter 16 109

Chapter 17 112

Chapter 18 119

Chapter 19 126

Chapter 20 131

Chapter 21 137

Chapter 22 143

PART 3 – ACTION! 146

Chapter 23 147

Chapter 24 153

Chapter 25 161

Chapter 26 174

Chapter 27 180
Chapter 28 188
Chapter 29 194
Chapter 30 202
Chapter 31 213
Chapter 32 218
PART 4 – CUT! 221
Chapter 33 222
Chapter 34 225
Chapter 35 238
Epilogue 245

About Elle Croxford

Despite coming from humble beginnings with an abusive father, divorced parents, a household surviving on a single mother's pension barely sustaining five kids and losing her mother to cancer at 17, Elle refused to let adversity define her. Growing up in optimistic 80s Australia, she found escape in feel-good entertainment, envisioning a life of infinite possibilities.

Believing that out of something bad always comes something good, Elle was resourceful and enthusiastic, excelling in various roles across the screen industry, government and creative industries, from distribution of iconic movies (*The Silence of the Lambs*, *Terminator 2: Judgment Day* and *Strictly Ballroom*) and games (SEGA and Electronic Arts); to securing movies and TV series productions to Queensland (including *Inspector Gadget 2*, *The Thin Red Line*, *Peter Pan* and *Scooby Doo*). She was a VFX & post-production executive producer (for films such as *Hacksaw Ridge*, *The Age of Adaline*, *Pirates of the Caribbean: Dead Men Tell No Tales*, *Thor: Ragnarok*, *Aquaman*, *Kong vs Godzilla*), and business development manager and consultant.

As a successful screen industry executive, consultant and leader with 30-plus years of experience, Elle transitioned from senior roles in sales and marketing; business development; VFX and post-production; and distribution to becoming a respected writer, producer and entrepreneur.

As a writer and producer, Elle is inspired to develop popular, feel-good IP franchises that captivate mass niche audiences with universal, positive and benevolent storytelling with happy endings.

As Chief Vision Officer/Co-Founder/Producer of Mixing It Up (MIU), Elle collaborates with a talented team, including the creator of the *High School Musical* franchise, an Emmy award-winning music supervisor, and Kpop producers and composers with credits including BTS and BlackPink, and MIU's advisory board comprises award-winning entertainment, business, and finance professionals.

ELLE CROXFORD

Elle is the author of the *Better Now Than Never* book series and has received prestigious awards such as the Lord Mayor's Creative Fellowship 2023 and the Queensland Writers Centre Fishbowl Writers Residency 2023.

Her entrepreneurial spirit and business legacy extend beyond feel-good entertainment to include a wellness focus. After experiencing family and friends suffer various cancers and health issues, Elle is committed to making the world a healthier place, focusing on longevity, prevention and women's health. Elle actively seeks opportunities that align with her vision of fostering holistic wellbeing in body, mind and spirit.

Inspired by her role on the board of a non-profit raising money for homeless women and their children, memories of her mother's need for charitable assistance and her own marriage breakdown in her fifties, Elle is dedicated to establishing a foundation to support women over 50 and contribute to affordable housing for Australia's fastest-growing demographic of homelessness.

Elle's commitment to being a positive and inspirational agent of change through storytelling, entertainment and wellness drives her multifaceted career and extraordinary life. By living her extraordinary life, Elle continues to inspire others to do the same.

To learn more, visit: www.ellecroxford.com

THE SENTIMENTAL BLONDE

Also by Elle Croxford
Books
Better Now Than Never: Book 1 Why
Better Now Than Never: Book 2 What
Better Now Than Never: Book 3 How
Better Now Than Never: Book 4 Mind Body Spirit Integration
Online TV Series
Life of Jess (5 episodes)
Theatre Playscript
The Sentimental Blonde

Copyright

The Sentimental Blonde

First published 2024

Published by ISEEC Pty Ltd., PO Box 1701, COORPAROO DC QLD 4151 AUSTRALIA. ABN 83 653 134 075

Copyright © Elle Croxford 2024

ellecroxford.com

ISBN 978-0-9874792-4-2 (ebook)

ISBN 978-0-9874792-5-9 (printed)

Author's Note

This book is based on the screenplay and theatre play script, *The Sentimental Blonde*, both written by Elle Croxford.

In the realm of historical fiction, this narrative was inspired by the lives and love that intertwined in the legendary figures of Lottie Lyell and Raymond Longford, protagonists in this cinematic journey based on true events of the making (and rediscovery) of Australia's long-lost silent era masterpiece, *The Sentimental Bloke*.

In the spaces between fact and fiction, the blurred realm of truth and invention, *The Sentimental Blonde* emerges. This narrative pays homage to history while letting the creative juices flow freely.

Lottie Lyell, a figure shrouded in the enigmatic silence of bygone eras, left no diaries or memoirs. *The Sentimental Blonde* takes some liberties to shape the narrative, weaving its fabric through the warp of historical threads. This is not a work of history, nor does it venture into the limitless realms of pure invention. Instead, it is a narrative that teeters respectfully on the edge of a distant reality, following real people's lives and events that Lottie would have experienced during what has been described as the greatest romance on and off the screen of Australia's silent-film era.

This story entwines the threads of past and present, and above all, extols the indomitable spirit of one whose determination transcended the boundaries of time, weaving through love, tragedy, and triumph.

The Sentimental Blonde was inspired by the tenacious Lottie, a woman of remarkable courage who became a fearless trailblazer of her time. It chronicles her trials, her industrious resolve, and the challenging experiences she endured, while staying true to the radiant authenticity of her essence.

The Sentimental Blonde is a tale that seeks to honour the legacy of Lottie Lyell while inviting you to lose yourself in the grand theatre of her life and times. She was a woman with an unquenchable thirst for something beyond the mundane. Her insistent pursuit burns brightly in the archives of Australian cinematic history, beckoning us to follow the trail she blazed.

THE SENTIMENTAL BLONDE

FADE IN

Prologue

New York, 1973

'Here you are,' declared the weary taxi driver, his utterance proof of the ceaseless grind of New York City's streets, as his sun-faded yellow taxicab screeched to a grinding halt. The taxi, a tired veteran of countless urban journeys, bore the scars of its service on the bustling asphalt and ceaseless hardship of urban life.

Ray Edmondson, a young Australian film archivist in his thirties and on a singular mission, emerged from the depths of the cab. His attire was a vibrant canvas of 1970s fashion—flaunting flares and an audacious clash of colours—that reflected the era's rebellion against convention.

With a congenial nod, Ray extended a gracious hand toward the cab driver in the unspoken acknowledgment of a journey in common, a brief interlude in their shared lives. 'Thanks, mate,' Ray uttered words infused with the quintessential Australian camaraderie, acknowledging the taxi driver's role as a temporary companion on his days-long journey across continents and time zones.

The taxicab retreated into the distance, its tyres tracing a solitary path down the driveway and leaving Ray standing in splendid isolation before a formidable and imposing presence—a stately, neoclassical Georgian Revival mansion. It is a sentinel of a bygone era and now a treasured artifact of history.

The architectural masterpiece stood as a hallowed monument to the legacy of George Eastman, the visionary founder of Eastman Kodak. Decades earlier, upon Eastman's departure from this world, the mansion was bequeathed to the University of Rochester and entrusted to posterity to become a beacon for future generations. It metamorphosed into a stronghold of film preservation and the meticulous art of photographic conservation. A shrine of images captured on celluloid through the preservation of film and conservation of the art of photography.

With unhurried steps, Ray embarked on a contemplative pilgrimage, moving towards the mansion's imposing front entrance. Each stride was a respectful acknowledgment of the occasion's significance. It would be his first time stepping foot inside 'the' George Eastman Museum, affectionately known as GEM. With reverence, his discerning eye captured every intricate detail—the Corinthian columns, the intricately carved mouldings, and the timeless elegance that had withstood the constant march of time. At that exact moment, man and mansion converged, united by a shared purpose—a profound commitment to the preservation of history's captured points in time.

Deep in the colossal expanse of the climate-controlled vault, Ray found himself surrounded by an awe-inspiring spectacle. The hallowed halls of the repository, with towering shelves stretching from the floor to the vaulted ceiling, formed a labyrinth dedicated to the meticulous cataloguing and preservation of the world's cinematic and photographic legacy. Ray made his way to the section dedicated to the Australian collection. Immersed in a sea of celluloid, the profound depth of the collection struck Ray with reverential awe. Each shelf bore a staggering compendium of film artifacts, in an attestation to a nation's rich and storied filmic heritage.

The vault was a cinematic sanctuary unlike any other he had encountered in his esteemed career, holding an abundance of cinematic stories awaiting their resurgence.

Ray slipped on a pair of pristine white cotton gloves in a mark of reverence for the historical treasures within his reach. Before him, a mosaic of film titles from decades of Australian cinematic history beckoned, each a chapter in the nation's cultural narrative. His eager fingers journeyed through time as they traced familiar titles such as *The Story of the Kelly Gang*, *Sons of Matthew* and *Forty Thousand Horsemen*—echoes of Australia's cinematic past. In all his years as a film archivist, he had never encountered such an extensive private collection of Australian movies.

An unexpected discovery halted his methodical checking of the collection against his meticulous manifest. Eight film canisters prominently labelled 'THE SENTIMENTAL BLONDE,' stood out, calling to him with a whisper of intrigue. With stirred embers of curiosity and a furrowed brow, Ray ran his eyes down his paper list only to find an unsettling absence. A double-check revealed the same results. *No match.*

The GEM film archivist, a conservatively dressed middle-aged woman named Peggy Dunbar, emerged from the rows. The embodiment of grace, she greeted Ray with a smile that bore the warmth of shared passion.

'Hi, Ray. Thought I'd check in with you. How's the search going?'

Ray, his energy undeterred by jet lag, responded with enthusiasm, 'So far, so good, Peggy. It's great to focus on something after all the travel and my jet lag.'

Sympathetic to his long journey, Peggy offered her perspective. 'I guess you can expect some jet lag after travelling halfway around the world. I can only imagine how long the flight was from Australia to New York.'

Ray grinned, his youthful Aussie optimism shining through. 'I lost count with all the flights. It's worth it now that I'm here.'

The GEM archivist replied with equal excitement. 'I am happy to have you here and help you crosscheck the Australian catalogue. The George Eastman Museum has quite the collection.'

Ray nodded and replied, his voice imbued with excitement. 'I can see that. I understand why Australia's National Film and Sound Archive sent me here. You've got everything!'

Brimming with delight at his enthusiasm, she revealed, 'And this is only the Australian collection.'

A broad grin spread across his face. 'It's like I've died and gone to archive heaven.'

In the camaraderie of shared passion, the GEM archivist realised she had found a kindred spirit in Ray. 'I do love my job... which doesn't feel like a job.'

Ray, resonating deeply with her sentiments, responded in kind. 'I can relate. What's your favourite Aussie film?'

Without hesitation, she said, 'I'd have to say *The Story of the Kelly Gang*.'

Ray, incredulous yet impressed by her enthusiasm for Australian cinema, remarked, 'Whoa, classic.'

Clearly in her element, she continued, 'The world's first feature-length movie, I believe.'

Ray gazed at this living encyclopaedia of Australian cinema with awe before expressing his admiration. 'Impressive. You know your Australian movie history.'

Her cheeks flushed a shade of crimson, betraying her modesty at his acknowledgment. 'Thanks. Well, I'll leave you to it.'

Before she could retreat, Ray extended one of the eight film canisters towards her, a puzzle to unravel. 'Hey, before you go, is it possible to see this film?'

Curious, she scrutinised the label. '*The Sentimental Blonde*. Sure.' With dexterity born of experience, she transferred the stack of eight film canisters to a nearby trolley equipped with a film projector. She prepared the first 35 mm reel for projection, gracefully spooling the film onto the projector reels.

Ray assumed a position on one side of the projector. The GEM archivist switched off the main overhead lights, plunging the room into near-darkness. The intimate cocoon of cinematic anticipation built as the flickering light of the projector illuminated their faces, etching the canvases of their expressions with shades of wonder.

The first intertitle card materialised on the bare-walled makeshift screen, stark white capital letters etched upon a black canvas:

THE SOUTHERN CROSS

FEATURE FILM C$^{\underline{O}}$ L$^{\underline{TD}}$

Presents

"THE SENTIMENTAL BLOKE."

C. J. DENNIS.

PICTURISED AND DIRECTED

By

RAYMOND LONGFORD.

Ray's eyes sparkled with excitement, his wide smile betraying his mounting anticipation.

'Do you realise what this is?'

PART 1 – QUIET ON SET

Chapter 1

Sydney, 1918

Lottie Lyell, a pocket rocket figure of energy and excitement for life, emerged from her post behind the camera and made her way to an intertitle card propped on a painter's easel with the stately declaration:

THE SOUTHERN CROSS

FEATURE FILM C^{O} L^{TD}

Presents

"THE SENTIMENTAL BLOKE."

C. J. DENNIS.

PICTURISED AND DIRECTED

By

RAYMOND LONGFORD.

With her purposeful stride, she embodied a seamless fusion of focus and efficiency, both the creator and curator of motion picture dreams. With a deftness that demonstrated her expertise and energetic passion, she exchanged the intertitle card for the next opening credit:

Australian Production

Cinematographed

By

Arthur Higgins

With a distinguished grace and dressed in a three-piece suit, matched elegantly by a homburg hat and shoes polished to perfection, Raymond Longford consulted his fob-watch, a cherished timepiece bearing an engraving of hidden sentiment on the back that whispered affection: *With love, LL*. It was a token that bound him to Lottie in the most intimate of ways.

Raymond's cultivated theatrical tone, resonant and commanding, sliced through the ambient hum as he intruded upon Lottie's artistic focus. 'Time to go, Lottie,' he declared. Lottie responded with an artist's tenacity, her voice carrying a note of dedication as she captured the final intertitle card. 'Almost done.'

Raymond issued a gentle but earnest warning, reminding Lottie of the normal world outside their cocoon of creativity 'We've only got a narrow window of time between police patrols.'

'I'm questioning my gifting of that fob-watch to you,' teased Lottie.

'I'll treasure it forever.' His eyes crinkled into a genuine smile. 'Although right now, we've got to go. We've still got to fit in your interview with the *Picture Show* magazine.'

'What are you thinking for that?' Lottie asks.

Raymond's response was righteous and matter-of-fact. 'Keep it about our work and *The Sentimental Bloke*. It should be straightforward.'

Tentatively, Lottie queried, 'Do you think he suspects anything?'

Raymond sensed her trepidation and sought to ease her disquiet, 'I'm not sure. If he does, he's being a good chap by keeping mum about it.'

'Hopefully, it stays that way,' she said, more to reassure herself.

'Mr Carhall, and every other journalist for that matter, loves you,' Raymond assured.

'You mean the *public* me,' Lottie corrected.

'Just as well. And we need Mr Carhall more than ever,' asserted Raymond, with a resonance of certainty.

'We're going to be okay,' Lottie exudes ardent optimism in her cheerful manner.

'Is that *public* Lottie talking?' Raymond looks at Lottie expectantly.

Lottie paused, deliberating her words. 'The *private* me, *your* Lottie, would ask, "We're going to be okay, aren't we?" '

Raymond enveloped Lottie, pressing a tender-hearted kiss to her lips. Their embrace intensified into a passionate entanglement, lingering as they slowly and reluctantly separated.

'Does that answer your question?' Raymond asked.

Still savouring their shared chemistry, Lottie smiled, acknowledging that their kiss conveyed more than words could express. 'And then some.'

Raymond reluctantly consults his timepiece, 'As much as I would love to spend more time with my own *private* Lottie, we have a crew waiting for the *public* Lottie.'

Lottie playfully frowned before responding with a triumphant flourish and announcing, 'We can't keep them waiting.'

Relief washed over Raymond, and a warm smile graced his features. 'That's *my* Lottie,' he declares, his pride and relief evident.

Lottie, affectionate and spirited, rose on tiptoes to plant a fleeting kiss on his cheek—a gesture that carried their shared passion and purpose. Raymond, enveloped in the warmth of that gesture, couldn't help but return her infectious smile with an adoring smile of his own as he followed her out of the room, closing the door behind them.

Within the heart of Sydney, nestled in the middle of the metropolis's hustle and bustle, lay a sanctuary of tranquillity—the botanical gardens. Local Sydney-siders sought refuge in the inner-city parkland, where verdant natural beauty flourished. Yet, as with all windows of respite, civility in the idyllic haven was a fleeting illusion.

Within this horticultural sanctuary, a small crew of five dedicated individuals descended upon the serene landscape to immortalise a scene from the poetry of C J Dennis's *The Songs of a Sentimental Bloke*. The story centres on a loveable larrikin, Bill, from the working-class streets of Sydney, who embarks on a heartfelt journey of romance and redemption that transforms him from a rough-around-the-edges scoundrel into a devoted husband, in what C J Dennis envisioned as a timeless tale of love, humour and sentimentality.

This scene sought to capture the essence of the rough yet endearing Bill, portrayed by actor Arthur Tauchert, who perfectly embodied the larrikin spirit so characteristic of the time.

Arthur, as Bill, entered the scene through the botanical garden gate, meant to be a simple yet profoundly symbolic act. His movements and gestures were studies in exaggerated expression, reminiscent of the silent film legend, Charlie Chaplin. He crossed the grounds to settle onto a time-worn park bench, his silent presence imbued with melodrama.

In the periphery, as a silent sentinel beside the camera, stood Raymond, the director and visionary responsible for bringing the cinematic tableau to life. He called out, 'And cut!' Raymond appeared satisfied with Arthur's performance. His face lit up with a beaming smile, radiating his joy for a scene well-captured.

Surrounded by the serene expanse of the botanical gardens, Raymond's restless gaze wandered nervously, and his fingers sought solace in the rhythmic ticking of his fob-watch. He advised the film crew, 'And that'll do,' his words were laced with a subtle tension, a sense of urgency hanging in the air like a fragile thread.

Behind him, a voice rose up, strong and impassioned in its certainty, 'Raymond, we need another.'

This seemingly simple request sent ripples of tension through the small film crew, a collective of dedicated individuals led by the cameraman, Arthur Higgins, who was assisted by Arthur Cross and Clive Marsh. Their gazes turned to Lottie, who stood motionless, her displeasure at Arthur's performance evident and proof of her untiring commitment to capturing the essence of their vision.

With a graceful stride, Lottie moved to stand beside Raymond, their partnership a demonstration of their shared creative vision, comfortable intimacy and mutual respect.

Raymond, ever the pragmatist, cautioned, 'We're pushed for time.' His plea sought to delicately balance her artistic perfection with the constraints of reality.

Lottie's reply conveys her expertise and persistence and is laced with empathy. 'I understand, but—'

Raymond, in a gesture of resigned affection, nodded, and yet he cut her off, advocating his own perspective. 'Lottie, Arthur's an original individual. Honest and likeable. That's what attracted me to him when I saw him perform,' he reflected, affirming his loyal belief in the authenticity of their chosen larrikin, Tauchert.

Lottie paused, finding herself at a crossroads. She chose her words carefully to strike a delicate balance between critique and empathy. 'I'm not questioning the man. Maybe he can't do more than vaudeville.' Her words hung in the air. Bearing the full burden of truth, it was a candid admission of Bill's artistic boundaries.

Raymond felt the grip of frustration tighten around his heart. He knew, deep down, that Lottie's assessment was accurate. With a deep breath and gritted teeth, he called out to the crew. 'Alright then. Another one.' His declaration carried a touch of resignation as he surrendered to the necessity of yet another take to capture their vision.

Arthur, now on the receiving end of this artistic recalibration, wore a mantle of discontent. His frustration bubbled to the surface. 'What was wrong with that one?' he asked, his mood edged with curiosity and irritation.

Lottie, the joint orchestrator of the creative vision, stepped forward to engage Tauchert in a dialogue about his performance. Her words, kind-hearted and unhurried, conveyed a simple request. 'Could we try no melodrama on the next take, please?'

It was a plea for subtlety, an appeal from actress to actor to strip away the layers of excess and reveal the raw authenticity beneath the surface—an earnest demonstration of her faithful commitment to the art of storytelling.

Arthur rankled, frustration simmering beneath the surface and revealed as a tempestuous undercurrent in his expressive look. Seeking a lifeline, he turned towards Raymond with a silent plea for support or understanding, only to find none forthcoming. The responsibility for his artistic challenge rested solely upon his own shoulders. Fuelled by a stubborn grit, he pressed his point with hard and fast self-assurance. His words sliced through the air like a well-honed blade. 'I just gave you less vaudeville, girlie.'

Raymond's keen gaze did not miss the subtle cringe that temporarily graced Lottie's features upon hearing Arthur's gendered reference. Her patience stretched to its limit by such a subtle yet potent affront to her. It's a pointed reminder of societal norms she has long outgrown. In that split second, a cascade of unspoken emotions passed between Lottie and Raymond. It affirmed their deep understanding and the silent solidarity that bound them. It was a shared recognition of the irksome nature of such outdated terms and recognition of the progress Lottie had made to distance herself from the conventions of the past. With a knowing look, Raymond conveyed his unspoken support, a silent assurance that they were united in their pursuit of cinematic excellence.

Notwithstanding her irritation, she rose above Arthur's verbal dig. 'When you're ready,' she said, her note carrying an air of patience and resilience. She returned to Raymond's side, an implied symbol of their united front.

Arthur, his frustration unabated, relented, rolling his eyes in exasperation. He prepared to go through the motions once more, a reluctant participant in Lottie's ceaseless quest for cinematic perfection.

The unassuming cameraman, Arthur Higgins, executed his duties with a quiet diligence, commanding the crew in hushed tones. 'Cameras rolling.'

Next in line, the assistant, Arthur Cross, assumed his role with a quiet authority, announcing, 'Quiet on set,' as a reminder of the sacred hush that enveloped an exterior set.

At this point of heightened anticipation, all eyes and ears were attuned to the director's call, the occasion of action drawing near. With a sense of timing honed through years of experience, Raymond commanded, 'Action.'

Arthur embarked on the familiar routine once more. This time, his performance bore the mark of restraint, a noticeable departure from the melodramatic vigour of previous takes. However, Raymond's discerning eye could still detect a hint of overacting in his portrayal, it was an evident remnant of the vaudevillian style that characterised his earlier efforts.

With an air of hope tempered by uncertainty, Raymond turned to Lottie for reassurance, searching her face for approval.

Lottie, instincts finely attuned to the nuances of performance, bit her lip in contemplation. She regarded Arthur's efforts with a critical eye. For her, regardless of the improvement, Arthur's performance was still not where it needs to be. With an even pitch, she issued her verdict, 'One more.'

Raymond, resigned to Lottie's uncompromising quest for perfection, nodded in understanding. His voice carried a mix of acceptance and weariness as he said, 'Okay, one more.' In an atmosphere of mounting tension, Raymond, unable to meet Arthur's gaze, sought solace in the intricate engraving on his fob-watch.

His decree weighed heavily on the tired crew, who collectively released a quiet sigh of frustration. Their exhaustion was evident in their furrowed brows and weary expressions.

However, Arthur took Lottie's critique the hardest. His growing frustration and resistance could no longer be contained by the bounds of professionalism. He found his target in Lottie. With a delivery laden with anger and defiance, he challenged her authority with a pointed question. 'For years, I've been acting. Who are you, girlie, to be telling me how to act?'

The question hangs in the air, a stark reminder of the complexities woven through the fabric of the prevailing norms of their time.

As if on cue, the entire crew pivoted their collective gaze towards Lottie, their anticipation hanging in the air like a heavy curtain waiting to be lifted.

In the emotionally charged situation, Lottie's entire comportment transformed. Her countenance shifted as the unwanted moniker 'girlie' struck a discordant chord deep within her. She summoned every ounce of her strength to veil her inner turmoil, ensuring Tauchert would not perceive the storm of frustration swirling beneath her calm exterior. She let his challenge wash over her like a passing storm.

Regaining her composure, Lottie marshalled her emotions and gave a consummately professional and equable reply. 'It's a suggestion to be smaller.'

Tauchert, undeterred and perhaps fuelled by his own irritation, aimed his retort and challenging glance at Raymond. 'Who's directing this picture?' The tension in the air crackled, an incontrovertible standoff that tugged at Raymond's heartstrings, leaving him to navigate the treacherous waters between two formidable forces as the standoff between Tauchert and Lottie escalated.

It was up to Raymond to find a workable solution. He attempted to defuse the escalating confrontation. 'As producer, Lottie's offering her opinion.'

Her professional pride wounded, Lottie stood her ground, her words carrying a subtle edge of offence as she pointedly reminded Arthur, 'We're making pictures, not theatre.'

Trying to bring the heated discussion back to a simmer, Raymond was equally conflicted by his own constraints, 'Although, we can't afford the time—'

'For this girlie's perfection,' Arthur, strong-willed and uncompromising, interjected with a final, defiant verbal dig.

The standoff extended to a three-way impasse. Each party was entrenched in their position, the tension unmistakable in the charged air.

In the absence of an immediate solution to the three-way impasse, Higgins took it upon himself to be the peacemaker. Stepping forward, he positioned himself between the trio. His words, steady and calm, emerged as the voice of reason and diplomacy, bridging the divide and rekindling the collaborative spirit while extending a lifeline to each of them. 'How 'bout we bang out one more?'

Chapter 2

Within earshot of the tranquil park bench, Raymond's only son—the sprightly eighteen-year-old Victor Longford—stood guard. Straddling the precipice of adulthood, Victor retained a youthful essence while earnestly striving to project an aura of worldliness. He was a vigilant lookout for the film crew, positioned strategically to ensure their work amid the idyllic surroundings went on undisturbed.

Victor stood watch but was distracted when he became the object of attention. His presence drew the curiosity of a young lady, captivated by the activities of the film crew. In a flirtatious gambit, she ventured a compliment, her words infused with admiration.

'I'm impressed that you get to work with Lottie Lyell.' Her flirtatious style betrayed her interest in the enigmatic world of cinema unfolding before her eyes.

Emboldened by her attentiveness, Victor seized the opportunity to extend an invitation with a subtle promise of shared experiences. 'Yep. You'll have to come and see it at the theatre... with me.'

Her blush set the stage for an enchanting exchange, a dance of words and glances that spoke to the timeless allure of young love.

Lottie, the embodiment of grace, could not help but notice the youthful couple ensnared in the throes of innocent flirtation. A knowing smile played upon her lips in silent acknowledgment of the enduring allure of young love in its purest form. She beamed a maternal smile at the young couple's exchange.

Her attention on the budding romance was diverted when a new take of the same scene unfolded.

'Let's take it from Bill sitting on the park bench,' Raymond instructed.

Tauchert assumed his position on the park bench, preparing to reshoot the scene.

Higgins, a paragon of professionalism, issued the directive with practised ease. 'Cameras rolling.'

Cross, his manner filled with authority, followed suit by solemnly announcing, 'Quiet on set.'

With that, the stage belonged to Raymond, the auteur of their cinematic endeavour. With an air of anticipation, he called forth the pivotal point in time, his command booming with the essence of artistic expectation. 'And action!'

In this iteration, Tauchert delivered a performance that bore the mark of authenticity. It was a clear departure from the exaggerated theatrics of previous takes. When the scene was complete, he waited.

All eyes turned to Raymond, seeking his judgment, although his uncertainty was apparent.

Reaching a point of an artistic crossroads, Raymond's gaze found solace in Lottie. She met his uncertainty with an affirming smile and a decisive thumbs-up. A surge of relief washed over Raymond, and his expression transformed from uncertainty into a radiant smile as he declared, 'And cut!'

There was relief all around for the crew, grateful that the latest take was acceptable to Lottie and Raymond.

Tauchert's discontent simmered beneath his breath, and his voice carried an undertone of disillusionment as he grumbled, 'There's nothing remotely different to real life.'

Lottie, ever the astute observer of words and emotions, snared the sly comment that slipped from Arthur's lips and returned it with an arched eyebrow and a subtle nod, her retort resonating with profundity, 'Exactly.'

In the middle of all the glaring tension and while the theatrical crew remained riveted on Lottie and Tauchert, Victor's attention on the young lady was somewhat distracted by the unexpected arrival of a uniformed returned soldier who strode past.

Victor's gaze, once firmly tethered to the young lady, wavered, following the soldier's path on an involuntary shift of focus.

The returned soldier, acutely aware of Victor's uninvited scrutiny, didn't appreciate the attention. He took Victor to task, his words crackling with an intensity that cut through the hushed ambience. 'What are you staring at?'

Victor was caught off guard by the unexpected confrontation. The soldier's challenge leaving him disarmed. His eyes descended in humble submission as he apologised. 'I beg your pardon. I didn't mean any offence.'

The returned soldier, not satisfied, pressed the issue further with a hard line interrogation. 'Where, then, is your uniform?'

Caught between the duress of the soldier's scrutiny and his own unpreparedness for this unexpected exchange, Victor faltered, lost for words. His response was hesitant and searching as humiliation washed over him. Victor was exposed.

As the curtains of Victor's composure were drawn back to reveal a vulnerable young man, the returned soldier, emboldened by Victor's capitulation, adopted an air of self-importance. As if to impress the young lady, the soldier summoned the mantle of his service. His words, heavy with accusation and entitlement, reverberated through the temperamental atmosphere when he said, 'It's an offence, you standing here, approaching this young lady when it should be men like me who have served for our country.'

Sensing the gathering tempest, the young lady took a graceful step backwards to execute a strategic retreat. It was a subtle dance of disengagement that conveyed a significant message: she desired to evade the impending storm.

Victor, now a captive of his own regret, extended an olive branch into the turbulent ether. His words were a plea born of apprehension, 'Look, I don't want any trouble.'

Undaunted by Victor's appeal, the returned soldier, bolstered by his own bravado, leaned in, closing the distance between them. Their faces converged in an instance of profound tension. Victor, though intent on holding his ground, couldn't mask the subtle tremors of intimidation coursing through him. Victor mustered his waning perseverance to meet the soldier's steely stare.

Sensing the young man's fear, the soldier's stance assumed an air of mocking condescension as he sneered. 'Sounds like you were afraid to fight for King and Country.'

Victor struggled to reclaim the resonance of confident vocals, and his words emerged as a stammer, a hesitant preamble to his defence. 'I-I-I'm not really—'

With almost cruel exultation, the returned soldier interrupted, challenging Victor's very essence. 'Not really what? A real man wears this uniform. A real man would be fighting in the Great War.' The words, dripping with forthrightness, carried the fervent creed of one who had borne witness to the crucible of battle.

A spray of the soldier's saliva punctuated each word, misting Victor's face with a chilling reminder of his own inadequacy. In a reflexive motion, Victor's trembling hand moved up to his face to dispel the unwelcome residue of this altercation. However, the returned soldier's instincts kicked in. In a blaze of innate feral aggression, he launched an unforgiving swing, solidly connecting with Victor's face in a resounding collision.

An ear-splitting scream, a primaeval wail of alarm, erupted from the young lady's trembling lips. The raw lamentation of shock and terror shattered the fragile peace of their chance event.

In the thick of the chaotic spectacle, the scene's coiled tension found its release in the form of Victor's bright red blood, streaming from his battered nose in a grotesque and haunting portrayal of human frailty.

Victor heard Lottie, who up until this point had been a silent witness to this cataclysmic drama, gasp in anguished disbelief at the ghastly display. Driven by a visceral instinct to protect Victor, Lottie rushed to his side, her steps echoing with urgency in the face of the unfolding never-ending chaos.

As the crimson tide flowed and cries of alarm filled the air, two uniformed police constables approached the unfolding melee. Their shrill whistles pierced the mounting commotion, raising the alarm.

The returned soldier, perhaps sensing the encroaching reckoning, made a hasty exit, vanishing into the labyrinthine folds of the city parkland. In a parallel escape, the young lady melted into the shadows, leaving a lingering, enigmatic memory of a turbulent encounter in the dramatic theatre of life.

In the aftermath of the violent altercation, Victor, his ego wounded, was trapped in a flurry of emotions. A familiar cocktail of embarrassment and physical pain coursed through his veins. His pride marred by the bright stain of his own blood.

Victor took a knee and accepted Lottie's help to curb his bleeding. She held out her hand for the handkerchief he always kept in his pocket. She gently inspected his nose. Her delicate touch was a balm for his wounded pride. As Lottie tended to his bleeding nose, a humble act of care in the thick of the chaos, Victor's gaze remained fixed on the nearby path. He detected an impending storm in the form of police constables fast approaching.

Lottie followed his alarmed gaze. She shared a concerned look with Victor and helped him to his feet. Recalling their agreed-upon warning, Lottie cried out with a note of urgency in her voice. 'Cooee!'

It was a call for aid that also acted as a signal. The word was a discreet beacon of caution that alerted the film crew to the impending arrival of the authorities and climax of their tumultuous narrative.

Victor and Lottie, in a portrayal of distress and disorder, made part of an indelible scene as a vivid tapestry of chaos and confusion unfurled around them. The film crew scrambled in frantic disarray, their hurried efforts to dismantle the camera and flee the scene enduring the disconcerting rhythm of haste.

Covered in the stark red evidence of Victor's injury, Lottie and Victor were the focal point of the theatre of chaos. Their sprinting figures, a stark contrast against the backdrop of the botanical garden's serene beauty, punctuated the scene as they navigated passers-by, hightailing it for the botanical garden's exit.

28

Chapter 3

Outside the botanical gardens, the crew stood in a dishevelled assembly—faces flushed, still buzzing with the residue of adrenaline—and drew in long, ragged breaths. A collective sigh of relief swept through their ranks as they took a short respite, a stolen pause in the unfolding drama.

Clive Marsh, ever the harbinger of the obvious, voiced the sentiment in the air, 'That was close.'

Arthur Cross echoed Clive's sentiment with unreserved agreement, his inflection conveying the distress of their shared brush with danger. 'Too close!'

Breathless laughter, a cathartic release, rippled through the crew as a shared liberation of tension and celebration in the exhilaration of their narrow escape.

'They tried to stop us by denying us the permission and threatening us with police action if we attempted to set up the camera,' Raymond's response punctuated the scene. Ever strong-minded and not giving way to the pressure, Raymond remained staunch, his voice sturdy and adamant as he made the pointed declaration.

Amongst the camaraderie and fleeting nanoseconds of levity, Lottie struggled to catch her breath. 'Don't they know we always find a way?' She asked before being ensnared by a persistent fit of coughing and wheezing.

Raymond cast a concerned glance her way. His eyebrows inched together, wrinkling his forehead and betraying his unease. Lottie, struggling to regain her composure, offered a reassuring signal to Raymond.

Yet beneath her genteel façade and concealed from the world's gaze within the depths of her voluminous skirt, Lottie held a secret. Small droplets of blood marked her palm, an unsettling confirmation of the price exacted by their daring endeavour.

Outside the garden's confines, Arthur Higgins cradled their cherished camera. Lottie watched closely as he cautiously examined their treasured apparatus. His contemplative words conveyed the wisdom of experience and a hint of caution, 'Well, best we don't do too many of those locations.'

Raymond, who had weathered many a storm in his ongoing crusade, explained their position, 'The head of police doesn't like pictures and has a personal objection against me. I can't wait for him to see the film.'

Higgins, pragmatic and quick-witted, proposed a solution to their mounting predicament, 'Best we find a workaround.'

Raymond, with a sense of dogged purpose, affirmed their need to find a solution. 'We'll work around it by using the Commonwealth Police dockyard and the old Woolloomooloo watch house.'

Lottie, with a perceptiveness that eclipsed their collective resoluteness, zeroed in on Victor's blood-smeared face. Her tone, dipped in genuine concern, delved into the heart of the matter. 'Are you alright? What happened back there?'

Victor, though physically injured, carried a burden of embarrassment that overshadowed his physical pain. His response, drenched with shame, betrayed the ongoing struggle that defined his existence, 'Same old story.' He brushed off her inquiry with a fleeting, evasive gesture in a silent acknowledgment of the burden of humiliation that had long shadowed his path.

Raymond felt for his son. 'Come on, son, I'll take you home. God knows what your mother is going to say this time.'

Chapter 4

Melena Longford, a woman approaching her late thirties, bore an unremarkable expression, her appearance steeped in conservatism. Her attire, meticulously chosen, conveyed propriety and conformity. When she swung the front door open, it was akin to being granted ingress into the very heart of the Longford family home, a realm where convention and tradition held sway.

Raymond, a figure of fixed purpose, ushered Victor, his face besmirched by a torrent of crimson, into the austere sitting room. His instructions, edged with paternal concern, resonated with an authority born of experience. 'Put your head back, son.'

The harrowing spectacle of Victor's blood-streaked face jolted Melena out of her staid routine. Her response was instinctual, marked by shock and immediate fussing. With an eruption of maternal anxiety, Melena hovered over Victor like a protective shield, her eyes pools of disquiet. Her voice, laced with a profound sense of concern and frantic for details, trembled as she said, 'Oh, Lord! Not again! What happened this time?'

Acutely attuned to his mother's inclination to overreact, Victor endeavoured to soothe the situation with a composed attempt at reassurance. 'Mother, I'm okay.'

Melena, a portrait of deep-seated concern, remained unswayed. Her maternal instincts, a force as unceasingly intense as the tides, compelled her into immediate action. 'You don't look okay. Here, let me.' With a swift and single-minded motion, she snatched the blood-soaked cloth from Raymond's grasp with trembling hands.

Raymond, though veiled in a façade of bravado, recognised the seriousness of the situation. He also attempted to infuse the atmosphere with a sense of assurance, his expression a declaration of faith. 'He's going to be fine.'

Unbelievable! She found herself staring at Raymond, incredulous. Did he not see the blood? Could he not sense, like she did, Victor's discomfort? How could he be so self-absorbed as to not realise their only son is hurt physically and emotionally? No, she would not accept his layman's assessment. Their son was clearly not fine!

Melena's sudden cessation was akin to the pregnant pause before a storm, her simmering indignation unmistakable. Her words, steeped with an aggrieved fury, cut through the room like a well-honed blade. 'You're meant to keep him safe.'

Raymond, standing his ground, countered with the unassailable logic of a man who did not want to be swayed by emotion alone, 'He's not a child.'

The force of her attitude remained undiminished as the tempest of emotions surged within her. She fixed her gaze on Raymond as she vented her pent-up fears, her words resonating with vehement intensity. 'I should have never let you involve him in your picture-making.'

Raymond, affronted by the accusation, his words layered with the depths of genuine certainty replied, 'He's my son too, Melena.' With that statement, the complex weaving together of their shared history and enduring bonds was threaded into the fabric of their conversation. It was an unspoken acknowledgment of the intricate bonds of their familial journey.

Caught in the crossfire of his parents' unspoken tension, Victor took on the uncomfortable role of mediator, compelled to intercede on his father's behalf. His admission, a reluctant but powerful assertion, signified the importance of reason. 'Mother, it wasn't Dad's fault.'

'It never is.' Weary cynicism pervaded Melena's response and her words drip with the bitter wisdom of her past experience. Her gaze then shifted to Raymond, her expression devoid of pretence as she asked, 'Will you be staying for dinner?'

Raymond replied in kind, his announcement stripped of sentiment, 'No, I must get back to work.' He regretted the words the second they left his mouth.

'It's always your precious work,' Melena's spite cut the air with precision.

Raymond, wounded and besieged by emotions, asked, 'How else—'

Melena gave him no reprieve. 'You chose to support two families.' Her venomous words hung heavy in the air, poisoning the atmosphere.

Endeavouring to rise above Melena's anger, Raymond attempted to conceal their war of words from Victor, 'I don't think this is the time or place for this discussion.'

Melena basked in her triumph. Sensing Raymond's symbolic defeat, she delivered a final, cutting blow to her beleaguered adversary. 'It never is.' She paused to let her sarcasm-soaked words land soundly. 'Go. Don't let me stand in the way of your art.'

Raymond, eager to conclude the conversation, shifted his attention to Victor. 'Son, are you okay?'

Victor, buoyed by a sense of personal resilience, sensed that the storm had abated. He aimed to alleviate the incontestable unease lingering between his parents. 'Yeah.'

Raymond offered his parting words with a paternal touch that conveyed unspoken reassurance. 'I'll check on you later.' With that, he donned his hat and departed, leaving the echo of familial complexities in his wake.

Melena, incredulous, was not at all surprised by Raymond's departure. It was not the first time she had been left to pick up the pieces while his work took precedence over their family's needs.

Chapter 5

In the languid hours of the afternoon, a group of businessmen gathered at the resplendent Moncur Street residence shared by Lottie, Raymond, and Lottie's mother and younger sister. Their meeting unfolded within the chaotic charm of the masculine study, a realm where intellect and ambition coexisted.

Sir David Gordon was the first to grace the room with his presence. A conservative financier, he was the quintessential distinguished businessman, with lines of fortitude etched gracefully upon his features as proof of his years. He occupied a leather Chesterfield armchair with a patience that indicated a lifetime of astute negotiations.

By his side, E J Carroll, of similar vintage, emanated a charismatic energy, his presence a magnetic force that beckons attention. E J was a consummate salesman, his manner an interplay of charm and persuasive brilliance. Alongside him sat Dan Carroll, who carried himself in a way that directly contrasted his brother's extroversion. Dan, the quieter of the two, was the Yin to E J's Yang, an opposite in temperament and presence within their business partnership.

The three men shared an anticipatory vigil, their gazes converging upon Raymond when he entered with an air of self-possessed authority. Lottie followed close behind Raymond. She greeted the men with her usual self-assured smile.

Sir David studied Raymond intently. As a man of notable influence, his words, stately and restrained, were a forewarning. 'Raymond, we need to talk.'

Raymond, anticipating the direction of the conversation and impending negotiation, summoned his most assured tone. He infused his words with a firmness of purpose. 'We're already working to a shoestring budget.'

Lottie, fully aware of their precarious financial circumstances, aligned herself with Raymond, a bastion of reassurance in the presence of these distinguished businessmen. 'If this is about the money you paid to come to terms with C J, you're going to make that and more back, based on what we've captured so far.'

However, whether by intent or circumstance, Sir David summarily dismissed Lottie's comment. His words, curt and to the point, were a gentle dismissal. 'It's not that.'

Lottie bristled at the brush off. This was not the recognition she had sought nor the validation she expected after her trying day. The unsettling undercurrent of discontent pervaded the room.

Sensing the rising tide of frustration within Lottie, Raymond steered the conversation. 'What can be so pressing?'

In his indelible style devoid of sentiment, the financier replied with unfaltering practicality, 'The Puglieses.'

For the first time since setting foot in the room, Raymond shifted his weight attempting to not betray the fatigue that settles upon his shoulders. With a sigh that indicated a great deal, he conceded, 'We can't ever go back to Humbert and Caroline Pugliese as investors.'

Sir David, a paragon of pragmatic thinking, explained the course they must navigate. 'Indeed. But we need to lessen the impact of the plagiarism charge as the court case becomes public.'

Regrettably, Raymond found himself speechless. A silence hung heavily in the room, serving as an unspoken admission to the seriousness of their predicament. In this shared lull, the unspoken truths that underpinned their collective understanding were starkly illuminated, looming as a formidable challenge to be confronted head-on.

E J stepped forwards, his words laced with insight. 'People get scared.'

Dan, never one to indulge in sentiment, supported his brother's sentiment. 'It's a business.'

Raymond, reproachful, said, 'An American business.'

E J, with his trademark optimism, shifted his approach, seeking a glimmer of hope. 'Any luck with your quota system idea?'

Raymond's weary manner manifested in a posture that portrayed that he'd had enough. He was a beaten man. His voice acknowledged the futility of his efforts. 'No, they're not interested. We're swamped by imported films while being refused screenings in favour of the Hollywood packages.'

Lottie advocated for a different course. 'We need more of our own films.'

Dan, not one to retreat into total introversion, was the archivist of the assembly. He refreshed the collective memory of the gathering with a mild reminder of the passage of time. 'Nothing happens overnight. It's only been two years since J D Williams shared C J Dennis's poetry with you.'

The men, their expressions marked by shared acknowledgment, nodded.

Lottie, no stranger to asserting her presence, reiterated the unvarnished truth of their shared history. 'You mean since I convinced him we have to make a picture!'

The room resonated with shared laughter, a harmonious acknowledgment of their collective oversight.

Raymond, echoing Lottie's sentiments, took the opportunity to shed light on the multitude of impediments that loomed large in their path. 'You laugh... Seriously, the American Combine takes aim at me personally.'

E J, disposed to a favourable view and yearning to uncover a viable solution to their quandary, attempts to allay Raymond's concerns.

'Look, we know it's a tough market. The American Combine is nothing more than a cartel.'

Raymond, however, delivered a candid yet sobering assessment of their predicament. 'We don't stand a chance against the American studio system.'

Dan, consistent in his role of chief supporter, countered the prevailing pessimism with an unswerving staying power. 'They may have refused us exhibition, but we're not giving up.'

However, Raymond's mood was immovable, his conviction hardened and doubts firmly entrenched. 'They think Australians don't want projects of the ilk championed by Lottie.'

Lottie, ever the optimist, offered a potential path forward. 'These higher than almighty politicians, religious leaders and police don't get it. *The Songs of a Sentimental Bloke* is well-loved because of its humour and simple love story.' Her words carried the undertone of aspiration, a beacon illuminating the path through the trials that stood before them.

E J aligned himself with Lottie's view, though he swiftly introduced an additional hurdle. 'That's all well and good, but what about the battle with the censorship board?'

Sir David, with a nod of agreement, underscored the importance of avoiding a recurrence of past misfortunes. 'We can't afford a repeat of what happened with *The Woman Suffers*.'

Dan agreed with the respected and powerful businessman, 'Too right!'

E J recounted a stark example of the film's reach. '*The Biggest Show on Earth,* brought in nine hundred pounds in six days and yet it's censored in New South Wales!'

In the wake of this discussion, Lottie suggested, 'Maybe the censorship board needs a woman's perspective.'

Raymond, without pause and possibly without consideration, delivered a scathing rejection. 'Women are too illogical to serve on boards!'

Lottie, initially taken aback, considered challenging this entrenched belief. Given the discernible collective agreement in the nods from Sir David, E J and Dan, not to mention the pervasive viewpoints and unconscious biases of the time, Lottie opted for sustained restraint. The room remained steeped in this sentiment until E J detected the fierce tenacity etched upon Lottie's face.

Sir David, with a direness befitting the occasion, pronounced, 'This picture business is high risk for all of us.'

In a fit of frustration, Raymond vented his ire at his long-time adversary. 'Damn Joseph Marks and his manufactured controversy with the Church and censorship board.'

The name of Joseph Marks, who had caused no end of trouble for Lottie and Raymond's filmmaking endeavours, was uttered with a fervent resentment.

E J Carroll, characteristically direct, summed it up. 'Bloody publicity stunt gone wrong.'

'Clever on their part, leveraging confusion off your film, *The Church and The Woman*, for his film, *The Monk and The Woman*,' asserted Sir David, the ever-astute financier.

Dan said, 'However, now it affects our film by sheer association.'

Sir David reinforced the severity of their predicament. 'Exactly. Plagiarism is a serious charge.'

Raymond, exhibiting a weariness that couldn't be dismissed, raised a question of great consequence, 'Do I stand down?' The seriousness of the question was unmistakable, bereft of jest or the pursuit of sympathy.

The response from Lottie, the Carroll brothers and Sir David was of astonishment, as the Carroll brothers protested in unison, 'No!'

Sir David was the first to rally behind Raymond and offer his support. 'Don't get ahead of yourself, old chap. You're contracted to deliver *The Sentimental Bloke*.'

A resounding knock reverberated through the interior of the tranquil dwelling. A moment later, the indistinct murmur of incoming voices reached them, signalling the presence of an unexpected visitor.

Lottie, attuned to these subtle cues, ventured out to investigate, allowing her head to gently peek from the study's threshold. With a subtle gesture and silent nod, she discreetly conveyed her message to Raymond before gracefully withdrawing. Sir David and the Carroll brothers, sharp to the unspoken signals, discerned their host's intent and prepared to depart.

'We best take our leave. I'm sure you've got plenty of work to do on the film.' Sir David excused himself.

Raymond, exuding a tireless determination, extended a final reassurance to his departing companions, 'I won't let you down.'

Raymond proceeded alongside Sir David and the Carroll brothers as they made their exit, while Lottie assumed the role of hostess, guiding the family doctor into the living room, where the secrets and revelations of the day may yet unravel.

Chapter 6

Within the spacious confines of the Moncur Street living room, a peculiar duality unfolded, where the ordinary cohabited with the extraordinary. It was a realm divided, where the customary trappings of a living area harmonised with the sombre vestiges of a makeshift infirmary designed to accommodate the needs of Lottie's younger sister, Lynda Cox. In the bloom of her early twenties, Lynda's once-vibrant vitality had been usurped by the insidious grip of illness. She lay in solitude upon a single bed nestled beside the window that served as her solitary portal to the outside world.

Charlotte, Lottie's mother, a woman in her late fifties, bore the appearance of one marked by the passage of years and the unrelenting trials of life. She extended a weary yet gracious welcome to the family doctor.

The distinguished gentleman, adorned in regalia befitting his noble profession, arrived with the gravitas of his calling and clutching a traditional doctor's briefcase. His presence within the makeshift triage assumed an almost sacramental significance as he embarked upon ministering to his ailing patient.

Charlotte assumed the protective stance of a compassionate yet devoted guardian over her stricken daughter, whose pallor and feeble appearance indicated her fragile state. As Doctor Wilson commenced his examination and treatment, the air within the room became a tapestry of sounds. Lynda's respiration, once deep and robust, exhibited a fragile shallowness punctuated by an unmelodious symphony of wheezing and rasping coughs in a sombre reminder of her ongoing affliction.

Even though the doctor went about his thorough examination of Lynda's rattling cough, his attention was drawn to Lottie, gaze transfixed by her vivacity and youthfulness. He was somewhat starstruck, and her presence eclipsed all else. He was compelled to humbly seek her pardon. 'I do apologise for arriving early.'

Lottie quickly reassured the doctor. 'We were finishing up anyway.'

Charlotte, too, endeavoured to express their gratitude for his attendance to Lynda. 'We appreciate the house call.'

The doctor, with a gracious nod, reciprocated their warmth. 'It's the least I can do.'

Lottie's genuine concern shone through as she asked the doctor about her ailing sister. 'How is our patient?'

The doctor offered his professional assessment. 'Her condition is not the best. She's stable. I suggest keeping up with the current treatment of bleedings. She must rest, eat well and exercise outdoors.'

Across the expanse of the sickbed, Charlotte and Lottie shared identical expressions of apprehension. Their worry for Lynda demonstrated the love that united them and attested to their enduring devotion to one another.

Frustration coursed through Lottie as she desperately implored, 'There must be something else we can do?'

'Trust the doctor, Lottie,' Charlotte soothed.

With concern etched in his kind eyes, the doctor asked, 'How are you, my dear?'

Lottie, intent on putting on a brave face, offered a semblance of assurance. 'Good as gold.'

Although the doctor had previously succumbed to the charms of Lottie's star presence, he remained unmoved by her bravado.

Responding to his unspoken concerns, Lottie hurriedly added, 'I'm fine. Really.'

Leaning close to Lottie, the doctor offered his sage advice. 'You must take care, my dear. If not for your own sake, think of your mother.'

Her family's welfare rested heavily on Lottie's shoulders, which she did not need to be reminded of. With austere intent, she conjured her most reassuring smile, striving to reassure everyone in the room that she was indeed well.

When the family doctor concluded his visit, Charlotte accompanied him to the door, leaving Lottie and Lynda to their thoughts.

In this private interlude, the sisters engaged in a heartfelt conversation. Managing a garbled giggle, Lynda uttered a few strained words, 'Australia's star of the stage and screen strikes again.'

Lottie responded with a warm smile. 'I'm so much more than that. You'd think after all these years, he'd not be so...'

'Starstruck? If only they knew how jolly-well complicated life has been for us.' Lynda's speech wavered when her words were interrupted by a fit of coughing. Lottie offered support as Lynda struggled to clear her throat.

Lottie encouraged her sister, her words carrying a strong indemnity. 'No one need know about us. Besides, we're not Father or Rita. You will beat this.'

Lynda returned the encouragement. 'As will you.'

Lottie embraced her sister with all her might, though a hint of doubt lingered in Lynda's eyes.

Chapter 7

The following day, Lottie and Raymond's modest film crew once again set up to film on location, this time transforming a local Sydney watering hole into their backdrop—a quaint, charming pub.

During a brief respite from filming, the comedic duo of Arthur Tauchert and Gilbert Emery, portraying Bill and Ginger Mick in the film, seized the opportunity to undertake a spirited escapade of amusement and tomfoolery. Arthur, always the showman, engaged in acrobatics and serenaded the patrons with Irish songs, hoping to elicit laughs and admiration. Their intent was to leave an indelible impression upon one particular member in their presence—the journalist from the *Picture Show* magazine, Mr Carhall.

However, undeterred by the uproarious merriment around him, the journalist was utterly absorbed by Lottie. No matter what antics the comic duo displayed, Carhall's attention remained steadfastly riveted upon the ethereal figure before him. Lottie was in the middle of an interview, and her presence cast a captivating spell over the journalist's senses.

Carhall, ensnared by Lottie's enchantment, hung on her every word. He skilfully orchestrated a premeditated pause, prolonging his stay within her orbit. His inquisitive mind, desiring to probe the depths of Lottie's artistic essence, unfurled the next question, designed to elicit profound revelations. 'You've had a long career in theatre and now pictures. Which do you prefer?'

With an adept knack for playing to people's adoration, Lottie responded with the theatrical lilt of someone who had captivated audiences in both arenas. 'I prefer the pictures. Besides being highly interesting, it is mostly open-air work. I think myself very fortunate to be acting in pictures telling our own Australian stories.'

Mr Carhall, seasoned in the craft of peeling back layers of the human experience, perceived a deeper sentiment beneath Lottie's words. With a subtle shift in his questioning, he delved into the depths of her passion. 'So it's not just art for you?' His question hung in the air, casting an inquisitive shadow.

Nearby, Raymond, an ever-watchful spectator to the captivating interplay of words, listened intently. His anticipation mirrored that of the journalist as they awaited Lottie's answer.

'Of course, art's important, but it's also a business choosing stories that make a difference to everyday Australians.'

The journalist, spurred by the subtle shift in Lottie's perspective, probed further into the relevance of Australian stories in the global cinema landscape. 'Do you think Australian stories have a place in world cinema, especially amongst American pictures?'

Raymond, impassioned by his own perspective, capitalised on the opportunity to share his point of view. 'Let me tell you about the Americans! They drive a wedge between art and business. They're systematically taking out independent filmmakers by monopolising distribution globally.'

The abrupt change in mood and direction of the interview alarmed Lottie. Sensing the conversation could veer well off course, she acted swiftly to realign it. 'What Raymond is trying to say is that Australia has a rich history of storytelling. Pictures combine art and narrative in a way that has the potential to reach not only all Australians but audiences around the world. Pictures allow us to do what the Americans are doing. We have a responsibility to choose stories that Australians are eager to see alongside those American pictures.'

Raymond sighed, a load lifted off his shoulders, recognising Lottie's artful skill in steering the interview back onto its intended course.

Lottie had employed that skill many times when Raymond's feelings about the American film industry had arisen at awkward times.

With an air of unshakeable confidence, Lottie pressed on, 'Personally, I'm attracted to work that has a seriousness to its subject matter. Acting provides the vehicle for me to take on more roles in my work—writing, producing, editing—and to tell stories about women.'

Carhall, enamoured by Lottie, was powerless to resist her charm and couldn't restrain his admiration. 'Like the successful *The Woman Suffers*. I enjoyed it immensely.'

Lottie's smile radiated warmth and sincerity as she replied, 'Thank you. Many people, not just women, have connected to the morals of the story. And of course, the revenge and sexual betrayal amongst the characters. Raymond and I are immensely proud of its success and its potential to change women's lives.'

The journalist's gaze flickered briefly towards Raymond. A subtle undercurrent of disappointment flickered across his face as he was reminded that he was not the sole recipient of Miss Lyell's attention. Nevertheless, he expertly concealed his desire for a more intimate conversation with Lottie. 'Yes, you have an incredible partnership.'

Raymond took the lead in the conversation. 'It's hard work, picture making. Finding stories, writing the photoplays, financing the production, then marketing and exhibition all take great effort. I'm constantly working hard to make each one a success.'

Lottie, privately taken aback by Raymond's statement, experienced a surge of surprise and annoyance at his omission of her pivotal role in their shared success. His claim seemed to relegate her contributions to the periphery as if she'd had nothing to do with their success. Her annoyance simmered beneath a veil of restraint.

Carhall, unaware of the underlying tension, redirected his attention to Raymond.

Raymond, his enthusiasm growing, continued. 'I'm the producer and director. First and foremost, though, I'm a family man. In fact, my son, Victor, over there, is also learning show business.'

Lottie steered the conversation toward more familiar territory. 'Of course, none of us would be here if it weren't for that colourful American, J D Williams. J D gave C J Dennis's *The Songs of a Sentimental Bloke* to Raymond.'

On more solid ground, Raymond took the opportunity to pitch their project. He enthusiastically embraced the role of storyteller, seamlessly transitioning into his salesman mode. 'After reading it, I knew immediately that we would do this picture!'

Caught off guard, Lottie couldn't conceal a brief expression of surprise.

'I had no doubt that it would transfer to the screen,' Raymond proclaimed with indomitable confidence.

Lottie's intentional cough was a discreet cue. Raymond, attuned to her intentions, smoothly relinquished the role of orator. He deftly passed the conversational baton back to his partner. 'Of course, I handed it to Lottie for her opinion.'

'I have nothing but praise for the contents and am positively certain the picture will be as successful as the book of poems. Its simple love story of Bill and Doreen will be key to its success,' Lottie declared with infectious enthusiasm and sincerity.

Carhall found himself thoroughly bewitched by Lottie's poise and self-assurance. 'As I'm sure you... I mean *it* will be,' he stammered, temporarily overwhelmed by her presence.

'You are too kind,' Lottie replied, her modesty adding to her undeniable charm.

'Speaking of that colourful American showman, J D Williams, how is his campaign to woo you away to star in American pictures coming along?' The journalist's eager inquiry dangled in the air.

Lottie paused, knowing any mention of the Americans could trigger another less than helpful rant from Raymond. She must choose her words carefully to avoid inflaming a festering sore point between her and Raymond. More than just the American Combine threatened their livelihood. While J D's consistent efforts to lure her away to star in American films was an exciting prospect for her career, it was a frightening possibility on a personal level for Raymond. Given J D would likely read the article, Lottie searched for an answer that would appease J D without hurting Raymond.

Carhall avidly awaited Lottie's response and both he and Raymond trained their eyes on the star before them.

Before Lottie could articulate an answer, Raymond masterfully commandeered the conversation. 'Speaking of our star,' he said, 'we should really get her back to work.'

With that suave intervention, the interview that had held the journalist spellbound reached its conclusion, leaving the lingering question unanswered.

For Carhall, however, it scarcely mattered. The journalist departed the set with a heart brimming with satisfaction, his forthcoming feature story destined to sing the praises of Miss Lottie Lyell, captivating star of stage and screen.

Lottie, discreetly but forcibly, pulled Raymond aside as the commotion around them subsided. The burden of the unspoken issue pressed upon her, and her voice carried a subtle reproach as she said, 'Really, Raymond?'

Raymond meets her gaze squarely, his expression obstinate. 'He brought up America, not me.'

Their eyes locked in a silent exchange, each acknowledging the complexities that remained unspoken. Lottie did not waver. 'That's a conversation for another day. I meant, "I'm constantly working hard to make each one a success." ' She cleverly mirrored his earlier response to Carhall with a touch of irony.

'I said "we," ' Raymond asserted.

Lottie, adamant and clear-cut, shook her head, exposing the fissure in his recollection and calling out his selective memory. 'No, you said "I." '

Raymond reassessed his recollection, instantly doubting himself. 'I'm sure I said *we*.' '

The longstanding tension between them, though familiar, remained conspicuous. Lottie, fixed on securing his acknowledgment, pressed on. 'Different to our previous films, you need to acknowledge my work on *The Sentimental Bloke*.'

Raymond took a deep breath. This was a conversation they had revisited countless times. He addressed her with a bearing softened by understanding, attempting to console her. 'Lottie.'

She replied with a wilful, 'Yes?'

Raymond, now earnest, reminded her, 'We've talked about this.'

Lottie conceded, though her discontent was incontestable. 'Doesn't mean I have to like it.'

'You know it has to be me out the front and you in the shadow.'

Lottie's frustration softened as she absorbed his words. Even though she knew Raymond was right, the complex nature of their business and the importance of their shared ambitions brought little comfort.

Chapter 8

On a new day of filming, Lottie surveyed the small, yet dedicated film crew as they diligently readied the practical open-air shed. It would present the vital stage for the day's scheduled sequence—the action-packed two-up raid from *The Songs of a Sentimental Bloke*.

Lottie, as stunt choreographer, coached the two actors who would portray the characters fleeing from the dogged pursuit of the heroic policeman through the intricate mechanics of the planned caper. They indicated their readiness with a nod and nervous smile. A lot depended on their perfect timing. The pressure was immense for the actors, as they didn't want to let Lottie down. With the actors in position, Lottie, also an adept horsewoman, took a serene moment's pause with a horse. She whispered softly into its ear and tenderly patted its muscular neck.

After giving the horse a parting rub, Lottie nimbly scaled a nearby fence to the shed's rooftop. The trio of actors, their expressions a blend of reverence and trepidation, gaped in wonder at Lottie's brilliance.

Unable to contain his admiration, one actor commented, 'Cor, is there anything this woman can't do?'

Lottie's radiant smile was a beacon of her boundless capability. Lottie always found herself perfectly in her element among the hustle and bustle of a film set, her spirit awakened and thriving.

The attentive gazes of the actors remained fixed upon her as she orchestrated a seamless stunt performance. With a graceful, running leap, she executed an astonishing somersault, landing with impeccable precision upon the waiting horse.

Once more, the three actors were in a state of awe and adulation, their mouths hanging open. After a moment of reverence, they whooped and cheered in appreciation of her talents. Eager to impress Lottie, they scaled the fence and took their positions.

With practiced skill, Lottie deftly manoeuvred the horse back to its designated position and dismounted gracefully. She called out in encouragement to the trio of actors perched on the shed's roof. 'Okay, now you try.'

One of the actors, emboldened but hesitant, launched himself towards the edge only to halt abruptly, teetering precariously on the precipice. His sudden cessation and loss of balance nearly caused a misstep, inciting the unrestrained laughter of the second actor.

Offended by the mirth, the first actor issued a challenge. 'If you find it so amusing, then I dare you to give it a go!'

Lottie was determined to iron out the details of the stunt choreography. However, as a producer, she also wanted to adhere to the schedule as she knew time equated to money. With a kindly and persuasive manner, she extended an offer to the other actor. 'You can do it.'

Motivated by their desire to leave a positive impression on Lottie, the two actors switched positions. However, although the second actor dashed toward the edge, he too, was unable to take the leap.

Lottie continued soothing the horse, ensuring the animal remained calm and in position as her concern grew. But it wasn't the horse that concerned her, it was the human aspect she needed to rally. With a tinge of frustration, she cried, 'It's a straightforward stunt.'

Always ready with a wisecrack, Arthur Tauchert couldn't resist offering a sardonic remark. 'For you, maybe.'

The disharmony in the group led to the horse stunt rehearsal attracting a substantial audience, with extras from the two-up game converging to witness the spectacle. The rehearsal had ground to a halt, and a distinct sense of impasse hovered over the group.

Lottie, visibly vexed, threw her hands up in exasperation. Addressing the burgeoning crowd of onlookers, she asked, 'Does anyone want to give it a go?'

Keen to leave an indelible mark on Australia's cinematic queen and demonstrate his prowess to the assembled men, another actor shimmied onto the rooftop. There, between the crescendo of anticipation and exuberant cheers from the enthusiastic crowd below, the man inhaled deeply and boldly took on the challenge. He sprinted toward the edge and leapt from the shed roof.

However, the outcome was a spectacular failure as he narrowly missed the horse stationed below.

'At this rate, we won't have anyone left to do the scene,' taunted Tauchert.

The actor's landing frightened the horse, sending it into a frenzied bolt, its hooves pounding the earth with a thunderous urgency.

Like a Greek chorus of one, Tauchert cast out his candid thought. 'Wish that horse would have run like that last week at Randwick.'

His witticism triggered an eruption of raucous laughter and hysterics among the crew and extras.

Undeterred by the mirthful chaos, Lottie took charge. She employed soothing whispers and gestures to calm the agitated horse and skilfully led the animal back into position. When the animal had settled under Lottie's guidance, Raymond stepped up authoritatively.

'The stunt's gone.'

The crew—as well as the actors perched atop the shed roof—breathed a collective sigh of relief, acknowledging the wisdom in Raymond's decision.

With a sense of urgency, Raymond drew Lottie closer and guided her away from the crowd.

Lottie protested, 'I need more time.'

Raymond pragmatically conveyed the unavoidable truth. 'There's no more time for this.'

Frustration surged within Lottie. 'Damn it, Raymond! If I can do it, surely one of these men can.'

'None have been able to, and truth be told, you shouldn't either. We're out of time, Lottie.'

She remained headstrong and asserted, 'Well then, you've got not only a continuity problem but a logic problem with the chase scenario I wrote.'

Raymond, in a bid to appease Lottie while adhering to the constraints of budget and schedule, hastily offered a solution. 'Then you can revise it. Let's get them running across the roof and simply jumping off.'

Lottie briefly contemplated protesting before opting to turn and walk away, leaving a lingering tension in the air.

A short time later, a disgruntled Lottie, her frustration now concealed, rubbed the horse's neck while she stood out of camera range.

Arthur Higgins prepared to capture the scene. 'Camera rolling.'

Arthur Cross issued the pre-emptive notice to the enthusiastic crowd of extras and curious spectators. 'Quiet on set.'

All eyes shifted expectantly toward Raymond, who called, 'Action.'

Raymond's condensed and refined stunt unfolded seamlessly. The two actors raced across the roof and made their daring descent. The pursuing policeman dashed across the rooftop but stopped at the edge.

'And cut! I'm pretty happy with that. Lottie, you'll need to update the scenario and photoplay,' Raymond instructed.

Smouldering with irritation, Lottie seethed, exasperated that the potential brilliance of the stunt had been squandered, leaving the audience bereft of an opportunity to marvel and applaud the characters' artful escape. A tangible sense of deflation hung in the air as she strode away.

Meanwhile, Raymond, ever watchful of the schedule, scrutinised his fob-watch and issued directives to the waiting ensemble. 'Let's move on to the scenario where Bill gets pinched by the two policemen.'

'I'll get the camera set up,' Higgins said, moving the tripod.

Tauchert, ever the merry provocateur, ventured toward Lottie's impromptu office, replete with a small table and chairs. He observed Lottie's intense typing, the keys clattering as she updated the photoplay.

Arthur Tauchert plucked the copy of the *Picture Show* magazine from the table. He sat in a chair opposite Lottie and leaned back, nonchalantly propping his feet on the edge of the table.

'Well, that's a bit of alright, girlie.'

In no mood for more of Tauchert's mocking, Lottie tried to ignore him. She continued her rhythmic tap, tap, tap on the typewriter. Yet, she was compelled to raise her line of sight from the typewriter, her fingers momentarily stilled, when he started reading aloud.

' "It was so easy to see Miss Lyell as one woman in a thousand. Enthusiastic, original, possessing charm and common sense. The sort of woman who will go far in the work she has chosen and will be a big factor in Australian production generally. I could see now what they meant when they said she had brains," ' recited Arthur, with flattering eloquence.

Lottie focused on Tauchert, her attention captured by his words. He relished having her full attention and continued reading, ' "Her mind is keen. She grasps things quickly and is clever enough to avoid reminding you that she is clever." '

'What's your point, Arthur? I have to get these pages corrected.' Lottie was wary of Arthur's intent and disinclined to tolerate more of his teasing.

Undeterred by Lottie's imperative to concentrate on her corrective work, Arthur offered his sincere assessment. 'It's more than a puff piece, girlie.'

Even with the now familiar 'girlie' reference, Lottie deemed it necessary to enlighten Tauchert about the importance of articles transcending superficial praises. She clarified her stance, 'If you must know, other magazines give us minimal press coverage—they're in favour of those pictures from America. The *Picture Show* has been very supportive of Raymond and me.'

Enjoying their spirited verbal exchange, Arthur took pleasure in winding Lottie up further. 'Oh, Mr Carhall mentions him too. "Raymond Longford is a man in demand as director and producer, family man and dedicated father, instrumental in bringing the C J Dennis love story to the screen."'

As Lottie's ire mounted, she redirected her staying power to her task at hand. Furious, she pounded the typewriter keys with growing intensity. Tap. Tap. Tap. Finally, she wrenched the page from the typewriter, rose and stormed off with the fierce purposefulness of a tempest. This small triumph left Tauchert wearing a contented smile.

The actors, poised for their cues, stood in silent anticipation. Arthur Higgins aligned the camera, ready to immortalise the impending scene on film.

'All set when you are,' he informed Raymond.

Raymond checked his fob-watch and eyed the sky, monitoring the fading afternoon light before moving to Arthur's side.

With a determined stride, Lottie approached Raymond, her steps unafraid and pages clutched in her hand. 'Here.'

Raymond met her overture with preoccupation and dismissal. 'What? Not now. We're losing light.'

Unperturbed and unwilling to be disregarded, Lottie persevered, pressing the pages assertively against Raymond's chest. 'I think it's some of your best work.'

Raymond remained uncomprehending. In response, Lottie pivoted on her heel and retraced her steps to her makeshift desk.

Lottie seethed as she approached Tauchert who watched the unfolding drama with eyes peering just above the magazine's edge. 'Ain't love grand?' He said to himself and anyone within earshot.

'Arthur, we need you over here,' commanded Raymond.

Tauchert snapped up, discarding the magazine on Lottie's typewriter. Lottie, trapped in a spiral of frustration and dogged determination, fiercely drew the line at shedding a tear, especially in Tauchert's presence.

Lottie watched Tauchert closely as he complied with Raymond's summons. Together with Arthur Higgins, they went through the customary motions of preparing the scene. A small assembly of eager onlookers congregated, drawn by curiosity and the promise of witnessing cinematic magic.

The worrisome plight of insufficient light continued to trouble the cameraman. Higgins voiced his distress to Raymond with worry etched across his brow. 'I'm still concerned about getting enough light into the scene.'

Raymond, equally troubled, considered postponing the shoot until the following day. He paused, an index finger tracing the contours of his fob-watch as he surveyed the sky as if seeking guidance from the waning sun. Finally, he asked Arthur, 'Should we push to tomorrow?'

Lottie resigned herself to finding a solution. She left her improvised office, released a heartfelt sigh and turned her attention to the gathered assembly of curious onlookers. She navigated through the modest crowd towards a woman resplendent in white. With genteel grace, Lottie took the woman's elbow and said, 'Could I ask you to come with me?'

The woman, her enthusiasm unbridled, eagerly acceded to Lottie's summons. When they reached Higgins, Lottie tapped on his shoulder to draw his attention, and indicated her plan. 'Let there be light.'

'You always find a way.' Higgins genuinely admired Lottie's problem-solving abilities.

'I learned from the best, Arthur.' Lottie held mutual respect for the cameraman.

Higgins welcomed the lady by shaking her hand. The woman's excitement surged as she envisioned herself gracing the silver screen in this instance of extraordinary serendipity.

Higgins positioned the woman in the last of the fast-fading sunlight. Her radiant white dress channelled the vanishing rays to where they were most needed—on Bill and the two policemen. Higgins gave a thumbs up and said, 'Camera's rolling.'

The woman dressed in white radiated joy and exhilaration, the embodiment of the unexpected starlet.

Cross, the arbiter of silence, issued the call to order, 'Quiet on set.'

A hush of silence descended over the expectant crowd.

'Action!' Raymond called, and the scene played out.

Bill was nabbed by the policemen and led away.

'Cut.' Raymond exhaled a sigh of relief, echoing the collective sentiment of the crew.

The final scene of the day had been captured.

Lottie, her heart brimming with gratitude for their impromptu saviour, approached the woman in white. Her gratitude, fervently expressed, was conveyed with a simple squeeze of her hands and a gently uttered, 'Thank you so much,' before Lottie gently returned her to the embracing crowd of enthusiastic admirers. Lottie and the delighted woman were enveloped, becoming indistinguishable from Lottie's exuberant fans.

Chapter 9

Arthur Higgins's masterful eye was singularly focused on capturing the unfolding narrative. The sequence involved capturing a long shot of the character of Bill seeing Doreen for the first time at a busy market stall.

A man acting as the stallholder and Bill, the bearer of longing, cast their watchful gazes upon Doreen, portrayed by the magnetic Lottie. Nearby, a female actor, an unassuming figure in the middle of the bustling market, portrayed a prospective customer.

Fully in character, Lottie engaged in a silent exchange with the stallholder; no words were spoken, yet sentiments were shared. Bill, unable to contain his longing, attempted to initiate a conversation, yet Doreen, possessed of an alluring mystique that was both confounding and beguiling, gracefully eluded his advances. In that fleeting encounter, an emotion akin to love at first sight engulfed Bill, rendering him a mere spectator of Doreen's continued travels around the market.

'And cut!' Raymond cried, then bestowed his approval. 'Perfect, Lottie and Arthur.'

Raymond's gaze traversed the scene, seeking an echo in the eyes of Higgins, whose face exuded a subtle satisfaction, evidence of the power of the captured beginning of Bill's inspired love affair with Doreen. In the wake of commendation, Tauchert, the eager vessel of adoration, absorbed the accolades, his spirit buoyed by the resonance of praise. Lottie smiled at Raymond's acknowledgment, finding herself inexorably drawn to him, her heart an unspoken devotee of his creative vision.

Having captured the love-at-first-sight moment, Higgins advised Raymond, 'I'll set up for the close-ups. Give me a few.' With intentional precision and unfaltering hands, Higgins readied the tripod.

In response to the instruction, Clive Marsh called out, 'Everybody, take five!'

The collective assembly—artists and crew alike—acquiesced to the call for a brief respite.

Victor approached Raymond and Lottie. 'Dad, Lottie, Sir Gordon is here.' Victor's hushed announcement hung in the air like a lingering note of disquiet, knitting concern across Raymond and Lottie's faces. They shared a fleeting glance of concern before making their way over to where Sir David Gordon awaited their arrival.

Raymond extended a welcoming hand, which the financier grasped solidly. Sir David then acknowledged Lottie with a tip of his hat. 'Raymond. Lottie. More bad news, I'm afraid.' Sir David's words were heavy with regret, mirroring the severity of the disconcerting news.

Raymond and Lottie's shared uneasiness was etched in their furrowed brows and evident in their glances as the financier presented them with a newspaper article. Together, they took a short time to absorb the contents, their expressions shifting from concern to a simmering disquiet.

Sir David's continued his sombre narrative. 'All your talk of the American Combine, Raymond, has my investors rattled.'

Raymond's indignation swelled like a tempest. It did not take much to ignite his short fuse when it came to the American Combine. Clearly incensed, Raymond flared. 'Well, if I don't raise these issues, who will?'

Sir David was sensitive to Raymond's principled position. However, he was there to represent his business interests. 'Our investors are wary enough without articles like this giving them cold feet.'

Lottie, sensing the mounting tension, tried to placate their financier. 'But Raymond speaks the truth.'

The atmosphere grew tense as Sir David dismissed Lottie, his gaze and words aimed squarely at Raymond and decreed, 'It doesn't matter. You have to stop, Raymond.'

Lottie bore the brunt of the financier's snub. Her wounded expression was a manifestation of the hurt within her. Yet, in that vulnerable resemblance of reality, Raymond saw her pain. He stepped up, a sturdy pillar of support and emerged as her staunch defender. His words were a shield against the sting of rejection. 'This affects Lottie too. We're partners in this film, in our company.'

Lottie brightened, a glimmer of hope shining in her eyes. Buoyed by the renewed strength she found with Raymond's assertion, she chimed in, 'This is our livelihood. We're invested as much as you are, if not more.'

Intrigued by Lottie's spirited defence, Sir David offered her an inquisitive glance, silently prompting her to elaborate. It was an invitation Lottie needed no second bidding for. She grasped the opportunity without hesitation, her worldview unshakeable and her words balanced.

'We may be a small-scale independent set-up, but it allows us to work on pictures addressing a range of important issues, including those affecting women.'

Raymond, too, caught the fiery thread of her passionate response and wove it into his own words. 'Which also leaves us in a precarious existence of being undercapitalised.'

The advocate within Lottie forced her to press on, her voice iron-willed, 'That's why we need quotas.'

Raymond's plea to their financial backer resonated with urgency, each word heavy with the direness of their circumstances, 'We need protection from the Americans so our economic and cultural interests can survive Hollywood.'

Lottie, his stalwart companion in the battle, lent her spirited support. 'We can't do it on our own.'

Lottie and Raymond made a formidable team.

Sir David inhaled sharply, his response edged with reluctance. 'Our investor's interest is not with battling American dominance.'

Raymond's fieriness in the matter was incontestable. He wore the badge of truth-teller, unafraid to challenge the status quo. 'It's a complete monopoly.'

While Sir David Gordon personally concurred with Raymond's assessment of the American Combine, his role as an envoy of the financiers demanded a more cautious stance. 'That may be. Our investors need assurance that *The Sentimental Bloke*'s distribution will be favourable enough to guarantee their returns. They want to make their money back.'

The tension surged between them. It is like waving a red flag at a bull—Raymond. 'How? When the Australian independent producers are squeezed out by the major Hollywood studios?'

As the conscience of reason and optimism, Lottie attempted to calm the state of affairs and bridge the divide by offering what she believed was the only solution. 'By making better films!'

The two men stared at Lottie. They recognised the irrefutable wisdom in her words.

Sir David, almost won over by the sheer conviction in Lottie's eyes, conceded. 'I wish I had your confidence, Lottie. You need to see something.

That evening, after finishing filming for the day, the trio of Lottie, Raymond, and Sir David, cloaked in darkness, gathered in the dimly lit picture theatre. The intermittent glow of the silver screen bathed their faces. It was a full house, every seat claimed by eager spectators, each one a starry-eyed pilgrim immersed in the latest Chaplin offering.

The theatre breathed as one before erupting into uproarious laughter at the master comedian's capers. Lottie, too, succumbed to the intoxication of collective joy that swelled within the theatre.

In an utterance scarcely above a whisper, Sir David shared his sage counsel with Raymond, offering an admonition carried on a breath of caution. 'This is your competition.'

Raymond looked around the audience. Their faces were illuminated by the mesmerising flicker of the black-and-white silent movie playing on the grand canvas before them. Raymond's chest tightened and he forced a breath in through his mouth, easing the tension in his body. With another breath, he admitted to himself, *it will be a formidable challenge, indeed.*

Outside the picture theatre, a bustling throng of moviegoers cascaded out onto the street, Lottie, Raymond and Sir David among them.

Raymond surveyed the lengthy queue of patrons waiting for the next showing, carrying a veritable tide of expectation and shared delight. It snaked down the street and around the corner in tribute to the irresistible allure of the latest Charlie Chaplin masterpiece.

Sir David gestured toward the long line. 'They're all here to see the latest Chaplin picture.'

Raymond, feigning indifference, half-heartedly offered, 'He's not that great. A flash in the pan.'

Neither Sir David nor Lottie believed Raymond's bravado. His feigned indifference could not obscure the obvious. Lottie cast a quizzical glance in Raymond's direction and gave a disdainful shake of her head in silent rebuke of his artless charade.

A handful of astute individuals waiting in the serpentine queue recognised Lottie. Warm smiles and appreciative waves punctuated their exclamations of admiration to attract Lottie's attention. Within a moment, a multitude of inquisitive gazes fell upon Lottie, and she was swamped by adoring fans. Their various questions, earnest and brimming with hope, sought insight into Lottie's destiny.

One asked, 'Will you go to Hollywood and do a picture with Chaplin one day?'

Ever gracious, Lottie responded with a smile as radiant as the sun at its zenith, her words gentle as an evening breeze. 'You never know what the future holds.'

Her response left an indelible impression that swayed hearts and stirred dreams. Raymond, however, couldn't deny the pronounced unease coursing through him. Both the question and Lottie's innocent-enough answer shook him to his very core. Why was everyone obsessed with America? Couldn't everyone see what the Combine was up to, or was he the only one conscious of the existential distress caused by the monopoly? The questions were an enigma he struggled to unravel.

Ever the consummate saleswoman, Lottie didn't miss a beat in trying to put the financier at ease. 'They're the same people who will see *The Sentimental Bloke* when it's released.'

Sir David, a man of discerning countenance, arched an inquisitive brow, his thoughts hidden beneath a veneer of contemplation. 'You'd better be right, for all our sakes.'

With those words echoing in the air, Lottie, encircled by her awestruck admirers, departed the scene, leaving her retinue of devotees in a state of enchantment. Sir David and Raymond followed in her wake, the shadows of uncertainty and opportunity trailing them.

Chapter 10

The day after the Chaplin showing, the modest troupe reconvened on a quaint local street. The team was in full-steam production mode with Raymond at the helm orchestrating a Chaplin-esque performance from Arthur Tauchert, who was bedecked in attire that included Chaplin's emblematic top hat and cane. The scene had Bill returning to the pineapple cart.

'Okay, Arthur, like your vaudeville act. Try a little funnier.' Raymond instructed with an earnestness that belied the comedic nature of the scene.

Tauchert, a seasoned thespian, absorbed Raymond's direction with equanimity, retracing his steps to his mark to start the scene over. Under his breath, he released whispered currents of exasperation. 'One tells me no vaudeville, the other wants more.'

Higgins, the custodian of the moving image, called the crew to attention, 'Camera rolling.'

Victor, assuming his mantle as assistant for the day, added, 'Quiet on set.'

'Action!'

Upon Raymond's cue, Tauchert went through the motions, infusing each movement with his vaudevillian genius as he took a basket of produce from the moving cart. Laughter erupted from the crew and a gathering of intrigued onlookers like an unrestrained fountain.

When the scene reached its end-point, Raymond's resonant voice cut through the frivolity. 'And cut. Great job, Arthur!'

The words reverberated like a benediction, and Tauchert responded to the ovation of Raymond's praise with a gracious nod.

Lottie's arrival coincided with the end of the scene. Brow wrinkled, she posed a question that carried an air of intrigue laced with disapproval. 'Why's Arthur dressed like Charlie Chaplin?'

Raymond's response is a measure of panic and wavering uncertainty. 'I, ah, well, you see...'

Tauchert chimed in with a touch of impish humour, 'If you can't beat 'em, join 'em.'

Lottie, her patience strained, grabbed Raymond and dragged him away from the expectant crew. They huddled in a hushed but charged intensity.

'I leave you alone for the morning to shoot the scenario as we planned together, and you've turned it into a Chaplin homage!' Lottie felt her expression and demeanour oscillate between perplexity and annoyance. How could Raymond think that this was acceptable? Perhaps he was not thinking at all! Did he not consider how this would be perceived? She was grateful she had arrived in time—who knew what he would have done with the other scenes.

Raymond, quick to defend himself, responded with the unease of one unaccustomed to chastisement, especially irked since the scene had so favourably resonated with the onlookers. 'That's not fair.'

Recognising the urgency of the matter, Lottie reminded him of the looming spectre of plagiarism. 'Raymond, you've already been accused of plagiarism.'

'This is not that.' Raymond retorted.

Lottie underscored the importance of faithfulness to the original vision. 'Well, it's certainly not being true to C J Dennis's vision. It's our story. It's got to be Australia's story.'

In pursuit of Lottie's approval and awakened by her wisdom, Raymond promised, 'It will be.'

With a respectful yet vigorous firmness, Lottie reiterated that their tale demanded authenticity. 'Not like this. We have an original idea. That's what we're capturing.'

Acknowledging the significance of her insight, Raymond's response was genuine. 'You're right.' Sincere in his recognition of Lottie's wisdom, he instructed the intrigued crew, 'Switch it back, boys, for another take.'

Higgins and their adept crew efficiently reconfigured the set, wheeling in the produce cart and making necessary adjustments. The seasoned cameraman turned to address Lottie and Raymond, his voice resonating with calm assurance. 'Ready when you are.'

Relief washed over Lottie, blending with a newfound sense of purpose as she approached Tauchert. Determined to sidestep any drama or chaos, she moved with deliberate swiftness, mindful to avoid delays that might cost precious time, while also treading lightly to avoid offending Tauchert. With a calm, steady hand, she gently lifted the Chaplin-esque top hat from his head and deftly plucked the cane from his grasp. These subtle adjustments, executed with minimal fuss brought them back on point, restoring a sense of balance and direction.

Tauchert, still in good humour but slightly exasperated, raised an eyebrow and, with a bemused smile, quipped, 'I wish you lot would make up your minds.'

Single-minded in her vision, Lottie turned her attention to Higgins. 'Arthur, you all set?'

Higgins, in turn, sought confirmation from Raymond, who nodded. Higgins readied the camera. 'All set.'

'Action!' Raymond called, and the scene came to life.

Much to Lottie's relief, they depicted a scene true to the original vision of the C J Dennis poem.

Raymond, cognisant of the ever-pressing hands of time and wanting to maintain the production's momentum, consulted his fob-watch and cried, 'Cut! And straight into the long shot for the street scene where Bill and Doreen are introduced by Ginger Mick.'

The production seamlessly moved to the next street. The scene unfolded with seamless precision.

'Cut! Arthur, let's set up for the close-ups.' Raymond's authoritative pronouncement held an air of satisfaction. He was on a roll.

'Got it, boss.' Higgins, the embodiment of efficiency, made fast work of setting up for the next shots.

'Everybody, take five,' called Victor, the diligent assistant overseeing the day's shoot.

As the crew dispersed, Tauchert and Lottie retreated to the cool shade of the surrounding buildings. Their brief time of respite from filming couldn't be spent more differently. Lottie, her mind entwined with her art, adjusted her costume with meticulous care. Her movements were methodical, each fold and seam receiving her undivided attention. In contrast, Tauchert delved into the day's news, perusing the newspaper articles with an initial glance of casual observance until he stumbled upon a particular report that commandeered his attention.

'That's not good,' Tauchert said.

Lottie, curiosity piqued by Tauchert's remark, asked, 'What's not good?'

Tauchert couldn't resist savouring the anticipation he cultivated within Lottie. 'You really want to know?'

Lottie, now a captive of her own curiosity, implored, 'Yes, Arthur. Don't keep me in suspense.'

Arthur obliged by reading from the newspaper article. ' "The Judge, after hearing all the arguments during the six-day hearing, has not only ruled with an injunction against Pugliese exhibiting the picture, *The Church and The Woman*, but also to an account of the profits and an order to deliver up the films and negatives." '

Lottie's shoulders slumped as her breath caught in her throat. She sat motionless, the weight of the moment pressing down on her chest. The pounding of her heart loud and quick. The world around her blurred, and a profound silence enveloped her. ' "Edmund Finn, the novelist of *A Priest's Secret*, published thirty years earlier, believes that Raymond Longford and Humbert Pugliese closely derived the photoplay from his novel. The Judge found in favour, in restitution of the novelist's rights." '

Upon absorbing these distressing revelations, Lottie experienced a profound sense of desolation wash over her, almost to the point where she felt physically ill.

Unaware of her inner discomfort, Arthur continued, paraphrasing the newspaper's statements, 'Says here that Pugliese will appeal it.'

Lottie's countenance reflected her deep distress. She snatched the paper out of Arthur's grasp and, in little more than a strained whisper, said, 'I'll be back in a moment.'

Arthur, the inadvertent provocateur of Lottie's emotional tempest, relished this atypical sight of Lottie fleetingly derailed by the torrent of emotions that cascaded from the written word. 'I'm sure you will, girlie.'

Anger coursed through Lottie's veins in the seething aftermath of the unexpected revelation. She strode purposefully down the street, her gaze fixed sharply on Raymond, who stood observing Higgins meticulously set up the camera. She beckoned Raymond aside, withdrawing to a secluded spot beyond the prying ears and gawking faces of the crew. In the confines of their intimate conversation, she unfurled the damning newspaper article, its words like poisoned arrows that had a very real potential to pierce their tenaciousness.

Raymond scanned the article, moving across the damning verdict etched upon the pages. He voiced an almost irrational hope, 'That's good news about the appeal.'

But Lottie, unflinching in her role as guardian of integrity, was taken aback. 'Raymond, it's anything but good. You and Humbert have been found guilty of stealing from the plaintiff's book. This is devastating to Pugliese's position, not to mention your own reputation.'

Feeling the pressure of a poignant 'what if', Raymond, unable to mask his frustration, doggedly replied, 'Things might have been different if they at least let me testify.'

Lottie, with a furrowed expression, reminded him of the potentially dire financial consequences, 'What if Pugliese comes after us for damages? We can't afford this on top of everything else.'

Raymond sought to temper her unease. 'It won't come to that. He'll win the appeal.'

With her sullen gave fixed on the newspaper in Raymond's hand, Lottie delivered the gravest of ultimatums. 'He better win, and we better hope that Sir Gordon and his investors don't see that news in Adelaide.'

With a solemn nod, Raymond could only agree.

Chapter 11

In the solemn confines of her home study, Lottie laboured long into the night, a solitary maestro of ceaseless toil. These were the nocturnal hours where time was like a persistent companion. Lottie's roles transitioned seamlessly with grace, each a note in a symphony of dedication. That night, she lent her artistry to crafting props as she prepared for the following day's shoot. At the sewing table, the costumes took shape, mirroring her artistic vision.

Subsequently, she relocated to the sturdy desk, where she immersed herself in a world of words while bathed in the delicate amber glow of lamplight. Every keystroke and every character etched upon the photoplay's pages was a tribute to C J Dennis's poetry.

When the unceasing hands of time marked the passage of another hour on the clock above the fireplace, Lottie put on yet another hat. With scissors and tape in hand, she undertook the role of the editor, threading fragments of film into a coherent tapestry of storytelling. Her hands moved deftly among the scattered remnants of celluloid, each splice a considered decision in weaving the segments into a narrative.

The hours unfurled like tendrils of fate. When the embers of her creative ardour had burned low, she emerged from the study, extinguishing the solitary lamp.

In the depths of the moonlit corridor, the house's serenity was gently broken by one of Lynda's coughing fits. Driven by sisterly devotion, Lottie carefully crossed the moonlit room. When she reached her ailing sister's bedside, she saw Lynda, restless and pale, lost in a troubled sleep. Lottie, with a gentle touch, smoothed the blankets. Each movement imbued with tender care, like a guardian angel hoping to relieve her ailing sister's fitful sleep.

And then, as if by some unspoken understanding, Lottie passed the torch of caretaking to Charlotte, who stepped forward in her night clothes.

In the tranquil embrace of the night, Lottie softly whispered, 'Go back to bed, Mother.'

Charlotte took the towelette from Lottie's hand. The women held each other's gazes, their unspoken communication conveying a wealth of information. Charlotte spoke with genuine love and concern when she said, 'She's not the only one I'm worried about.'

In response to Charlotte's sensitive confession, Lottie offered her mother a more prolonged and profound embrace than they usually shared. Charlotte felt the tremor in Lottie's embrace. Without a word, Charlotte wrapped her arms around Lottie, returning the hug. Its warmth offered an unspoken reassurance, an implicit recognition of their shared emotional burdens. As mother and daughter clung to each other, the weight of the world seemed to lessen, just for a moment.

Eventually, Charlotte gently disengaged herself from the embrace but held fast to Lottie's hands. Charlotte's gaze penetrated deep into her daughter's eyes. 'What's going on?'

Lottie hesitated, torn between the urge to shield her mother from the harsh truths of their world and the pressing need to unburden herself of the emotions that built with the latest developments. 'The usual,' she began cautiously, her observation a mere whisper. 'A lot rides on every picture.'

But Charlotte was quick to interject, her worry evident. 'You're working too hard.'

'Mother—'

'Remember what the doctor said. You must get proper rest and take care of yourself.' Charlotte insisted, her concern for Lottie's well-being evident.

In a bid to alleviate her mother's concerns and lighten the mood, Lottie offered a bright smile. 'There'll be plenty of time for that when this picture is finished.'

Charlotte's response was a profound and searching inspection. 'Promise?'

With a steady gaze to assure her mother, Lottie vowed, 'I promise on Father and Rita. I have to get it right. It must be a success, not only for Raymond and me, but for you and Lynda too.'

The burden of their shared dreams and aspirations hung heavily over them, a solemn pact binding mother and daughter in their quest for a better future.

The mere mention of her departed husband and their beloved daughter, both cruelly claimed by the unforgiving clutches of tuberculosis, stirred a tempest of emotions within Charlotte's heart. How she missed them. The heaviness of her grief pressed upon her heart, a constant reminder of the loved ones she held so dear. But Charlotte knew she could ill afford the luxury of getting lost in a melancholic reverie. She was a mother, powerful and purposeful, with two daughters who depended on her indefatigable strength.

Charlotte's voice trembled when she next spoke. 'I'm sorry you've become the breadwinner for this family. It was not the intention.'

In response, Lottie candidly revealed her innermost sentiments. 'I wouldn't be doing it if I didn't love it.'

There was pride in Charlotte's expression. 'Such drive, my girl,' she said, her words awash with warmth and approval.

Lottie, the spirited daughter who sustained the commitment to the aspirations and dreams of their small family, opened a window into her inner world by revealing the complexity of her existence. 'Some days are more frustrating than others. It's like there's three of me. The public me that must show restraint for fear of being judged, then there's the character me, perceived as who I play in the film. It can be quite overwhelming.'

Charlotte, her motherly concern undiminished, gently probed, 'And the third?'

A solitary tear, untamed, traced a delicate path down Lottie's cheek. She briefly closed her eyes. She inhaled deeply, steadying herself against the surge of emotions. 'The private me... with the freedom to speak my mind and be myself. Oh, to be that authentic version of me all the time.' Lottie's vulnerability unveiled the depths of her yearning.

Lottie hugged her mother again, and their warm-hearted embrace sealed their silent pact of love and support.

PART 2 – CAMERAS ROLLING

Chapter 12

I n the quietude of morning and the gentle clinking of utensils and porcelain, Charlotte tended to the morning breakfast rituals.

With the sun's subdued rays filtering through the curtains, Charlotte and Raymond took their customary positions at the well-worn dining table. Raymond, the master of the house, assumed the position of authority at its head while Charlotte occupied her customary place to his left.

Charlotte broke their silence. 'She's doing too much. You're going to kill my girl.'

Raymond's countenance was serious as he defended Lottie's unrestrained spirit. 'I can't make her stop any more than you can.'

Initially, no words came to her lips. How could she argue with the truth? She conveyed her acknowledgement of Lottie's unbridled energy. 'From that time her father and I agreed to put Lottie in your care for the theatre tour all those years ago, I've seen our outgoing little girl blossom into a vivacious young woman who knows her mind, but doesn't know when to take a break.'

Raymond cradled his teacup. Its warmth seeped into his fingers as he sipped the brew thoughtfully. He pondered the profound depths of sacrifice that love demanded. Balancing Lottie's public persona with her private self was a delicate dance for Raymond. He had been captivated by her inhibited spirit from the moment he first saw her on stage, drawn to both her talent and her allure. Leaving behind his family—his wife and son—for Lottie underscored his deep commitment to her. Now Lottie's tuberculosis threatened her health, their relationship and their livelihood, and Raymond risked everything, including his own life, by staying at her side. The sacrifice weighed heavily on him, not just in practical terms but in matters of the heart.

As Charlotte voiced her concerns, Raymond understood her intentions were good. Yet he felt the need to remind her of the immense personal risks he had taken to remain steadfastly by Lottie's side. He considered his words carefully, needing to make his position clear to Charlotte, while not offending her. 'We've all risked a great deal. She does the work of three mean for the picture, we couldn't afford to replace her.'

Charlotte, with a wearied determination, emphasised her plea, 'Then, for all our sakes, stop her pushing so hard.'

Raymond placed his teacup onto the saucer. 'I want Lottie around as much as you do.'

Charlotte needed Raymond to understand their situation fully to convey the precariousness of it. 'I see that now, although it wasn't like that in the beginning. You know her father and I didn't approve of your affair when it started. A married man with a child being unfaithful in the eyes of God. What sort of life would that be for our daughter? To be judged by those in ignorance of the love and respect you and Lottie share. You've more than proved your commitment, which is why I don't want you to experience the abandonment, the grief, of losing the one you love. God knows I've done it twice.' Charlotte, close to tears, busied herself with straightening the cutlery on either side of her place setting.

Raymond placed a hand on Charlotte's trembling one, providing a momentary solace in the face of their shared concern. Charlotte's hands settled.

'You have my word that I'll look after Lottie. No matter what happens. I will make sure you and Lynda will be okay, too.' Raymond's declaration echoed with sincerity. His affection for Lottie and his profound sense of duty for her reverberated in his voice. How could he not? He loved Lottie and all that came with her, including the onus of responsibility for her mother and sister.

'For that, I'm forever grateful.' Charlotte dabbed at her moistened eyes.

His eyes blazing with unfaltering intensity, Raymond declared. 'I promise to—'

Just as the emotions of the morning tableau reached their zenith, Lottie, a portrait of weariness and tenacity, made her entrance. Her query, echoing from the hallway, demanded an explanation, 'To what?'

She lightly kissed Raymond's cheek and took her seat to his right. 'Are my two favourite people conspiring against me?' Lottie joked, although her joviality masked her seriousness.

Charlotte's cheeks flushed with embarrassment, and Raymond, unable to meet Lottie's stare, acknowledged his complicity. Neither enjoyed being caught out by Lottie.

'I don't need special treatment,' admonished Lottie, her posture demonstrating jest and earnestness as she poured her tea.

'We were only—' began Raymond, embarking upon an explanation.

'This is who I am. Of all people, you both know that.' Lottie took her teacup in hand and departed, leaving her presence lingering in the room.

On the tranquil shoreline, Raymond and his dedicated crew laboured to immortalise the love story of Doreen and Bill, their silhouettes painted by the pale moonlight as they paced along the sand.

Raymond turned to Higgins. 'Happy with that, Arthur?'

With the wisdom of countless frames behind him, Higgins replied, 'I am if you are. It's sure going to look romantic.'

Raymond took hold of the megaphone and instructed the two protagonists, 'Okay, Lottie and Arthur. Come over, and we'll get the kissing scene done.'

Tauchert goaded Lottie with a playful dare. 'Race you, girlie.'

Lottie accepted the gauntlet thrown by Tauchert, and they commenced their mock race along the shoreline. Yet, as the race unfolded, Lottie's strength faltered, and her breath escaped her grasp. She lagged behind Tauchert, her attempts to catch her breath proving futile.

Tauchert jested, 'Come on, girlie. You're making it too easy.' Despite his teasing, concern began to creep into his expression.

The light-heartedness of the adventure took an abrupt and devastating turn when Lottie struggled, gripped by a fit of coughing and wheezing. She expelled crimson droplets upon the sand. And then, in an instant of cruel fate, she collapsed.

Tauchert, his jests vanquished by horror, sank to his knees beside Lottie, eyes widening at her distress. Aghast at the sight of the blood, he uttered a heartfelt exclamation, 'Jesus, girlie.' Arthur recoiled. He saw her fear followed by the sting of hurt from his reaction.

In his helpless concern, he offers her his handkerchief and asks, 'Is it—'

'Please, Arthur. Not a word,' pleaded a distressed Lottie.

Arthur's voice cracked with a blend of frustration and anxiety. 'For Christ's sake, we're about to do a kissing scene! Should I be worried?' His questions hung in the air, weighted down by his raw vulnerability and unspoken fears.

'I've been very careful,' Lottie reassured a worried Tauchert.

Tauchert accepted her assertion. What choice did he have? His mind raced to Raymond. Was Raymond even aware of Lottie's condition? Surely not if she was working despite being infected. Was he also at risk?

Tauchert's initial concern deepened as he inquired, 'Does Raymond know?'

Lottie nodded, her eyes betraying the weight of the secret she had carried alone until now. Tauchert, observing the subtle relief in her expression, recognised the unspoken burden she had shared with him, her unintended confidante. Despite his attempt to remain composed, a sense of betrayal gnawed at him. He had worked closely with Lottie and Raymond, yet neither had seen fit to confide in him about her condition. Their secrecy stung, leaving him feeling like an outsider in their carefully guarded world.

'Of course he does,' Arthur, still grappling with the revelation, shook his head in disbelief, his voice conveying a mix of astonishment and bemusement. The responsibility of bearing such a secret would be staggering. Coupled with their professional obligations, the pressure they were under must have been immense. He felt for them, empathising with their plight. Navigating life under such ominous circumstances and living with such an uncertain future couldn't be easy. He offered her his handkerchief, which she accepted gratefully.

'He must never know that you know.' She warned. 'Promise me."

Tauchert shook his head in disbelief. 'You two are full of surprises.'

Tauchert watched as relief flickered across Lottie's face. Her guarded demeanour easing slightly as she finally shared her burden with someone outside her family circle. 'It doesn't usually impact my work.'

At that moment, Arthur understood she was right. The disease had not hindered her on-camera work or her behind-the-scenes production duties. While some days were probably more challenging than others, overall, the impact was negligible. She and Raymond had been business as usual.

'Maybe your work is impacting it,' Tauchert offered, his modulation full of concern.

He could see her struggling, refusing to expose her vulnerabilities. Lottie downplayed the magnitude of her condition. 'It complicates things.'

Tauchert offered his candid perspective with a hint of jest, 'That's one way to describe it.' He expressed his frustration at the circumstances. 'You should've told me... you should've told all of us.'

'You're right.' Lottie admitted.

'You've put us all at risk,' cautioned Tauchert, not meaning to chastise but to make her aware of the risk she posed to him and the rest of the small cast and crew.

His words hit Lottie like a sledgehammer. Did she fully comprehend the consequences of her actions? Arthur understood that Lottie likely never imagined that her condition would be revealed in this manner, let alone to the public. He had to give it to Lottie and Raymond, they kept it a closely guarded secret among the chosen few.

God only knew what she'd been dealing with after having witnessed her father and sister battle consumption. Tauchert didn't understand what she had been grappling with since she tested positive for tuberculosis. How could he? He had only heard how the disease could be emotionally and physically unrelenting. He could only imagine that the toll of keeping her diagnosis a secret had been a burden of equal magnitude.

'Would you have told me?' Lottie asked.

This line of questioning took Tauchert by surprise. After a moment, he replied, 'Ah hell, probably not.'

'Now imagine that you're me... and times your reaction by thousands,' Lottie instructed Tauchert.

He knew that she was right. The stigma surrounding consumption was pervasive.

Lottie, earnest in her concern, brought the relevant issue forward. 'I understand if you don't want to continue.'

Tauchert, with a mock expression of shock, retorted, 'What? You think I want to quit now? I'm finally getting the whole natural acting thing!'

Their shared laughter provided a short period of relief against the background of their newfound secret, but it was short-lived. Lottie's laboured breathing served as a stark reminder. 'I'm serious.'

Tauchert, matching her manner, leaned in and reassured her. 'So am I, for a change. Look, if Raymond hasn't got it from you after all this time, then I think I'm good.'

Appreciative of Tauchert's understanding and loyalty, Lottie had but one earnest request, 'I only ask that you... If people find out... I mean, it could make it very difficult for Raymond and me. It would mean a death sentence for my career. Please, I beg you, no one can—'

Tauchert promised, 'Your secret's safe, girlie.'

Lottie visibly relaxed. No doubt her anxieties were temporarily alleviated by his sincerity.

'Thank you,' Lottie responded.

Raymond approached with a mix of concern and haste. 'You two good? We've got to get these last scenes.'

Arthur saw Lottie's panic as she hastily scattered sand to conceal the blood stains.

Tauchert came to Lottie's defence, reassuring Raymond. 'Good as gold, boss. Good as gold.'

Kneeling, Raymond fussed over Lottie. He noted their actions and the traces of blood, prompting him to ask, 'She told you?'

Tauchert replied bluntly, 'No need for words when you see someone coughing up blood.'

With an air of resignation, Raymond conceded, 'Well, I guess you know now.'

Tauchert, his perspective changed by this revelation, nodded thoughtfully. 'A lot of things suddenly make sense.'

Raymond, overwhelmed by the implications, vented his frustration, 'Goddammit... No one can know. It would kill the picture.'

Lottie, acutely aware of the stakes involved in keeping their secret intact, pleaded, 'Please, Arthur—'

Tauchert, perturbed by the implication that he might betray their secret, asserted with impatience, 'I already told you that I wouldn't tell anyone.'

Raymond expressed his gratitude. 'Appreciate you doing that.'

Scratching his head and contemplating a way to improve the situation, Tauchert offered a different perspective, 'I think you underestimate Lottie's star power.'

Raymond responded swiftly, 'It's too much of a gamble. We've got too much at stake.'

Raymond rose from the sand and tenderly lifted Lottie into his arms. 'I'm taking Lottie home. Arthur, go tell the others that we're done for today.'

In the face of Raymond's determination, Lottie raised her objections, her voice laced with a wilful purpose. 'Raymond, no. I'm fine.'

Raymond's patience dwindled, his disposition urgent as he reiterated, 'Now, Arthur.'

Tauchert, a touch disoriented by the abruptness, sought clarity, uncertainty etched across his features, 'What do you want me to tell them?'

The expiration of Raymond's patience is evident in his strained retort. 'You're an actor, improvise.'

Acknowledging Tauchert's predicament, Lottie intervened, offering a pragmatic solution, 'Tell them I've sprained my ankle, and Raymond is taking me home.'

Arthur set off up the beach.

Lottie's focus returned to Raymond. She endeavoured to alleviate his worries. 'I'll be okay. I just couldn't catch my breath.'

Raymond maintained his protective hold around her, and his expression showed a jumble of persistence and frustration in the face of circumstances beyond his control. 'It's too much.'

She felt her body's weakness descend upon her. She was unable to remain awake.

He punctuated his declaration with a vehement shake of his head and exclaimed, 'Heaven help me. Charlotte's going to have my head.'

Chapter 13

The living room in the Moncur Street residence had undergone a bitter transformation, now appearing more like a sombre hospital ward. A second makeshift infirmary bed had been hastily assembled next to Lynda's and held Lottie's wan form.

Deep in conversation, Charlotte and Raymond, guardians of their fragile universe, hung upon each of Doctor Wilson's hushed words. 'I can't rule out a relapse of the disease.'

Raymond, still gripped by the shock of the recent events, ran trembling fingers through his hair. His internal dialogue was an unrelenting litany of self-reproach and self-interrogation that tormented him without respite. *Could I have finished shooting earlier? Granted Lottie more breaks between scenes, or altered the shooting schedule to spread her scenes over more days and thus provide her with the respite she so justly deserves? What have I done?*

Raymond finally lamented aloud, 'It's all my fault.'

Charlotte's anger, a perceptible presence in the room, raised a tempestuous response to Raymond's torment. 'You promised,' she reminded him, her voice trembling on the precipice of raw grief.

The severity of the situation dawned upon her in all its sombre hues. Her cherished daughter, Lottie, could have met her demise upon the moonlit shore the previous night. The inescapable bitter truth could not be denied, and Raymond's assessment of the blame as being one hundred per cent his own, was a testimony to his actions.

Raymond was the author of their current sorrow.

It was his fault.

The brevity of Charlotte's accusation landed a profound and indelible blow upon Raymond. Her transient anger was a tempest he could weather, but her deep disappointment was harder to deal with. It lacerated his soul and presented a far more formidable adversary that might not pass so easily, or at all. In her reprimand, he sensed the inexorable pressure of his failure to honour his commitment to protect Lottie from harm. The expression of fiery rebuke emanating from Charlotte's eyes, too searing for him to confront directly, left him no choice but to bear her admonishment.

The physician's stern edict delivered yet another blow to Raymond's conscience.

'Until that girl recovers, she's on a total work ban,' Doctor Wilson advised.

Distraught, Raymond's face tightened, the pressure compounding monumentally. His eyes darkened with turmoil as each passing moment added to the invisible weight crushing his spirit. Lottie's fate, the indefinite halt in production, and Charlotte's unforgiving reprimands converged, forming a colossal load of responsibility now threatening to drown him.

Raymond caught a glimpse of Charlotte's small, triumphant smile. That flicker of relief, though a fragile ember, offered a shared sentiment with the doctor. At last, someone sided with her about Lottie's workload. Raymond understood Charlotte's solace in the support, a lone ally in alignment with her profound concern for her daughter's well-being.

Beside them, a faint voice defiantly declared, 'That's not possible.'

Raymond, overcome by a tidal wave of emotions, lowered himself to kneel beside Lottie's bed and clasped her hand in his. Lottie mustered a fragile smile.

The family doctor, seeing Lottie awake, allowed a sigh of relief to escape his lips. A warm smile graced his face, veiling his recent concerns. He moved to the other side of the bed and gently checked her pulse.

The fleeting relief that washed over Charlotte's face swiftly surrendered to a mother's apprehension. 'At some point, you must listen to the doctor,' she admonished with maternal tenderness. It was a modest yet firm reminder.

Raymond, whole-heartedly anchored in his role as the guardian of their shared dreams, strengthened his grasp on Lottie's hand, his face etched with worry that scarcely remained veiled. The spectre of her disease encroaching upon their creative enterprise added a new layer of dread.

While this was not their first brush with the disease, it was the first time it had impacted their work. He could lose her, not only from the production, but from his life. Raymond's voice was layered with tenderness and trembled slightly as he said, 'Lottie, Doc's right. We need you better.'

In the silent language of their intertwined fingers. The depth of his concern was not lost on her, and she deciphered the nuance in his emphasis on 'we.' Yet Lottie refrained from descending into the depths of their apprehension. With the dawn of a new day and feeling rejuvenated by the restorative embrace of the night's rest, she strove to reassure them. 'I feel right as rain today.'

Raymond, recognising the delicate balance between his concern and their shared ambitions, turned to the family doctor. 'How long, Doc?'

Doctor Wilson's response was matter-of-fact. 'At least a week.'

Lottie and Raymond, each grappling with the doctor's unforeseen recommendation, revealed a spectrum of emotions. Lottie's face paled, her breath catching in her throat, while Raymond's jaw tightened.

'A week!' they exclaimed in unison.

The doctor's suggestion of a week's respite stunned Raymond. Lottie noticed Raymond's fists clenched. She sensed his mix of anger and helplessness as none of them had anticipated Lottie would require a full week of rest. That was beyond the scope of their wildest invention. The sense of urgency that drove their creative enterprise clashed with the harsh reality of Lottie's condition, casting an uncertain shadow over their grand scheme.

In her turn, the seemingly excessive prescription for bed rest flummoxed Lottie. Her face displayed a myriad of emotions as she grappled with the impending hiatus from work. The notion of an entire week devoid of work gave rise to a tumultuous ocean of emotions, as Lottie contemplated the ramifications on her well-being, along with the implications for their business of picture-making.

Her musing was interrupted when Charlotte, eternally watchful and protective, imparted a gruff reminder, 'A week is a blip in the bigger scheme of things.' With those words, Lottie knew that Charlotte had directed her anger at Raymond, reminding them that the present act was a fleeting interval in a greater, unwritten epic within life's grand theatre.

Lottie's vexation reverberated within the room, characterised by an intense emotional current surging through her words. 'Might as well be eternity.'

Sensing the imminent quagmire of a family conflict, the doctor opted for a strategic withdrawal. 'I'll be back tomorrow to start the bleedings,' he announced, while methodically stowing his stethoscope.

With a courteous farewell, he took his leave, bidding the ladies adieu before extending a cordial handshake to Raymond.

'Thank you, Doc. I'll see you out.' He then returned his focus to Lottie. His restrained parting gesture, a peck on Lottie's cheek, carried an unspoken understanding of their shared plight. 'I'll go explain that we're shooting as many scenes as possible without you,' he advised. He was not happy with the situation, yet there was no room for self-pity; the show must go on.

In her bedridden frustration, Lottie reached out to grasp Raymond's hand, capturing his gaze. She wielded humour as a coping mechanism. 'Must have been quite a sprain.'

Raymond heaved a sigh. He empathised with Lottie, a sentiment that extended, in truth, to both of them. This predicament marked uncharted territory in their shared professional journey, and he grappled with the unsettling notion that the production might falter irreparably in Lottie's prolonged absence. But what to do?

'What else would you have me tell them?' He asked flatly, with the silent expectation that Lottie, more than anyone, would comprehend the complexities of his predicament.

Raymond was confounded, wrestling with the mounting difficulties of the circumstances.

Lottie paused, her thoughts swirling as she reconsidered her stance. A moment of reflection led her to acknowledge the necessity for a shift in her approach. It wasn't like he could announce her condition to all and sundry. They must stick to their story. 'You're right,' she conceded, her delivery bearing traces of vulnerability. 'It's just that I feel so helpless.'

In this tender moment of shared vulnerability, Raymond keenly sensed Lottie's emotional turmoil. He felt her pain and anguish, yet knew he was powerless to alleviate her suffering. The demands of the day pressed upon him, leaving little room for respite. He had much to do and no time to waste. He donned a façade of fortitude. 'I'll see you later tonight,' he proclaimed, placing a gentle kiss on Lottie's brow before departing.

Lottie and Charlotte watched Raymond's figure recede. Their silent contemplation of his departure reflected a mix of emotions, with the tension from the morning's events still hanging in the air.

Charlotte picked up her needlework and sat down alongside Lottie and Lynda, exhaling a sigh as if to relieve herself of the morning's heaviness. Her sigh carried not only the exhaustion of recent events but also the depth of her maternal worry.

Throughout the doctor's visit, Lynda had maintained a respectful silence, no doubt harbouring her own thoughts and perspectives. Now, however, her inner musings emerged, suffused with a dreamy quality. 'It's kind of romantic.'

Lottie, ensnared in the maelstrom of her thoughts, belatedly registered Lynda's comment. She struggled to comprehend how, in the midst of their professional turmoil, Lynda could broach the subject of romance. The stakes seem overwhelmingly high, and the concept of romance feels irrelevant and incongruous. 'Romantic?' Lottie asked with frustration. She underscored the severity of the last evening's incident, stating, 'I might've become critically ill.'

Charlotte, her needlework briefly suspended, fixed a stern and cautionary look upon Lottie. Her admonishment was pointed. 'Please, no more talk of illness.'

Lynda, feeling guilt-ridden for inadvertently getting Lottie into trouble, hastened to clarify her perspective. She explained, 'No, I meant romantic as in Raymond is your knight in shining armour.'

Still nursing her annoyance and shouldering the repercussions of her mother's reprimand, Lottie delivered a curt rejoinder, 'I'm no damsel in distress.' Her posture stiffened with determination to demonstrate her autonomy and strength, even with the challenges confronting her. She was more than capable of looking after herself.

Charlotte, mindful of the evolving dynamics within their small family unit and their dependence on Raymond, sought to mediate the rising tension. While her anger toward Raymond for endangering Lottie's life was undeniable, she also recognised his role in the family. Their interdependence was beyond doubt, with Raymond serving as the head of the household and a crucial support for the women. She sought to guide her daughters, although her words were primarily for

Lottie. 'Be careful when you dismiss him like you do. Remember how much Raymond has done.'

Lynda agreed with her mother, and her words overflowed with admiration for Raymond. 'He's the love of your life. You're the love of his life. Mother's right. He's done so much since Father and Rita died. That's got to mean something.'

Raymond's contributions to their family loomed large, demanding respect. Both women looked expectantly at Lottie, their eyes brimming with hope that she might heed their heartfelt pleas on Raymond's behalf.

Caught in the crosscurrents of their fervent appeals and the complexities of her entwined personal and professional relationship with Raymond, Lottie contemplated the situation. Her mind tussled with an unspoken longing. *What would my life be like if I hadn't fallen victim to the insidious grip of tuberculosis?*

The disease was a shadow that loomed over her existence, casting its ominous influence on every facet of her life. It was an indefatigable companion who balked at being ignored and carried a sombre reminder of her father and older sister's harrowing fate.

Her introspection plunged her into the abyss of acceptance. *Who am I trying to fool? I have tuberculosis. There is no turning back the clock on that diagnosis.* Tuberculosis was not a mere presence in her life; it was a pervasive force that shaped her choices, her relationships, and her very identity. She stood at the precipice of her own revelation, recognising that, like the playful jest of Arthur Tauchert, if she couldn't beat 'em, she should join 'em. If she could not vanquish her condition, then she must embrace it.

With a solemnity born of acceptance, Lottie revealed her intention to confront the disease head-on, accept its place in her life, and cast aside the pretence that once shrouded it. 'Maybe I don't have to hide it anymore. I've accepted the disease.'

The unexpected turn in the conversation took Charlotte by surprise. She quickly interjected, her apprehension clear in her tone. 'The reality is that while you may have accepted your consumption, others won't. Are you truly prepared to risk all that you've worked so hard for?'

Lynda added, 'I agree with mother. I don't believe you're prepared for what I have endured with consumption. The loss of the ability to do normal things, your friends and the community turning their back on you and your family, feeling sick all the time, and—dare I even think about it—the very real prospect of death.'

Charlotte and Lottie exchanged glances, their eyes widening as Lynda's perspective sank in. It was a revelation, a glimpse into a part of Lynda they had never seen before. Her point of view on death, so candidly expressed, caught them off guard.

'And for someone who has never experienced romantic love, I don't feel that you have thought it through fully, Lottie. You're thinking about your future in the now as a relatively healthy Lottie, not as sickly Lottie. The disease will catch up with you, Lottie, just like it has me and it did father and Rita.' Lynda continued her stream-of-consciousness oration on the matter, 'Why can't you see how good your life is with Raymond as you are? Don't you realise how lucky you are to have a man stand by you and not run the other way, knowing that you have consumption? How many men would stay with a woman who had a death sentence, who could die at any time and infect him?'

'That's enough,' cautioned Charlotte.

'No, mother. Lottie needs to hear this.' Lynda turned to Lottie, 'The answer is very few. How can I make you appreciate what mother and I recognise in Raymond?'

Lottie absorbed Lynda's frank words. She opened her mouth to respond, but no words came; instead, Lottie found herself enveloped in a profound silence. She grappled with the truth Lynda had laid bare before her, fully attuned to the risks entwined with this matter, steered the conversation towards more personal terrain. She used Raymond's all-encompassing devotion as a powerful lever as she pleaded on Raymond's behalf. 'Raymond's risked everything in loving you.'

Lottie, acutely aware of the heaviness of these cautionary words, wrestled with the uncharted territory of revealing her condition to those beyond the protective cocoon of her family. No one knew how people outside her family would react when they learned Lottie had tuberculosis. It was an unknown quotient.

She was also fully cognisant of the lingering uncertainty and profound personal stakes held by her suitor. Lynda's reminder of Raymond's wholehearted commitment echoed within her. *And she is right. Raymond risked his own health to be with me.*

Her thoughts shifted to the path her life had taken, riddled with unforeseen complexities and unanswered questions. She shook her head as if to disentangle her turbulent thoughts and confessed, 'I want... No, I need honesty in my life more than ever.'

With wisdom, Charlotte counselled, 'Start with yourself.' It was a poignant reminder of the precious fragility of life and the capricious hand that fate could deal. Lottie, chastened by the wisdom, recognised the critical nature. She earnestly wrestled with the stark fact that her fate, or Lynda's for that matter, might easily have mirrored that of their father or sister, who had already lost their lives to the same unabating disease they suffered.

'You were very fortunate, my dear,' Charlotte implored Lottie to grasp the delicate balance upon which their family teetered. What she would give to have her darling husband and eldest daughter back with them. Charlotte did not want to confront the haunting prospect of losing either Lottie or Lynda—or both—to their merciless adversary. It was a scenario too unbearable to contemplate.

To shield her mother from further distress, Lottie endeavoured to deflect the exhausting seriousness that loomed over them all. 'You worry too much, Mother.'

Charlotte, however, deliberately upheld the burdensome severity of their circumstances, her response laden with the concern borne of a disease that lingered as an ever-present threat. 'Perhaps you give me too much reason to worry,' she countered.

Their conversation remained unfinished because Victor entered at that moment, his footsteps resounding through the entrance hall. He announced his presence with a casual, 'Only me.'

His arrival provided Lottie with a welcome diversion from the prevailing seriousness. She invited him closer, 'In here, Victor.'

Charlotte, summarily ceasing her needlework, offered Lottie a gentle reminder. 'As per doctor's orders.'

Lottie, her spirit immovable, asserted her need for a semblance of normalcy and the pursuit of her profession. 'I need to work. I feel trapped in here.'

Lynda, whose health was fragile, lent a touch of humour to her words as she jested, 'Oh, thanks very much.'

Realising too late that her words could be misinterpreted, Lottie hastened to amend her statement. 'I didn't mean it like that,' before breaking into a light-hearted smile. She then pulled a dramatic expression and added, 'But a total work ban? You might as well cut off my oxygen supply!'

Victor set down the prop table lamp he'd carried in and shared a heartfelt hug with Lottie. As they separated, it took all of her effort to adopt a brave face. She patted the bed, inviting Victor to sit beside her. Unable to restrain herself, she made a poignant plea, 'I need you to be my eyes and ears, Victor. Please tell me everything.'

Charlotte interjected before Victor could deliver his insights. 'Lottie. A total work ban—'

Lottie, her spirit undimmed by her mother's sternness, engaged in a playful verbal exchange with Charlotte, her pitch retaining its spirited edge. 'Doesn't mean we can't talk about it.'

Victor, witnessing the exchange between mother and daughter, was captivated by the interplay of their contrasting perspectives—one soundly anchored in seriousness and the other exuberantly light-hearted. Charlotte, displaying a fond smile, eventually conceded, realising that there was no restraining her spirited daughter. She returned her attention to her needlework.

Lottie, ever eager to grasp any morsel of information, signalled to Victor to divulge the details. Victor, bearing deep affection for Lottie, willingly obliged and shared, 'Dad said we're going to get through all the scenes that don't feature you.'

Relief swept over Lottie, her fears instantly allayed by the knowledge that the production was forging ahead in the face of her illness. 'That's good. Smart on Raymond's part.'

Victor, however, candidly acknowledges his father's limitations, adding a touch of humour to the conversation. 'Hopefully, it works. Dad's definitely not you in the organisation department... or the writing... or stunts.'

This frank admission elicited a restrained but shared giggle from Lottie and Lynda. Victor was content to see the women in good spirits, even at his father's expense. Charlotte, her heart warmed by her daughters' levity, found her contentment was marred only by Lynda's coughing fit.

Lottie, ever watchful and protective, held her breath, anxiously awaiting the end of Lynda's painful whooping. It was her unspoken prayer that her sister would emerge unscathed.

Lottie grasped Victor's hand, her advice carrying an air of urgency, 'Don't be too hard on your dad. Pictures are the future.'

Victor, offering a rueful smile, shared the burden of his father's expectations, 'He reminds me every day.'

In a gesture of empathy and reassurance, Lottie kindly squeezed Victor's hand, her gaze revealing the depths of her concern. 'He knows what he's talking about. He's seen war. He doesn't want that for you.'

The truth was that Lottie harboured an unspoken fear of Victor enduring the same fate as so many returned servicemen. If they did return, many good men were forever altered by the harrowing experiences of war, and not for the better.

'Could you please tell that to those who have a go at me for not being over there doing my duty for King and Country?' Victor's quiet seriousness underscored the pressure of prevailing societal expectations pressing down heavily upon him that had taken a toll on his mental well-being.

Lottie, to infuse hope and alleviate Victor's pain, offered words of encouragement. 'It's been four years. The Great War can't go on indefinitely.' Her words were a lifeline acknowledging the difficult path Victor had chosen that set him apart from his peers and subjected him to criticism from those unaware of his circumstances. To see his cohorts sign up and head off to war must be alienating. So much was expected of the young man, who until just recently was still a boy.

Lynda, unflinchingly honest, voiced the harsh truth. 'Because there'll be no young men left.'

Charlotte interjected with a glimmer of optimism. 'It must be near its end.' Yet none of them knew when the war would truly come to a close.

Lottie patted Victor's arm in a comforting gesture, delivering a final note of reassurance, 'Besides, you're needed here. We're lucky to have you on the crew.'

Accepting Lottie's reassuring words with a grateful nod, Victor rose from his seat. His gaze turned to the prop table lamp, and he said, 'Speaking of which, I better get back. They need this lamp for the night shoot.'

After embracing Lottie, Charlotte and Lynda in turn, Victor took his leave. As if rejuvenated by the smallest snippet of news from the film set, Lottie watched him go, her spirits buoyed by the connection to the world outside her confined quarters.

Chapter 14

Hours later, under the cloak of night, Raymond and his modest crew gathered to observe Arthur Tauchert enact a scene. Bathed in the soft glow of lamplight, Tauchert portrayed a character engrossed in study at a table.

'And cut! Good job, Arthur, exactly as planned.' Raymond commended before instructing the crew, 'Okay, next set up.'

Under the muted luminance, Raymond's discerning eye caught the figure of Sir David Gordon patiently awaiting his attention. Summoning his courage, Raymond strode over to the financier. 'Good evening. What brings you out at this hour?'

They shared a sturdy handshake, and Sir David said, 'I came to see for myself.'

Raymond reassured him. 'All is well given the circumstances. We're shooting as many scenes without Lottie as we can.'

Sir David delivered a cautious verdict. 'The picture will not sell without her. You've got until the end of the week. Lottie must be back, or we will have no choice but to shut you down.'

Raymond, besieged by desperation and the grim knowledge that such an outcome would ruin him and Lottie, strove to conceal his inner turmoil. He implored, 'Why not suspend the shoot for a few weeks rather than burn the money you've invested already?'

'Time is money,' stated Sir David. 'Get her back, Raymond, and finish the picture.'

As Sir David walked away, Raymond caught movement near the door as Victor emerged from the shadows. Raymond wondered how much of the conversation his son had heard.

In the depths of the night, beneath the watchful cloak of darkness, Raymond and Victor trudged homeward, bearing a collection of props employed in the evening's shoot. Victor shouldered the table lamp as they moved through the streets.

Raymond offered to alleviate Victor's load, 'You sure you don't want me to carry the lamp?'

Victor's response was laced with subtext. 'I think you're juggling enough stuff.' His words hung in the quiet night air.

Raymond stopped in his tracks, caught off guard by Victor's unspoken implications. 'Dammit, son. You weren't meant—'

'You said you want me to learn the business. Finance is a pretty important thing to learn about.' He awaited his father's response with a mixture of trepidation and anticipation.

Slowly turning to face his son, Raymond contemplated the profundity of the matter. 'You can't say a word to anyone, especially Lottie,' Raymond pleaded, effectively enlisting Victor as a confidant.

Victor's brow furrowed. 'What are you going to do?'

Raymond, bereft of a clear path forward, voiced his uncertainties. 'Not sure. We could recast. Lottie would be devastated.'

'As would the investors and audience,' noted Victor with an air of consternation.

'We could push for more time,' Raymond suggested.

Victor replied solemnly. 'Sir David was pretty clear that wasn't an option.'

'I think Lottie could be pretty convincing if she needed to be about time and reassuring Sir David,' Raymond mused, more to himself than Victor.

Victor highlighted the unspoken truth. 'But that requires you telling her.'

Raymond was burdened not only by the physical weight of the props in his grasp but also by the mental burden of his conscience. The rhythm of his speech intensified, rife with urgency, as he expressed his moral conundrum. 'Lottie is the key to everything. I've got to decide what's right for the picture, which may not be the best for Lottie. Or vice versa, what's right for Lottie is not right by the picture.' Raymond's his mind was a labyrinth of conflicting duties.

Victor brimmed with empathy. 'You should talk with her.'

Raymond dismissed the notion with a sombre shake of his head. 'No. Not a word. Not to anyone, you hear?' He waited for Victor's agreement, silently pleading for the young man's loyal discretion.

'Yes, of course,' Victor assured. 'But you can't be making decisions on your own. It's not right.'

Their footsteps led them to an intersection, a symbolic crossroads of their divergent paths.

'See you tomorrow, son.' Raymond, compelled by the load of his responsibilities, shuffled his props and reclaimed the lamp from Victor's grasp. With that final exchange of words, Raymond steered himself away to face his moral dilemmas.

Victor knew the door was still open for Raymond to talk with Lottie and the crew. Raymond would be thinking on it all night.

'Good night, Dad.' Victor watched his tormented father, enshrouded in the heaviness of his unspoken indecision, slowly retreat towards the home he shared with Lottie and her family.

A weary and ravenous Raymond, still bearing the pressure of the day's tribulations, reluctantly settled before the hot meal and frosted glass of beer Charlotte had thoughtfully presented. Dressed in her night clothes and looking like her normal self again, Lottie sipped from a cup of tea. Sensing their need for privacy, Charlotte wordlessly withdrew, leaving Raymond and Lottie to confront the matters looming between them.

Raymond consumed his dinner in silence, laboriously chewing each bite. Each mouthful of beer felt less like nourishment and more like an unwelcome cross to bear. The sustenance offered little solace; it merely added to his obligations. He was acutely aware of the pressing discussion he must have with Lottie that loomed like an unspoken shadow over the table.

'How was your day?' Lottie's question bore a quiet measure of concern as she sensed that all was not well with her lover.

Raymond kept his silence, the beer acting as a companion to his unspoken troubles. The unanswered question left Lottie to tussle with her own thoughts. Perhaps he didn't hear her, or perhaps he was lost within the labyrinth of his thoughts. Lottie extended her compassionate touch, enveloping his hand within her own.

Responding to her warm-hearted gesture, Raymond found his gaze ensnared by hers. Love flowed between them, an undeniable connection. He summoned a brave smile, a testament to his affection for her, even though the growing intensity of their impending conversation pressed heavily upon him. *God, how I love this woman. How on Earth will I be able to start?* Drawing a deep breath, he let the words unfold.

'My day was good. How was yours?' Though carefully chosen, the words belied the inner turmoil he struggled to contain.

Lottie, attuned to the discomfort etched upon Raymond's weary features, mustered her indomitable spirit and said, 'I reckon I'll be right by Monday.' Her tone carried an unshakeable confidence. She wore a façade she had meticulously crafted and gave a performance so good that she almost convinced herself.

This sudden declaration startled the fatigued Raymond, leading to an inadvertent misstep that sent his beer cascading across the table in an amber torrent. The resounding clatter disrupted the silence, and Lottie flinched and stifled a cry as the pain that coursed through her body threatened to overwhelm her. She strove to regain her composure, but she was not alone in her observations.

Raymond was no stranger to the deviousness they employed, and his heart ached deeply to witness the agony she endured while feeling compelled to play the role of never-ending performer to conceal her suffering for his sake.

Disregarding the spilled beer, Raymond moved to Lottie's side. He knelt beside her, eyes focused on the torment etched in her features. His touch was thoughtful and soothing as he delicately assessed her condition, and a noticeable flutter coursed through her body in response. She sought solace in the warmth of his hands, yearning to quell his profound concerns. Lottie wished she could dispel his anxieties and quell the torment that threatened to overwhelm their fragile equilibrium. Their hands entwined, and for a brief instant, the pain receded into the background.

'You're not alright,' he observed with an accentuation of unpacifiable concern, his hands tracing her form as if to assess the damage hidden beneath her brave façade. In her eyes, the depths of his apprehension were mirrored, they were caught in a desperate quest for answers.

She took his hands in hers, intertwining their fingers in a silent plea to alleviate his mounting anxieties. Her touch spoke of a longing for mutual understanding, a communion that transcended words.

'I have to be,' she asserted, her pronunciation losing none of its intensity. 'The picture won't... We'll never recover if we stop now.' It was a stark admission, a truth neither of them could deny, a choice that dangled her health and even her life precariously in the balance. Her unyielding stubbornness remained veiled beneath the façade of strength she presented.

Their eyes locked in a frantic search for a viable solution, an elusive remedy to their predicament. Lottie and Raymond stood on the precipice of an impossible decision.

Raymond was the first to relent, breaking their gaze briefly before looking back at her and cradling her face in his hands. 'We need you to be better.'

Lottie contemplated his meaning. 'We?' she inquired, a note of curiosity lingering in her phrasing.

Raymond affectionately caressed her cheeks. 'Yes, we,' he asserted with seemingly endless surety. 'Your family, the crew, the investors—'

Lottie held his gaze and whispered, 'And you?'

Raymond's unfaltering gaze met hers, as he proclaimed, 'I'd rather shut the picture down than lose you.'

His arms encircled her waist, and he rested his head on her lap. Lottie, hindered by pain, could not lean forward to kiss him, but her fingers moved gently through his hair in a gesture of deep affection.

'What do you mean shut the picture down?' Lottie was taken aback by the mere suggestion of this option. 'I'll be back on set tomorrow.'

'The hell you will!' Raymond exclaimed with fierce firmness, stubbornly refusing to change his opinion.

Lottie pulled herself up, insistent on proving her point as his equal.

He took her gently into his arms, enveloping her in a passionate embrace. He loved her profoundly, and the mere thought of life without her was inconceivable. He tightened his hold, and she let out a pained groan. Reluctantly, he loosened his grip but remained close, refusing to let her slip away. His concern was earnest as he gently kissed her forehead, demonstrating the love that bound them.

Chapter 15

The Sydney shoreline basked in the brilliance of a resplendent day. The very elements seemed to exult in Lottie's return to the set. It was a collective excitement that coursed through everyone present, a sentiment not lost even on Arthur Tauchert, who was typically reserved.

Leading Lottie to a chair, Raymond said, 'This is where I need to see you between takes.'

His eyes aglow with genuine happiness at Lottie's return, Victor approached the duo with a warm, sincere smile and said, 'Good that the old man told you.'

Perplexed by Victor's comment, Lottie glanced at Raymond, who directed a discreet look at Victor that urged him to desist. Victor appeared disquieted, yet his discomfiture paled in comparison to Raymond's profound mortification.

'Raymond?' Lottie asked, a questioning furrow on her brow. Her gaze flitted between the two men.

Victor, apprehensive and looking to leave the uncomfortable exchange, offered a diversion. 'Is that Arthur I hear calling for help?'

With a tinge of exasperation, Raymond retorted, 'You've certainly given more than enough here.' The impulse to throttle Victor remained buried beneath layers of affection and concern and would not see the light of day.

Victor, astute enough to decipher his father's frustration, swiftly departed in the direction of the crew gathered nearby.

Lottie sat in a simmering silence, her eyes fixed on Raymond, penetrating the depths of his soul, waiting for the revelation that lingered in the stifling air. It was a protracted pause, thick with discomfort and the distress of unspoken truths.

The point of reckoning arrived. Raymond laboured to find the best words to navigate them through the treacherous currents of their predicament. Raymond finally broke the suffocating stillness. 'Sir David visited the set the other night...'

'And?' Her alarmed expression underscored the significance of the events she had been kept in the dark about.

Raymond continued, driven by a sense of liberation and an overwhelming urge to disclose. 'If you weren't back by now, the film would have been shut down.'

The words cascaded from his lips, unburdening him of the financier's dire ultimatum. In laying bare the crux of the matter, he felt, for the first time, strangely relieved of his burden.

But for Lottie, the revelation landed an unexpected blow and bore the sting of betrayal. The shock of Raymond's concealment sent ripples of disbelief and hurt through her, shaking the foundations of their partnership.

Raymond's briefly shed discomfort reclaimed him as he gazed upon Lottie's expressive face. 'I wanted to tell you,' he implored, his murmur fraught with remorse and the desire to mend the rift.

Lottie, her inference brittle with the sorrow of revelation, charged forth with the pain of betrayal. 'But you cut that scene.' The accusation was borne of a deep-seated sense of injustice. The disbelief swirled in her eyes, a poignant reminder of the profound disappointment within her. Even in her turmoil, she knew Raymond's actions were intended to protect her, but the agony of not being trusted with this monumental decision sliced to her very core.

Raymond, caught between a fervent wish to explain himself and a throbbing awareness of the pain he had unwittingly inflicted, stumbled over words of justification. 'I did it for—'

He faltered, realising there was no easy redemption for breaching her trust. He faced a stark reality that threatened to cleave the bond between them.

Despite her aching heart, Lottie chose a path of quiet resolution over anger. She gathered her composure, a paragon of professionalism even in the face of personal hurt. Her words were laced with persistence as she reminded him of their objective, 'We have a picture to make. That's our only priority.'

Raymond sensed the transformation in Lottie's pitch and attitude. Chastened by her response, he was propelled into overdrive in a whirlwind of regret and determination to mend the rupture. He embarked on a fervent appeal, the words tumbling from his lips with an urgency born of his deep love for her, 'I did it for you. I did it for us.'

In response, Lottie, composed and undeterred, steeled herself against her emotions, seeking resolution. She did not let anger consume her; instead, she addressed the core issue with subtle courage. 'Good God, Raymond. I love that you care for me so much more than finishing the picture. But personal life aside... As business partners, we're meant to share everything that affects the delivery of this picture.' She struggled to maintain her sense of calm, her emotions swirling beneath the surface, threatening to engulf her.

Raymond, struggling with the consequences of his actions, attempted to explain, 'As the man, that's my—'

'Times are changing,' Lottie interrupted. 'That means you need to change too, Raymond.' Her words, bearing the weight of expectation and earnestness, carried an insistent plea for respect, both as a person and as an equal partner.

Raymond, his defences crumbling, started again. 'But—'

'You're not my guardian anymore. You're my partner,' Lottie cut him off again, then imposed her own ultimatum. 'If what you and I have is to work, you need to promise that you will not keep things from me.'

Raymond grabbed hold of the opportunity to negotiate and countered with his own condition. 'As long as you promise you'll focus on your health. Will you do that?'

'I promise.' Lottie nodded and a fragile truce emerged.

Raymond consulted his fob-watch, an ever-present companion in his role as a producer-director. With their understanding reached, he proceeded to his next task.

Later that day, Raymond embarked on a pilgrimage down a narrow laneway nestled in the heart of Woolloomooloo. The suburban setting was utterly at odds with the sun-drenched beaches of Sydney and delved into a working-class area of sinister reputation.

He arrived at a modest townhouse, its timeworn façade indicating a life marked by toil and hardship. He tapped gently on the weathered door.

After a pregnant pause, the door creaked open, revealing a woman whose face was etched by the hardships of the lower class. Her stare, piercing and appraising, swept over Raymond, taking in his three-piece suit and dignified hat with a mixture of curiosity and wariness.

'Good afternoon—' Raymond started.

'Whatever it is, we can't afford it,' her voice verged on a high-pitched screech.

Raymond, compelled to correct her misapprehension, offered his most genial smile. 'You don't know what it is yet.'

The woman sternly rebuked what she perceived as his planned exploitation of the impoverished. 'Don't need to. All dressed up in your fancy suit and hat, preying on us poor people.'

Unaccustomed to such a curt reception, Raymond found himself in a dilemma. He was in uncharted waters as he urgently needed a location for the forthcoming shoot. Taking another approach, he removed his hat and meticulously smoothed down his hair. Having heard their voices—and sensing a spectacle—a small gathering of neighbours collected and edged in, inquisitive ears tuned to the unfolding drama.

Seeking to mend the rift, Raymond employed his most persuasive charm. 'Perhaps we can start again. I'm Raymond Longford. Do you have any objection to my using your front door and a portion of these premises for filming?'

The woman, immediately taken aback, pondered the request. 'For filmin', you say? I'm not sure my humble home is near grand enough for the pictures.'

Recognising an opportunity, Raymond pressed forward and swiftly moved in. 'Oh, that's quite all right. Any old ramshackle house situated in a lane of disrepute will do.'

Moving even closer, her neighbours were increasingly drawn to the escalating drama.

The woman, taking affront, grew indignant. 'Let me tell you, it's my house, and what's more, if it's good enough to raise my five kids, then it's too good for your bloody picture!'

Raymond, faced with the surging ire of the neighbours who circled him like sharks, was clearly out of his depth. He conceded to the woman's opinion that her house, imbued with the struggles of life, should not be tarnished by the vanity of cinema.

'It's lucky for you, my husband ain't home!' The woman warned an embarrassed Raymond.

With the grace of an experienced diplomat, he executed a strategic retreat. With neighbours in hot pursuit of the unwelcome interloper in the sanctuary of their lives, Raymond made his escape.

A short while later, Raymond retraced his steps to the narrow laneway, this time with Lottie at his side. The distress of his previous encounter sat heavily on his shoulders, leaving him disconcerted.

'It's embarrassing...' Raymond began, his revelation laden with chagrin.

Lottie reassured him. 'Put your ego aside, Raymond. If you've got your heart set on this location, then let's see if we can convince the woman otherwise.'

Though his desire for the location remained unchanged, Raymond was sceptical about whether they would gain the woman's cooperation. Unlike their previous venture in the park, where they could skirt the watchful eyes of the authorities overseeing filming permits, they needed her permission. He issued a warning to Lottie, 'She's got a voice like a banshee.'

As she always saw the good in people, Lottie countered, 'I'm sure you just caught her on a bad day.'

The alley woman, spotting Raymond's return, called out to him in her shrill, disapproving tone, 'You again?'

In a whispered aside, Lottie murmured to Raymond, 'Maybe it's a bad week.'

He replied in an equally hushed manner, 'Or year.'

Lottie and Raymond cautiously approached the woman who made a pointed comment. 'Bring another with ya to see how the other half live?'

Raymond directed a knowing look towards Lottie, his expression signalling an unspoken, *I told you so*. Lottie, in response, took a beat to gather her thoughts and formulate her approach.

Turning on her charm, Lottie extended a welcoming hand towards the woman. Exuding charisma, Lottie introduced herself, 'Hello, I'm Lottie. Lottie Lyell.'

The woman, rendered instantly speechless, processed the astonishing reality that the luminous star of Australia's theatre and silver screen was standing before her. Furthermore, Lottie was engaging her in conversation. In that instant, Raymond, who had stirred her emotions earlier, seemed to fade into oblivion.

Overwhelmed and starstruck, the woman's demeanour transformed, and her voice assumed the modulation of a young, excited girl. 'As in Lottie Lyell, the star from the theatre and pictures?'

Lottie bestowed her most radiant smile and confirmed, 'The very same.'

'Gladys, did you hear that?' The alley woman excitedly cried.

Gladys and the other neighbours gather around the trio. Although they all gave the evil eye to Raymond, their reverence for Lottie's presence remained riveted.

The woman, transformed as though by magic, poured forth her adoration. 'Gladys and I loved *The Woman Suffers*.'

Gladys chimed in, 'Myrtle's right, it was like I was watching my life on the screen.'

Leaning closer to Lottie, Myrtle adopted a conspiratorial inflection as she said, 'Gladys' husband did a runner. Left her with four kids to raise on her own.'

Lottie, her heart brimming with empathy, recognised the trials faced by both women. While their circumstances were starkly different from her own, she understood how easily her mother and sisters could have faced a similar plight following her father's passing if it not been for Raymond's devoted support.

Myrtle's voice shed its rough edges. 'It really meant something to us.'

Lottie was deeply moved by the women's heartfelt connections to her earlier film. Similar expressions of appreciation had reached her ears from women in all walks of life. 'I'm touched. It has definitely struck a chord with audiences all over the country.'

'Especially here,' added Gladys.

Lottie beamed with pride as she explained, 'That's the type of pictures we're making. Ones that mean something to not only you and your neighbours in the city but also in country towns. Our next picture is based on C J Dennis's book of poems, *The Songs of a Sentimental Bloke.*'

Myrtle's voice became shrill again, and she pointed at Raymond. 'He didn't tell us that.'

Raymond, clearly ill at ease, rolled his eyes.

Understanding the challenge, Lottie executed a strategic diversion, capturing the women's attention with an earnest and heartfelt appeal. 'Our plan is to make the best Australian picture to date. We want this iconic love story to appeal to all the hardworking Australians like yourselves. We want Bill and Doreen to represent you and what all you stand for.'

Fortuitously, Myrtle and her neighbours, captivated by Lottie, embraced her words.

Lottie continued her impassioned pitch to the gathered residents. 'And that's why Raymond wants to capture the essence of life in this part of the country.'

In unison, the group redirected their gaze to Raymond, who squirmed under their collective scrutiny.

Myrtle, her harsh frame of mind softened, cast an approving look over Raymond and spoke more kindly, 'Well, if you're with Lottie Lyell, you're okay.'

The small assembly of residents enveloped Lottie, leaving Raymond with no alternative other than to witness Lottie doing what came naturally to her: bringing out the best in people.

Chapter 16

H aving secured the alley location and successfully averted the crisis, Raymond experienced a rare state of relaxation, almost buoyancy. Not even having to rise from the armchair to answer the door brought down his mood.

He answered the front door of the home he shared with Lottie and her family and was greeted by a young telegram boy. The boy handed over a telegram, which Raymond accepted with practised ease and rewarded the lad with a tip. He watched the boy pedal away from the scene on his bicycle before returning inside.

The telegram was addressed to Raymond and Lottie. It was from J D Williams. Raymond's curiosity was instantly stirred. He unsealed the telegram and read the missive. After taking in the words, he closed his eyes. His earlier sense of ease and buoyancy vanished, replaced with a mood that was far more sombre.

'Who was at the door, dear?' Charlotte inquired.

'Telegram delivery,' came Raymond's flat reply.

Charlotte picked up Raymond's downcast tone and scrutinised him. 'Everything alright?'

Aware of Charlotte's interrogating gaze, Raymond quickly recovered his composure, masking his emotions behind a cheerful disposition. 'Yes, yes. I have to take care of something. Let Lottie know I'll be back later.' Raymond forced a smile before donning his hat and briskly departing on foot, leaving a sense of mystery in his wake.

Raymond tried in vain to engage in a civil discussion with a conservatively dressed Melena in their conservatively decorated sitting room in the meticulously maintained conservative suburban home they had once shared as husband and wife.

Even with his best efforts, tensions escalated as Raymond and Melena faced off. Mid-argument, the atmosphere was suffocating, mirroring their intense hatred for each another.

'You call me selfish! You're making a fool of me and a mockery of our marriage,' Melena's shrill voice pierced the air with accusation.

'No, I'm asking out of respect for our marriage,' Raymond countered, pleading as he struggled to maintain his composure in the face of Melena's infuriating manner.

Melena scoffed. Her disgruntlement seemed to grow with each passing second. How could Raymond claim to uphold the sanctity of their marriage? He disrespected their marriage the day he started his affair with Ms Lyell. And again, he appeared in her home here asking for something she was morally against. She was mortified by his persistence on the matter. The more she considered it, the more anguish and anger she felt towards Raymond and his mistress. Anger built within her body, and her mind was a torrent of rage and melancholy. The mere mention of his mistress reignited the flames of anguish, intensifying her resolution not to give him what he so desperately wanted.

Raymond, seeing Melena's building ire, attempted to defuse the situation. Instinctively, he reached out to placate her, but she was in no mood to accept his attempt to quash her rage. She rebuffed his gesture, refusing to be pacified.

'Besides, the Church would never allow it,' hissed Melena, embodying the essence of a woman scorned.

Raymond, helpless in the face of her fury, was at his wit's end. 'I don't know what else I can do to lessen your hurt.' She brushed his hand away, further rejecting his attempt to calm her.

'You tell of your love for Lottie, but all you've brought me is pain,' Melena's voice quivered with emotion as tears welled up in her eyes. With persistent obstinacy, she closed the distance between them. Her gaze pierced Raymond's soul as she screamed, 'You abandoned us!'

'You know that's not true. I stepped up and married you. I've said I'll continue to support you.' Raymond's disclosure carried an inflection of strained patience as he struggled to maintain decorum in the face of her outburst.

'Get out!' She screeched. Her flushed face betrayed her inner turmoil as she pushed hard against his chest. As much as Melena wanted her husband permanently back in their matrimonial home, she wanted him gone at that moment.

Raymond stood moored, absorbing her fury. While he wanted nothing more than to get the hell away from Melena, he was immovable. 'Please. I beg you.'

Melena remained immovable, knowing full well her power in the situation. She defiantly growled, 'You stand here begging me, but you won't beg your precious Lottie to leave our marriage.'

Raymond fought to control the anger boiling like molten lava within him. He glared at Melena with silent frustration. The familiar pattern of her riling him up to a point where they wound up screaming at each other exasperated him, and he didn't know how to break the stalemate. He turned away and retrieved his hat with an air of resignation, silently acknowledging yet another futile attempt to bridge the divide.

A despondent Raymond walked out, his hands empty and heart heavy with conflicts unaddressed—and no closer to manifesting what he truly desired.

Chapter 17

Woolloomooloo bustled with activity. On a nearby wharf, returned servicemen alighted from a navy transport ship, and jubilant cheers erupted from crowds welcoming the men home from the Great War.

At the filming location, a sizable crowd had gathered, drawn by the allure of Miss Lottie Lyell. Word that Lottie Lyell was filming on the wharf had spread like wildfire, creating a stir of excitement. It was mayhem as the men, most of them in military uniform, jostled for a prime position to get a glimpse of Australia's sweetheart.

As Victor moved through the throng towards the set, he was heckled with taunts and jibes about his perceived lack of wartime service for King and Country. Witnessing the commotion and escalating tension, Raymond and Lottie exchanged concerned looks, wary that Victor may face further conflict because of Raymond's anti-war stance.

With a flash of inspiration, Lottie hit upon a plan. 'Follow my lead.' With nimble agility, Lottie ascended a stack of wool bales, cargo waiting to be transported, to rise above the tumultuous crowd.

Perched atop the makeshift stage, she began to serenade the crowd with the ethereal melody of *The Curse of An Aching Heart*. Slowly, the clamour of the crowd subsided as, one by one, the audience became enraptured by her angelic voice. She wove a spell of enchantment, and the crowd grew silent in appreciation.

Arthur Tauchert, emboldened by the magic and spontaneity, joined Lottie in song atop the wool bales. Tauchert's rich tenor vocal blended harmoniously with Lottie's voice. The crowd, captivated by the duet, swayed in unison, swept away by the song's haunting beauty.

Lottie motioned for Victor to join them. He shook his head, remaining firmly rooted in place, his reluctance evident. Undeterred, Lottie signalled to him again. Sensing the opportunity, Raymond added his good-natured encouragement, nudging his son forward to join Lottie and Tauchert.

Lottie orchestrated a transformative and memorable occasion atop the bales, coaxing a reluctant Victor to join her in the spotlight. Gently, she guided him into the rhythm of the popular melody. His initial hesitation seemed to melt away with each note.

The song had a hypnotic effect on the burgeoning crowd. Their collective gaze was fixed on Lottie as if under her spell. When they reached the chorus, the audience joined in, their powerful vocals rising in unison with an almost otherworldly harmony. Even Raymond and the crew were swept up in the joyous occasion and added their voices to the song.

During the musical esprit de corps, a photographer captured a fleeting instant of magic—Lottie and Victor united in song, framed by the backdrop of jubilant returned servicemen.

It was a snapshot of pure joy—where all was forgiven for Victor. As the final notes faded, any lingering tensions were swept away in the tide of celebration. Lottie's embrace of Victor gave a clear impression of a silent declaration to the crowd that, at that moment in time, all differences were set aside in favour of shared harmony.

As they descended from their stage atop the wool bales, Lottie and Victor were met with heartfelt congratulations rather than jeers.

Tauchert followed suit; however, his contribution seemed to have gone unnoticed in the music-induced euphoria. 'I was up there too, you know,' he said, but his words were drowned out by the revelry of the crowd.

When the crowd finally dispersed, Lottie and Victor were engaged in conversation with a small group of returned servicemen, their faces still flushed with the thrill of the impromptu performance.

'How would you all like to be in the two-up scenario we're filming later? Lottie asked, her manner warm and inviting.

The men's eyes lit up with excitement. To be immortalised on film alongside the beloved Lottie Lyell was an opportunity they had only ever dreamed of. How could they possibly refuse?

As the producer and protector of the filming schedule, Raymond consulted his fob-watch. He needed to get back on track if they were to complete this picture. He extended his hand and engaged in firm handshakes with each serviceman. 'Thanks for your help. Now Miss Lyell, Arthur and Victor have to prepare the next scenario.'

In a show of camaraderie and gratitude, the uniformed men reciprocated the gesture, offering heartfelt handshakes to Lottie and hearty pats on the back for Victor. With a wave and a smile, the dynamic duo returned to the fold of the film crew huddle.

Raymond lingered with the servicemen, silently listening to the tales of valour and sacrifice they shared.

One of the men, his eyes reflecting a depth of experience that belied his youthful appearance, turned to Raymond with a probing stare. 'You serve?'

Raymond's sombre response was matter-of-fact, 'Boer War.' The words fell from his lips with a sense of resignation. It was a period in his life that he preferred to forget.

The serviceman offered a sympathetic nod, his expression a dark reminder of the shared burden of wartime memories. 'Never leaves you, does it?' he remarked, the words resonating as more of a statement than a question.

Raymond's silence lingered, heavy with unspoken words until he finally nodded. 'Never.' His murmured response overlayed with the echoes of regret. 'I offered to go to the battle fronts and film, but the Government declined.'

The serviceman looked Raymond directly in the eye. 'You did the right thing for your son, keeping him here.' His manner was humble and ineluctable. 'If the war didn't get him, the Spanish Flu probably would.'

Raymond's expression softened. He appreciated the counsel of wise words of comfort as solace for the tumult of his inner turmoil. 'Unfortunately, he doesn't see it that way,' he confided, his revelation coloured with a hint of sadness.

The returned serviceman nodded in agreement, knowing all too well the distress of Raymond's torment. It was a silent salute to the struggles borne by those who had tasted the bitter fruits of war.

That evening, in the dimly lit confines of her meticulously kept living room, Melena waited in seething silence. Her fingers were clenched tightly around the edges of a newspaper folded in her lap. Her eyes fixed on the front door with an intensity that bordered on fury. The air was heavy with anticipation. She waited for Victor, a coiled spring of resentment and frustration.

Oblivious to his mother's presence, Victor bound through the front door. The carefree outlook he donned by the wharves that morning was still firmly in place, and he hummed *The Curse of an Aching Heart*. The joyful melody seemed out of place when compared to Melena's brooding silence.

A highly strung Melena confronted Victor, pouncing on him like a jaguar takes down its prey. She brandished the newspaper in his face like a weapon. Her eyes ablaze with fury and venom. The suddenness startled Victor, who recoiled and ceased his humming. His smile faltered, the warmth of his expression melting away in the face of Melena's ire.

Enraged, she thrust the newspaper in Victor's face and unfolded it to reveal a photo of Lottie and Victor. The image of them joyfully singing was plastered across the front page. Victor smiled at the fresh memory the photograph elicited.

'Have fun today?' Melena demanded, her words dripping with disdain as she gestured angrily at the damningly joyful image of Victor and Lottie. Victor's cheerful expression was crossed by a flicker of unease as he realised the magnitude of Melena's rage.

She fixed her wild gaze on Victor. 'You and the perfect Miss Lyell... if only her fans knew,' Melena threatened, her words laden with bitterness and resentment.

Shocked as he was with the onslaught of his mother's wrath, Victor was disinclined to let her tarnish Lottie's name without a fight. Collecting his courage, Victor steeled himself against his mother's menacing veiled threat and defended Lottie. 'She saved me from that crowd,' he declared, his voice trembling.

He braced himself, fearful of her reaction. Her geyser of fury erupted in spectacular fashion.

Filled with rage, her face contorted with anger as she spat, 'Well, I raised you, not her. Or your father, for that matter.'

A look of apprehension replaced his fearful expression as Victor struggled to find the appropriate words to placate her. Melena's disappointment bore down on him, adding to the pressure. His heart was heavy with sorrow at the sight of his mother consumed with rage. Attempting to allay her distress, he murmured, 'I know that, Mother.'

Melena was ensnared by the tangled web of her own conflicted emotions, her mind a maelstrom of discordant thoughts and bitter regrets. She didn't seem to hear Victor's calm life buoy thrown into the thick of the tempest of her ire, lost in a downward spiral of her conflicted thoughts. 'I wanted you saved from the war. Not pushed into their world. Lottie will never be your mother!'

Victor lowered his voice and softly said, 'Lottie's not trying to be my mother. You're my mother.' His words reminded her of the unbreakable bond that bound mother and only child together, even when in extreme adversity.

Victor's words seemed to pierce the veil of Melena's despair, drawing her back from the brink of her inner turmoil. Melena grasped Victor by the shoulders with fierce intensity and sternly instructed, 'You'd better remember that.'

In a somewhat misguided attempt at mediation, Victor tried to bridge the growing chasm between his parents. 'She's a great artist, and with all that's going on—'

Melena's steadfastness is unsympathetic, and she would not be swayed by Victor's plea. 'So now your father has you doing his bidding? I will never grant him that divorce.' Melena pushed Victor away, in a motion symbolic of the bitter rift that had torn her family apart.

Victor's shock quickly gave way to exasperation. In frustration, he pushed back against his mother's stubbornness. Shaking his head, he demanded, 'What's wrong with you? She's really sick, and you—'

'With what?' Melena spat back, her defences firmly entrenched, as she challenged her son to explain.

In that split second, Melena saw that Victor realised the futility of his action. His mistake was thinking he could make her understand the enormity of Lottie's condition. His attempt to bridge the gap between his parents had only widened the divide, leaving him feeling more helpless than ever. He needed to swiftly bring this cross-examination of a conversation to a close.

Melena knew her only child better than he knew himself. She detected the unease emanating from her son. A notable tension hung in the air. She sensed his heightened fear and that there was something he was not sharing with her.

She probed deeper, pressing him in a way only a mother knew how to do. 'A child has no secrets from their parent,' she said, her tone soft yet nuanced with an unmistakable undercurrent of concern.

Victor felt cornered and unable to evade his mother's penetrating gaze. He had reached a point of no return, leaving him exposed and vulnerable.

And Melena knew it.

Chapter 18

O n set for the factory entrance scene, a thick tension grew between a visibly shaken Victor and Lottie and Raymond who faced Victor with stern expressions.

Trying to keep his frustration under control, Raymond paced the length of the makeshift office, away from the crew and extras. 'Bloody hell, son, it wasn't your news to tell.' Raymond's comment carried a mixture of disappointment and exasperation.

Victor's heart sank even lower as he realised the extent of his mistake in trying to mediate the emotional minefield that lay between his warring parents. His eyes welled with tears of regret.

Lottie sensed the emotional turmoil enveloping both men. 'Well, she knows now.' Her words were laced with quiet strength and empathy as she attempted to defuse the growing tension between father and son.

Raymond remained steadfast, unwilling to let Victor off the hook so easily. Given Victor's first-hand experience with Melena's volatile nature, he had expected better from the boy. After all, he lived with Melena, and had seen her volatile and vindictive nature. The boy was a people pleaser.

Frustrated by the situation, Raymond grumbled, 'Still, the boy should have known better.'

Lottie picked up that Raymond was disappointed in his son. She couldn't help but feel for Victor, who was only trying to help. He had been caught in the crossfire of his sparring parents too often. Melena's attitude was not the boy's fault. It broke Lottie's heart to see the men in her life upset like this. Lottie inserted her thoughts, saying softly, 'He was only trying to help.'

If he could rewind time and take it all back—erasing the events of the previous evening—Victor would seize the opportunity without hesitation. He believed he was doing the right thing, but on reflection, Victor realised he had done everything but help on this occasion. He went too far, was too involved, and got in over his head. Regardless of being an adult in age, he realised he still had a lot to learn about complex relationships and personalities. He was intimately aware of his mother's volatility and realised he should have exercised greater caution. It wasn't like he didn't know. Like his dad rightly judged, he should have known better.

'I'm sorry,' Victor uttered with remorse.

'Maybe it's for the best,' said Lottie, offering a glimmer of positive perspective.

Buoyed by Lottie's optimism, Raymond dared to entertain the possibility of a silver lining. 'Now perhaps Melena will realise why I've been asking and stop being so angry about us.' Perhaps, with this revelation, Melena would finally understand his motives and relinquish her anger. Maybe, just maybe, this would pave the way for the dissolution of their strained marriage, granting Raymond the divorce he so desperately desired, the official end to their sham of a marriage, so he could finally marry the woman he truly loved. Lottie.

Victor's sobering revelation shattered Raymond's hopeful scenario. 'She's beyond angry.'

Arthur Higgins tentatively approached the huddled trio. He sensed the unvarnished tension like a foreboding cloud hovering over the fraught family dynamic.

He nodded to Lottie and Raymond. 'All set, boss.'

Raymond checked his fob-watch and released a heavy sigh. With a sense of urgency, he brought the impromptu family meeting to a close, 'We'll deal with this later. We've got a film to make.'

Victor, wiping away his tears, followed Raymond and Higgins towards the camera, leaving Lottie to contemplate the news of Melena's latest outburst, each more and more volatile than the previous.

Lottie redirected her focus back to editing the photoplay. She was deep in her creative process at her makeshift office, deftly tapping the keys on her typewriter, when a well-dressed man in his thirties entered.

J D Williams exuded an air of American charm—he was charismatic, larger than life and undeniably likeable—as he stopped before her, waiting patiently. It took a beat for Lottie to register his presence.

Surprised by his unexpected appearance, she jumped up from her seat and enveloped him in a warm embrace. 'What are you doing here?' she exclaimed, as genuine excitement lit up her face.

'I've been down in Melbourne checking on my Luna Park operation and thought I would see you and Raymond before I head back to America,' J D explained with a friendly smile, bringing a welcome burst of energy to the set.

'Oh, Raymond will be pleased to see you,' she gushed, her enthusiasm bubbling over. 'The picture is going so well.'

J D regarded her with an amused expression. 'That's not what I heard, but I'm glad you're feeling better.'

Caught off guard, Lottie realised her slip. She attempted to lighten the mood with a playful tease, 'Not much gets past you.'

Unfazed, J D continued their banter, his spirit light with a hint of seriousness underlying his words, 'Your answer to my telegram has. Unless, of course, you're not interested?'

Perceiving his earnestness, Lottie's interest is piqued. 'What do you mean?'

J D was straight up with her, clarifying, 'My telegram. You have an offer to star in what I hope will be the first of many pictures in America.'

Confusion clouded Lottie's expression.

Patiently, J D elucidated, 'I double-checked with the telegram company. It was delivered to your Moncur Street residence.' He watched her closely, waiting for a response.

Lottie's brow furrowed in bewilderment. 'I swear I didn't get anything. I would have responded,' she insisted.

J D was perplexed, his confusion deepening. 'I knew that you would have. That's why I checked on the delivery status. Raymond definitely signed for it,' he revealed, again searching her face for any indication of recognition.

He noticed a distinct change in Lottie's overall manner as a wave of realisation washed over her. Her cheerful way of carrying herself shifted. A sense of troubled disappointment settled upon her features.

'Excuse me for just one moment, J D.' She abruptly left the room, leaving J D standing there, bewildered by her sudden departure. His eyes tracked her moving towards the camera set up, leaving him to wonder what would happen next.

In the middle of shooting the factory entrance scenes, an exasperated Lottie strode up to Raymond. With a combination of frustration and controlled rage, she took a robust grip on his arm and steered him away from the now curious crew and extras.

'Damn you, Raymond. You promised,' she admonished him in a mood of simmering anger that caught everyone, especially Raymond, off guard.

He was shocked and confused by Lottie's outburst, for it was expressed during a take. Her fury was visible. He tried to placate her while simultaneously issuing instructions to the crew. 'What? Cut! Everyone break for five minutes!'

Undeterred by how her confrontation may be interpreted, Lottie issued her own stern ultimatum to Raymond. 'Make that forever if you can't tell me the truth right now!' Lottie warned, her eyes flashing with an intensity he'd rarely witnessed.

Aware of the prying eyes around them, Raymond turned his back on the growing number of immensely interested bystanders. He struggled to find a semblance of privacy.

'Ain't love grand?' Arthur Tauchert chuckled, oblivious to the severity of the conversation about to unfold.

'Shut up, Arthur,' Raymond and Lottie demanded in perfect unison. Their joint directive cut through the air.

Raymond reached for Lottie's arm. As the crew and extras observed with rapt attention, Lottie forcefully shook off Raymond's grasp. She was beyond wanting to be soothed.

Raymond, struggling to maintain his composure, pleaded, 'Please don't go.' He understood how desperate he must appear to her but didn't care.

Lottie's jaw tightened. It took all of her self-control to refrain from throttling him in front of everyone. With her trademark quiet strength of character, she challenged him with a simple yet important question, 'Did you ever think that perhaps I need to do this?

Raymond's brow furrowed in confusion. This was unknown territory for him as he'd never seen her like that before. Her sudden intensity made him unsure of where she was leading the conversation. He desperately wanted everything to just go back to normal.

Undeterred, Lottie pressed on, her eyes fixed on Raymond and her words coming with a sense of urgency as she laid out her vision for their collective future. 'This could theoretically set us up. Mother, Lynda, our company.'

Feeling the pressure of responsibility bearing down on him, Raymond desperately tried to reassure her. 'I can make things work here for all of us.'

Lottie asserted her authority with intransigent dogma. 'It's my obligation to look after my mother and sister.'

'The telegram—' Raymond started.

'It's not about the damn telegram!' Lottie cut him off with the sharp retort.

While a fog of uncertainty descended upon the crew and bewildered bystanders as to what Lottie was referring to, there was no such confusion for Raymond.

Raymond desperately pleaded, 'Don't do this.'

'Give me one reason why,' Lottie challenged.

Raymond searched for justification, a lifeline to grasp in the tumultuous cycle of emotions. With a heavy heart and a confession weighing heavily on his conscience, Raymond presented his truth. 'I was protecting you.'

But Lottie's patience had been worn thin by the emotional burdens of their relationships as lovers and business partners. She unleashed her frustration in a torrent of ire directly squarely at Raymond. 'We're meant to be in partnership.'

It was a sharp indictment of his shortcomings. She could hardly be much more direct, short of unleashing the full force of her pent-up frustration. Her desire to scream and rail against the injustices of their private and public union threatened to overwhelm her.

In very real fear of losing her, Raymond's heart raced with the urgency of the fast-imploding state of affairs. He immediately entered damage-control mode. 'What can I do?'

He, like the crowd of invested onlookers, awaited Lottie's reply.

Lottie paused, her mind racing as she carefully pondered his question. How could they navigate this treacherous path? What could he do?

She needed to consider the bigger picture—how could they survive this? Could she trust him again? A clear answer did not present itself. She needed time to think about her options.

Lottie took a deep breath and looked the somewhat panicked and flustered Raymond in the eye. 'Don't come home tonight.'

With those words, Lottie retreated, leaving Raymond to cope alone with the magnitude of his actions.

Crushed beneath the stress, Raymond was consumed by a flood of self-recrimination. What had he done? He couldn't believe it. How could he be so stupid as to think she wouldn't find out? How could he be mad with Lottie? She was right.

What gave him the right to dictate her choices, to impose his will upon someone as talented and amazing as Lottie? How could he have been so blind?

As the realisation of his numerous missteps dawned on Raymond, he was left to confront the harsh reality of his shortcomings. It was a sorry sight to witness, casting a sombre shadow over all those present.

The observers, Victor and the assembled crew, looked incredulous and uncomfortable. Even Tauchert, typically animated, sank down behind the veil of his newspaper.

Chapter 19

On the night of his exile, Raymond joined Arthur Higgins at their preferred local pub, where he found solace in the company of frothy beers and sombre reflections. They were quite a few beers into the wind by the late evening.

Raymond's spirits dampened, he lamented, 'I'm punching above my weight.'

Arthur concurred, 'Outclassed for sure.'

As Raymond contemplated his predicament, he despondently shook his head. 'How do I compete with a Hollywood offer?' he mused, before taking another generous swig of amber ale.

Leaning in conspiratorially, Arthur delivered a blunt truth. 'You're a right proper idiot, mate.'

As if overburdened by his troubles, Raymond slumped further on the bar stool. 'Of course, I don't want to lose Lottie for personal reasons. But I also can't lose Lottie professionally.'

Higgins slurred a reply laced with unfiltered sincerity. He declared to everyone in earshot, 'She's the best thing that's happened to you. Ever.' He slapped Raymond on the back to punctuate his words of wisdom.

'There's that. Thanks, mate.' As his thoughts drifted into a deeply sad reverie, Raymond spoke softly into his beer, 'It's another way the Combine wins.' He said, his words heavy with resignation.

Higgins didn't quite know where the conversation with Raymond was headed. 'Not following you.'

Despondent, Raymond sadly informed his mate, 'Talent drain... There'll be no one left to star in our pictures.'

Higgins, now caught up on their alcohol-induced musings, offered a glimmer of hope. 'They can come back, you know.'

'Maybe, if we're lucky. But then we can't afford them,' Raymond sorrowfully explained the dire straits of the fledgling industry.

His public broadcast was heavy with resignation, attracting the attention of the kind-hearted publican. In solidarity, or perhaps sympathy, the publican brought the men another schooner of beer each and joined in the commiserations.

'Another round, boys. To drown the bitterness felt at the way the Australian Government continues to legislate against the local film industry while the Hollywood Combine simultaneously destroys the Australian film industry through its American power base.'

Raymond, heartened by the publican's understanding, perked up. 'See, even he gets it.'

While punctuating his point with an exaggerated gesture, Raymond swayed precariously before losing his balance in a swift, ungraceful motion, toppling off his bar stool.

That same evening, Lottie paced before her confidantes, Charlotte and Lynda. It was not the first time Lottie had sought her mother's counsel on the matter of working in America, because she was torn about her decision.

'There's so much for you to consider. Perhaps it will do you good to take a break from everything here,' counselled Charlotte.

'Do I stay, or do I go?' asked Lottie.

'The answer will come to you, my dear.'

Lynda also voiced her opinions. 'Are you two really over? Raymond's the love of your life. You're the love of his life.'

Lottie knew that Lynda was right, as was Charlotte. 'Part of me wants to make the most of what remains of my life while I feel and look fine. Why not explore stardom in America? What do I have to lose?'

Both Charlotte and Lynda gave Lottie exasperated looks. Each had her own ideas of what Lottie might lose. Plus, not only Lottie would be impacted, they also worried about how they would feel in the aftermath of Lottie's choice.

Lottie's own internal dialogue dominated her thoughts. At worst, she died. At best, she made it, and her mother and Lynda would be looked after financially. Did she need Raymond for either of those options?

She felt betrayed by Raymond, who had sabotaged her career in the name of what he thought was best. He had controlled her career since she was sixteen. At first, his managing her career worked, as she was eager and had a lot to learn. But now his control, with the added influence of his love, was stifling. And he loved her on his terms.

Her terms were simple and unconditional: honesty and trust.

Loud banging drew the women's attention and interrupted their discussion.

They cautiously moved toward the front door and clung to each other inside the dimly moonlit front entrance hall, waiting.

After a moment, the pounding continued, rattling the women and the heavy wooden door. Their outright fear eased when a drunken cry accompanied the thudding and reverberated through the night. 'Lottie! Lottie!'

Raymond.

Charlotte cautiously stepped closer to the door but didn't open it. She called out, her frame of mind a mix of compassion and firmness. 'Raymond, you're in no fit state to be calling on anyone at this hour.'

A thud was heard, as if Raymond pressed his forehead against the rigid door. His voice strained with emotion as he cried, 'Lottie! I need to see you!'

Charlotte exchanged a worried glance with Lottie and Lynda before issuing another stern warning, 'She won't see you.'

Raymond's voice was muffled by the door. 'She told you.'

'Lottie shares everything. You know that.' Charlotte reminded him.

As he next spoke in what seemed like a resigned whisper, the women barely made out Raymond's muffled reply. 'No secrets.'

The sound of Raymond's sobbing reached Lottie, stirring conflicting emotions within her. Anger and hurt vied with compassion and empathy as she wrestled with her feelings. Even though she was incredibly angry with him for keeping things from her, she detested seeing him in this vulnerable state. She wanted to soothe his pain. She took a hesitant step towards the door, but Charlotte halted her advance.

Charlotte fired off a warning. 'Life is too short for secrets, my boy.'

Charlotte's even-tempered but firm admonition echoed in the stillness of the night. All three women held their breath as Charlotte's wise words lingered. Then, the sound of retreating footsteps broke the silence. Charlotte's warning seems to have worked. The sound of Raymond's sobbing eventually subsided.

A sense of relief washed over the women. Charlotte hugged both her girls. A fragile peace was restored for the time being.

An exhausted Lynda wearily retreated to the living room, her footsteps heavy with fatigue.

Perceiving the impact of the day's events, Charlotte reached out to grasp Lottie's hand. With concern and foreboding, Charlotte expressed her apprehension by cautioning her daughter. 'I hope you know what you're doing.'

Lottie was taken aback by her mother's solemnity. 'What do you mean?'

With a knowing gaze, Charlotte raised her eyebrows and met her daughter's eyes. She probed gently, 'Why are you running away?'

In a breath of earnest vulnerability, Lottie said, 'Maybe I'm running away to find myself. Who am I without Raymond?'

Lottie felt it was time to step out of his shadow, forge her own way and make her own decisions about what was best for her career. That was J D's suggestion of America. Sure, she would have the added pressure of being the sole breadwinner for her mother and sister. But it would be on her terms.

Chapter 20

A heavy sense of melancholy settled over Lottie and the small crew as they loitered near the pickle factory. They waited in a state of uneasy anticipation. All preparations for the filming were in place, but Raymond was conspicuously AWOL. Things on set were tense and strained, compounded by Arthur Higgins's hangover. Next to him, Lottie was exhausted and anxious.

Fearing calamity for the movie, she wrestled with the conflicted thoughts racing through her mind. Her fears gnawed at her peace of mind. She couldn't help but think the worst. What if something terrible had befallen Raymond? The mere notion sent shivers down her spine. She should never have let him leave the house last night.

No, her mother was right. He needed to go. Yes, he needed to go, especially after lying to her.

Then a darker possibility loomed. What if Raymond's absence was on purpose? What if this is all part of a calculated act by Raymond to deliberately sabotage and derail their film?

The force of uncertainty pressed upon her, and Lottie struggled with a profound sense of apprehension and foreboding. Every passing minute amplified her anxiety, leaving her to confront the daunting unknown with a heavy heart and a mind besieged by doubt.

Higgins couldn't stand Lottie's distress. He endeavoured to alleviate her burden and put her mind at ease. 'Victor's out searching for him.'

In contempt of her very real worry, Lottie's annoyance and resentment toward Raymond simmered beneath the surface. Her anger was still raw. 'The sooner we're done here, the sooner I'm gone,' she asserted, her words reflecting her inner frustration and resolution.

Raymond, nursing a severe hangover, appeared just as she spoke. His presence was a testament to the toll of the night before. Sensing the tension in the air, he attempted to defuse the mounting animosity. 'I won't keep you a moment longer than necessary,' he declared with a hint of contrition.

Lottie's response was curt, her resilience unbroken. 'Fine.' Her expression gave away nothing of her inner turmoil.

'Good,' Raymond countered, equally short and mirroring her terse attitude.

Locked in a silent standoff, neither gave any ground. Though each stood rigid and unmoving, a silent plea lingered between them. Unable to break their locked gaze, they stared longingly at each other with a yearning for reconciliation hidden beneath layers of pride and resentment. Equally stubborn, neither moved.

However, Arthur Tauchert was happy to oblige with his quick-witted assessment. 'Two hearts in love need no words.'

Raymond consulted his fob-watch. He was in go-slow mode, perhaps from his hangover or maybe because they were already so far behind for the day.

For all his inner turmoil, he still mustered the stamina to push forward, his delivery subdued yet commanding as he directed, 'Places.' Behind his façade of composure, his jaw clenched with the lingering pain of his self-inflicted ordeal.

Sensing the urgency of the situation, the crew and extras snapped to action at Raymond's command. Their movements were swift and precise, reflecting their relief that filming the pickle factory scene, where Doreen labelled pickle jars, was finally commencing.

'Cameras rolling.' Higgins was quietly reserved, subdued by his hangover. His usual enthusiasm was tempered by the throbbing ache in his head.

As filming commenced, Clive Marsh, mindful of his colleagues' hangovers, called out softly, 'Quiet on set.'

Lottie assumed the role of Doreen and diligently labelled the pickle jars. Her movements were precise and methodical despite the mounting tension.

Raymond's actions, whether intentional or not, prolonged the filming process, and he signalled for yet another take.

Raymond demanded another. Each additional request weighed heavily on Lottie.

She was not the only one affected. All of the crew members had frayed nerves from all the reshoots.

'Keep rolling for another take,' Raymond insisted, oblivious to the strain he was placing on everyone.

Frustration simmered beneath Lottie's composed exterior as she struggled to maintain her patience. In her opinion, they should have wrapped on the scenes hours earlier. 'Really, Raymond?'

Undeterred, Raymond asserted his authority as the director, publicly putting Lottie in her place, 'I'm still the director of this picture, Miss Lyell.' His declaration added fuel to the already intense fire.

Lottie stood her ground against Raymond's provocation. 'Yes, you are, Mr Longford.' Lottie refrained from succumbing to tears of frustration. She would not give him the satisfaction of seeing her falter or appear unprofessional in front of the crew.

'Now he stands up to her about directing,' Tauchert's inappropriate quip did little to relieve the mounting tension. But much more simmered beneath the jovial jibe, it masked his frustration with Raymond.

Raymond was unrelenting and inflexible. 'When you're ready,' he called to Lottie. His persistence with this scene only served to fuel the already fever-pitch tension on set.

Higgins took his cue and maintained the façade of continuity regardless of the unease permeating the atmosphere. 'Cameras still rolling,' he said.

'Quiet on set,' Marsh's instruction was almost unnecessary, yet underscored the precariousness of what was unfolding. The usually lively *The Sentimental Bloke* set was shrouded in a sombre silence. It has never been so quiet or tense. Everyone was either low-spirited, on tenterhooks or hungover—making for an unhappy team.

Upholding her professionalism, Lottie diligently acted out the scene, continuing to methodically label pickle jars. Over and over, jar after jar, her actions were a silent, moving meditation. She was fixated on seeing the production through, even with the challenges she was facing.

Raymond, fighting every unrelenting ache in his body, persisted. 'Keep rolling... And again.'

Lottie and the crew mirrored his indefatigability, executing his instructions to the letter. Their collective efforts were fuelled by the hope that this would be the take that that met the director's vision, bringing an end to the arduous chapter of production.

'And another,' Raymond demanded.

Lottie's fatigue and stress from the previous evening's events were evident in every movement as she repeated the actions. Her resilience was being tested by the demanding repetition.

Tauchert, usually quick with a jest to rib Lottie, was overcome with concern for her well-being. He was worried enough to broach the matter with Raymond, 'Mate, I think she—'

'Stay out of it, Arthur,' Raymond commanded, interrupting him. His curt inflection shut down further discussion as he returned his attention to Lottie, 'And again,' issuing the directive for yet another take.

Lowest of low, the crew went through the motions with weary resignation.

'Cameras still rolling,' Higgins announced robotically.

'Quiet on set,' Marsh echoed, his words a stark reminder of the tension on the once vibrant film set.

Even with the merciless cycle of repetitive actions, Lottie, ever the professional, remained committed to her role of Doreen. With each repetition, she surrendered a piece of herself to the task at hand, her movements becoming automatic. Though it was too close to call whether she would run out of bottles or labels first.

She was lost in the mindless task when finally Raymond called, 'And cut! That'll be all, Lottie.' Raymond's abrupt declaration broke the spell.

Lottie and the crew waited. Were they really done? Would he change his mind?

He sensed their silent questioning of his direction and commanded them to move on to the next scene. 'Set up for the workers leaving the factory scene.'

Lottie was relieved. She needed a break from work, from that Raymond. As Lottie moved off set, Victor made a beeline for her. She smiled at him. He leaned in to whisper in her ear, and she pulled back, searching his face. His solemn expression confirmed what he just divulged to her, prompting her to discreetly slip away.

Lottie's sudden departure didn't go unnoticed. Tauchert's frustration boiled over, and he admonished Raymond, 'Now you've gone and done it.'

Not one to be chastised without a retort, Raymond promptly put Tauchert in his place with an abrasive reminder. 'It's between Lottie and me.'

Notwithstanding Tauchert's exasperation with the couple, his respect for Raymond shone through as he acknowledged the complexities of the dynamic duo's relationship. But Tauchert wouldn't let it go. Out of respect, he attempted to make Raymond see reason, 'You've always done alright by me. You're a good bloke, Raymond. No doubt about it. Not many could do what you're doing.'

Tauchert's sincerity was enough to melt away Raymond's bravado and his words were enough for Raymond to recognise the depth of his commitment to Lottie even though the chaos of their personal and professional lives impacted him indirectly.

Raymond confided, 'I can't imagine my life without her.'

Not one to mince words, Tauchert took his cue from Raymond's vulnerability, adding, 'Life is short, mate.' When he saw that Raymond responded to his counsel, he went for the jugular, challenging Raymond's choices with a sobering reminder of life's fleeting nature. 'Is this how you want to spend what time she has left?'

Tauchert's pointed question cut to the core of Raymond's inner conflict. Raymond looked Tauchert in the eye. Tauchert held his gaze. In that silent exchange, both men knew the answer to the question.

Raymond broke the gaze, yielding to the immensity of Tauchert's wisdom. Raymond's inner turmoil, doubts and insecurities were laid bare by Tauchert's piercing perceptibility. Raymond's façade of certainty crumbled. He realised in that moment of profound self-reflection that the situation was not about him alone.

Life had a purpose extending far beyond the confines of his own desires.

He finally deeply understood the 'why' of life. Humans lived to experience life and discover their place in the larger narrative. It was not about him at all.

It was about Lottie.

Chapter 21

In the early afternoon, the Queen Street café exuded an air of tranquil solitude and only a sparse scattering of patrons dotted the tables.

In a secluded corner, Lottie and Melena engaged in a tense tete-a-tete. Melena, her face etched with concern, made a grand gesture of shielding her nose and mouth behind a delicate handkerchief.

With a discernible sense of urgency, a very concerned Melena broached the delicate subject of Lottie's consumption. 'Raymond might not care about his own health, but I'm worried for Victor's well-being, having to keep your dirty secret, not to mention being exposed to the white plague.'

Lottie was prepared for this response. Her expression betrayed a mixture of guilt and resignation. She knew full well the toll her secret exacted, not only on her own health but also on the precarious balance of her loved ones' lives.

When she was first diagnosed, Raymond and Charlotte had prepared her for these very same reactions from the public. Fortunately for Lottie, she had so far avoided that by successfully shielding those closest to her from those harsh truths. She needed to allay Melena's fear about her consumption without causing more concern for the already highly-strung woman. It would take every ounce of discipline for Lottie to keep her composure for both of their sakes, not to mention for the sake of her career and professional privacy.

With a quiet strength, Lottie gently and calmly said, 'I'm sure you mean consumption or tuberculosis.' Lottie paused, maintaining her serene composure, waiting for Melena's reaction to being corrected. When Melena remained silent, Lottie added, 'And Victor is a strong young man. He can make up his own mind.'

Beneath her somewhat composed façade, Melena harboured a lot of anger towards Lottie and fear for her precious Victor. It was a battlefield of conflicting emotions for Melena. How easy it seemed for Lottie to sit there and tell her how it was with her son. But Victor was her only child and the only remaining vestige of her relationship with Raymond.

To lose Victor would break her permanently. To lose him would constitute an irrevocable rupture in her heart, a wound from which she could never hope to recover. How could Lottie sit before her, knowing that her disease was highly contagious and death was inevitable. How could she be so selfish to put in danger what little Melena had remaining in her life? This train of thought made her furious.

With an intensity borne of maternal instinct, Melena spoke her mind. 'You stole my husband's heart. I will not let you take my son's life.'

Despite Lottie's earnest attempts to assuage Melena's fears, she saw that the woman was ensnared by the tangled threads of resentment, mistrust and hurting. Lottie tried to help her understand that such feelings shouldn't shroud their interaction and pleaded for Melena's understanding. 'I would never intentionally—'

'Expose my son, and I'll expose you.' Melena interrupted, delivering a dire ultimatum as her deeply rooted anger prevented her from seeing Lottie's perspective.

'We could be arguing a moot point,' Lottie suggested, trying to steer their conversation away from Melena's growing hysteria towards a more reasoned discourse.

Her effort had the opposite effect. Thinking the worst, Melena veered dangerously close to the brink of hysteria. 'Oh, God. You've already infected him.'

The few other patrons of the café cast furtive glances at Lottie and Melena. Melena pressed her handkerchief to her mouth and nose, her eyes wide with apprehension.

Lottie, not wanting to draw any further attention, leaned in to instruct Melena in discreet urgency, 'Will you keep your voice down? Of course, I haven't.' Lottie paused, then further allayed Melena's fears. 'I will be leaving for America as soon as we finish filming. I will be making the trip alone.'

Finally, she had laid bare her intentions. Lottie had not anticipated that Melena would be the first person outside her family to hear her decision.

Melena was taken aback by Lottie's revelation. Her initial shock gave way to a tumult of conflicting emotions. Could she believe her? Raymond must be furious that his prized star was leaving him. And yet, even with all the chaos of their fractured relationship, Melena sensed a glimmer of hope—a chance to safeguard her only child's future and perhaps win back Raymond's elusive affection.

As Lottie's candid confession sank in, Melena sent another snide barb across the table. 'You're full of surprises, aren't you?'

Lottie didn't react to Melena's taunting, choosing to ignore her venomous scepticism. She was unruffled and deliberate when she responded, 'It might also surprise you to learn that I didn't push Raymond to ask you for a divorce.'

Melena's eyes widened in surprise, caught off guard by Lottie's revelation. Lottie referencing Raymond in such a manner was a first, hinting at cracks in the once seemingly unshakeable foundation of Raymond and Lottie's affair. This is moment marked a significant turning point.

The usually united couple were showing fissures. Lottie's breaking rank with this disclosure was new territory for both women.

Lottie, unperturbed by Melena's incredulity, matter-of-factly explained her motives, 'I didn't have any intention of falling in love with Raymond,' she asserted, her words coloured by a note of regret. 'And equally, I don't want to be the reason a marriage ends.'

Melena's heart clenched at the mention of Lottie's unintended role in the dissolution of her marriage. The sting of betrayal cut deep, another bitter reminder of the deep divide between them. She issued Lottie—the other woman—a stern reminder of the secrets, lies and unspoken truths. 'And yet, here we are.'

Keen to reduce the tense atmosphere of their conversation and help Melena understand her own perspective, Lottie carefully chose her next words. 'I understand that being married gives respect to women. And I've seen what happens to divorced women in this country—'

'I'm not a character in one of your pictures. This is my life you're destroying,' Melena interrupted, deeply offended. Lottie surmising that Melena was like common folk and that her marriage was over struck a nerve. To Melena, the mere mention of divorce signalled that Lottie was doing Raymond's bidding.

She would never grant him a divorce.

Lottie was taken aback by Melena's vehement reaction. She had completely misread Melena and hadn't anticipated such a visceral response. Her attempt at empathy had backfired spectacularly. Melena's words hit Lottie like a slap to the face. She was still reeling when Melena set the record straight.

'It seems a man can do whatever he wants, including abandoning his wife and child for an affair with a younger woman.'

That comment landed like a one-two punch to the gut for Lottie. It was hard to stomach the until-now unacknowledged pain and betrayal that had brought them to this impasse.

Now Lottie was offended. She struggled with a surge of indignation at being called out as the other woman. It took her a second to recover her composure. She attempted to have Melena see her point of view. 'What Raymond and I share is not a fleeting affair.'

Melena remained unmoved. 'It's immoral, given how many years it's been going on.' Melena leaned in conspiratorially close, fixed Lottie with a penetrating look of judgment and asked, 'Are you so smug that you think it can't happen to you?'

There it was. Another verbal slap from Melena.

Lottie was breathless, stunned by Melena's words. In that instant, she realised the depth of Melena's pain, the profound sense of betrayal that had fuelled her anger and resentment.

Before she could respond, Melena delivered another verbal blow. 'The moment Raymond took up with you, he betrayed me.'

Silence. It took a period for that reality to sink in for both women. They were confronted by the harsh realities of love, loss and shattered illusions. They strained under the painful truth of Raymond's culpability in their shared tragedy. Where was Raymond while the two affected women sparred verbally, trying to maintain what shreds of honour they had left?

Melena's anger subsided, gradually giving way to introspection. 'Who am I without Raymond?'

Melena's vulnerability made Lottie ponder her own role in all this. It was unsettling. She also struggled with the question of her own identity in the absence of Raymond. Her response was equally contemplative, 'I've asked myself that exact question.'

Melena only just heard Lottie's response and was perplexed by the other woman's unexpected vulnerability. Her mind raced as she tried to figure out a reasonable explanation for another sudden break in the perfect couple's united front. Where was this coming from? What did Lottie hope to achieve with this newfound openness?

Melena didn't need to wait long to learn Lottie's motive.

'If you keep my consumption quiet, I'll leave without making a fuss,' Lottie announced in an even modulation that matched her controlled expression.

Melena mulled over this. She was torn. Deep inside, she was doing cartwheels. How long had she dreamt of ridding her life of Lottie once and for all? A nagging feeling gnawed at her, and Melena's initial surprise transitioned to suspicion. Where had this sudden turnabout come from? Why now? It was too good to be true. Was she being played? Her fear kicked in. Could she trust Lottie to uphold her end of the bargain?

Melena's fear threatened to overwhelm her. She desperately needed clarity but knew she must tread carefully. Summoning all her courage, Melena pressed Lottie for confirmation. 'And you won't make an attempt to take Raymond or Victor with you?'

Lottie, unwilling to make concessions, met Melena's steely gaze. 'Correct.'

Melena relaxed as she absorbed Lottie's assurance. The relief gave way to hope for a future free from the turmoil that had plagued her for so long. Lottie Lyell would be gone from her life for good. 'Then I accept those terms.'

As the reality of their agreement sank in, the women regarded each other with wary anticipation as if they had each done a deal with the devil.

A triumphant grin spread across Melena's face as she contemplated Lottie's imminent departure. A surge of vindication rose in her with the knowledge that she would soon see the back of the woman who had caused her no end of pain and anguish.

Lottie was relieved to finally regain control over her own destiny and excited about what was yet to unfold for her.

Chapter 22

On the Sydney headland high above the surf, Lottie assumed her directorial mantle with steely efficiency. Lottie was all business as she guided Arthur Tauchert and another male actor through the rehearsal for Bill's tragedy dream scenario. The trio were watched by the modest crew and Raymond.

Lottie explains the blocking to both men, 'Doreen and the other beau kiss while sitting here. Now, Arthur, you're going to come up from over here and spot them kissing.' With notable tension and emotion, Lottie further orchestrated the scene. 'This fills you with rage, and you grab him like this.' She forcefully took hold of the lapels of the actor's jacket. 'And a fight ensues,' Lottie instructed. Lottie manoeuvred the actor, dragging him perilously close to the cliff edge, only to lose her balance and career over the edge.

In the wake of the heart-stopping climax, the silent spectators were suspended in hushed disbelief. Was that merely a masterful display of stunt choreography, or had they unwittingly borne witness to a tragedy? Lottie had certainly elevated her stunt work to the next level in terms of adrenaline-fuelled action in recent weeks. Though, as seconds stretched into eternity in what seemed like an ultra-slow-motion movie, the grim reality dawned on them.

This was no staged performance.

With his heart filled with dread, Raymond was the first to rush to the ledge. He took in the scene below.

His precious Lottie lay motionless on a rocky shelf, her delicate form juxtaposed against the harsh, jagged surface. The sea breeze tousled her hair, the only part of her in motion, emphasizing the fragility of the scene

His mind was awash with regret. How could he have allowed that to happen? He silently berated himself for being swayed by Lottie's persuasive nature and agreeing to such perilous theatrics. She was so convincing and had it all mapped out. How could he say no to her?

In his fervent desire to honour her vision and give her the respect of co-director she so craved, he had unwittingly steered them into the abyss of danger.

His raw panic lit the collective fuse of concern among the others and the crew. With bated breath, the onlookers immediately converged on the ledge. Down below, Lottie lay very still as if frozen.

Stricken with disbelief, Raymond stood rooted to the spot, transfixed, until his anguished cry pierced the air. 'Oh, dear God! Lottie!'

Beside him, Tauchert's stoic behaviour belied the gravity of the episode. 'That could've been me.' It was a stark reminder of not only his own mortality but that of those nearby.

That was enough for Raymond. In a flurry of desperation, he sprang into action. He cautiously embarked on the treacherous descent, each step fraught with uncertainty and laden with trepidation.

Please be alive, he repeated to himself before more sombre thoughts dominated his internal dialogue. What if he was too late? What if she did not recover? What if she was already dead? Would his efforts be in vain? Was he making the descent only to retrieve her corpse? What if he killed himself trying to rescue her, thus sealing their tragic fate?

More and more melancholic thoughts echoed within his mind as he cautiously shimmied down the sheer rock face to the ledge where Lottie's still form remained unmoving.

It was a long wait for the others, and a sense of apprehension descended upon the crew and onlookers. The small crowd gathered in silent vigil, their concern increasing as more and more agonising minutes ticked by.

'Is she dead?' Tauchert asked the question on everyone's mind.

Their collective anguish was laden with existential introspection, and their unspoken fears underscored the fragile nature of life itself. A shadow of uncertainty settled over the gathering.

'You better pray she's not.' Higgins's voice was terse, his eyes glued to Raymond as he carefully made his way down to reach Lottie's motionless form on the small ledge below. With each precarious step, the tension tightened like a taut wire.

Cautiously, Raymond inched closer and closer to Lottie.

Minutes surrendered to the eternity of time as Raymond made his way back up the cliff with Lottie's seemingly lifeless form cast over his shoulder.

As Raymond approached the ledge, Tauchert stepped back to give him space to place Lottie's limp body on firmer ground. A collective sigh of relief swept through the small crew, and they all backed up a little. The unease lingers.

With a sweating brow and trembling hands, Raymond struggled to hoist Lottie's seemingly lifeless body to safety.

Out of breath and with the stress of the life and death ordeal still written all over his face, Raymond gently lifted Lottie's limp body up over his head. His instructions were strained, but urgent. 'Pull her up! Careful! Don't worry about me. Make sure she's okay.'

Higgins stepped forward and, with concerted effort, helped Raymond lift Lottie's body up and over the edge.

The small crew rallied around the young woman's unconscious form.

PART 3 – ACTION!

Chapter 23

L ottie was a fragile figure, unconscious on the bed.

Lynda maintained a solemn vigil, her fingers intertwined with Lottie's. An air of desperation permeated her hushed words. 'Please, please wake up, Lottie... Don't leave me, not like this. I don't want to be the only one left.'

The burden of past losses hung in the air. Lynda could not bear the thought of losing her older sister, not like this. Lottie had promised not to leave her like Rita and their father. The very thought of losing Lottie haunted Lynda's every thought as she clung to the hope of her recovery.

Lynda laid her head gently on Lottie's torso and sobbed quietly. There was a subtle movement beneath her as Lottie's free hand patted Lynda's hair. For several seconds, Lynda froze.

Did she imagine that?

But there it was again, Lottie's touch as her fingers stroked her hair. The caring gesture filled Lynda's heart with disbelief and relief. Lynda jolted upright. She couldn't believe it—Lottie was awake!

Lynda carefully repositioned Lottie, her movements gentle yet decisive. Each slight adjustment drew a wince from Lottie, and her face contorted with pain. The sight of her sister suffering so pierced Lynda's heart. She fought back her own tears, her fingers trembling as she tried to find a position that might offer some relief to Lottie.

'Oh, Lottie, thank God!' Lynda exclaimed, beside herself with joy. She hugged her sister with joyous abandon.

Lottie tried to move. Her discomfort bordered on severe pain.

Lynda sensed Lottie's body tensing. She recoiled in concern, not wanting to hurt her sister. 'Don't move,' she urged, her instruction imbued with urgency. 'The doctor needs to examine you.'

Lynda hollered at the top of her voice, 'Mother! Raymond! Doctor!' Her excited broadcast echoed around the room. 'She's awake. Lottie's awake!'

Struggling to articulate her thoughts, Lottie whispered, 'How long?' Even that level of effort was exhausting, leaving her feeling drained.

'Two days,' Lynda stated. 'You had us so worried. We all took shifts to be with you,' she continued, her dedication to her sister evident in her every word. 'I'm so happy.' Tears glistened in Lynda's eyes as she gently embraced Lottie, unwilling to let her sister go. She couldn't express her love and heartfelt relief at learning Lottie had awakened. Lynda's heart swelled with gratitude.

As Lynda moved aside, Raymond, Charlotte and Doctor Wilson converged around Lottie's bedside, each expressing their profound relief at Lottie's awakening.

Lottie welcomed a motherly embrace from Charlotte that was so emotionally charged neither woman could sustain it.

Lottie sought out Raymond in the flurry of emotions, and Charlotte graciously made way for him to kneel next to the bed. Raymond's bedside manner was loving and compassionate.

His heart burst at the sight of his beloved Lottie alive, albeit bruised and exhausted. A restrained smile graced Lottie's lips, sending a surge of dopamine coursing through Raymond's entire being, filling him with overwhelming relief and joy.

Ever so delicately, Raymond's fingers traced Lottie's scratched cheekbone. His eyes brimming with tears, he spoke in a soft, trembling voice. 'You really scared me this time.' He carefully laid his head on her chest.

Lottie was torn between the deep love she felt for Raymond and the pain inspired by the pressure of his embrace.

'You scared all of us,' Charlotte stated, her words carrying both genuine concern and admonishment. 'You could've been killed.'

'It's all my fault,' confessed Raymond. His sense of responsibility for what happened atop the cliff was profound. He acknowledged that allowing the stunt to take place was a grave error on his part. The consequences could have been much worse than what Lottie grappled with now. The thought of losing the love of his life was unbearable. He knew he would never forgive himself if Lottie had died.

In Lottie's eyes, Raymond's candid admission unveiled a depth of remorse over what happened that she hadn't anticipated. Taking responsibility for the incident entirely demonstrated his love and reverence for her. Though she believed her love for him was profound before, in that moment, it swelled exponentially, resonating with an intensity she had never imagined.

Lottie caught Charlotte's unimpressed look and her heart ached for her mother's silent anguish. Consumption was one thing, but it was a slower farewell, that allowed time for appropriate goodbyes. Hurtling herself off a cliff offered no such luxury—only a stark reminder of the words left unsaid and emotions left unexpressed.

This was her doing. She convinced Raymond to let her direct the stunt. She could not let him shoulder the full responsibility for her decision. 'If it was anyone's fault, it was mine, Mother,' she confessed, her explanation heavy with regret. 'It was an accident,' she further implored, desperate to absolve Raymond of guilt.

Raymond lifted his head. His gaze overflowed with love when he met Lottie's eyes. She didn't blame him. His love for this incredible woman deepened even more. And in that love-filled beat, the burden of the accident was shared as equals.

The doctor stepped closer on the other side of the bed from Raymond, his presence a reassuring anchor in the room's pensive atmosphere. He checked Lottie's vitals while Raymond gently held her hand, proving his reluctance to let her slip away.

Lottie's gaze was fixated on the doctor as he methodically assessed her condition.

The doctor was pleased with Lottie's responsiveness but guarded in his prognosis. His unsmiling words punctuated the air, cautious and yet hopeful, 'Well, given the circumstances, I recommend taking the next few weeks—'

Lottie's interruption was swift and decisive, 'No. This has already put us further behind.'

Surprise rippled through the room. In her denial of the acuteness of her injuries, she was not in the mood to yield, a blatant reminder that nothing, it seemed, could keep Miss Lottie Lyell down.

Lottie maintained her wilful mood as she continued addressing the doctor with quiet assurance. 'With all due respect, Doctor, I value your medical opinion, but we can't afford another total work ban.'

The doctor was struck by her indefatigable commitment. Who wouldn't be in awe of her work ethic? But, as a professional medical practitioner, he had to remain dedicated when performing his professional duties. She needed time to recover and heal properly from her injuries. Emphasising the severity of her injuries, he urged caution, 'This is much worse than that.'

This time, Raymond agreed wholeheartedly with the doctor. No film was worth what they'd just been through. He attempted to convince her to agree. 'We'll find another way, Lottie. You need—'

'Don't tell me what *I* need,' she said, standing her ground. 'What *we* need is to finish the damn picture.'

'Lottie! Raymond's right. You need to rest,' Charlotte interjected, her concern evident as she observed Lottie's increasing agitation.

Rest was essential for Lottie's full recovery. They all agreed on this much, except Lottie.

'Mother, there'll be time to rest later. A work ban would be disastrous. The picture and our business won't withstand it,' she persisted with her purposive reference.

'Lottie—'

'Oh, darling Raymond, we both know there's no other option. We've already lost another two days because of this,' she implored him with her large, dark, pleading eyes.

Charlotte turned away, her tears flowing freely. She was emotionally torn seeing her daughter in such a fragile physical state, yet she swelled with pride at hearing Lottie's tireless persistence. Her clarity of purpose was to be admired. She understood Lottie's perspective. Her well-being and presence were crucial to finishing the film and salvaging their business partnership, which underpinned their family's livelihood.

'Mother, please try to understand,' Lottie implored. 'We can't stop now. We're so close.'

'Are you sure?' Charlotte tentatively asked, already knowing what her daughter's response would be.

'Yes. We must finish,' declared Lottie. 'Sir David will shut us down otherwise. And we'll never recover from that,' Lottie explained with meek humility, pressing her point, 'We have no choice. We will lose... everything.'

The words were heavy, and Raymond searched Lottie's face for any sign of hesitation. An unspoken understanding passed between them. She was uncompromising, 'You know I'm right, Raymond.'

Raymond held her gaze, a hint of reluctance flickering in his eyes. 'Doesn't mean I have to like it,' he replied, a wistful smile playing at the corners of his lips.

It was more than a fleeting nanosecond of connection. Raymond and Lottie shared a knowing smile at their inside joke. Even with all the adversity of late and the strain on their working relationship, their connection remained unbreakable. A strong bond of love and partnership propelled them forward.

Summoning all charm and diplomacy, Lottie turned to the family doctor with a polite yet firm request. 'Doctor, I would love it if you could patch me up as best you can.'

Chapter 24

Lottie, portraying Doreen, was lying ill in bed. The young actress still felt the lingering effects of the clifftop stunt mishap.

Wanting to make sure that Lottie didn't overdo it, Raymond addressed the crew and cast in his theatrical tone. 'I ask that we give Lottie a little space. She's still on the mend,' he announced, his voice carrying a note of concern for his leading lady.

Arthur Higgins reassured his director, 'We'll take it slow, boss.' His words echoed the sentiments of the entire team. Truth be told, they were all relieved to see Lottie alive and well. It was quite the scare for the modest team, though now, with Lottie back on set, there was a renewed sense of camaraderie.

Lottie noticed their concern and offered them a reassuring smile. 'I'm okay, everyone. I'm happy to be back,' her confirmation was filled with positivity. 'We've got a picture to finish.'

They took great comfort in her confidence. They appreciated Lottie's brilliance and loved her courage. With her at the helm, they knew the show would, indeed, go on.

Raymond beamed with pride as he addressed the crew, 'You heard the lady.' His expression was infused with genuine warmth and encouragement. 'Set up for Doreen's ill scene.'

With a renewed purpose, everyone sprang into action, each team member taking their designated places with practised efficiency.

Arthur Tauchert, also happy to see Lottie back on set, took the opportunity to check in with her while the crew set up. 'It won't take much acting for this one, girlie,' he remarked with an affable smile. And while it hurt to laugh, her chuckle showed that she would let Tauchert's 'girlie' jest slide this time.

With skills honed by years of experience, Tauchert could detect good acting a mile away. He held her gaze as he asked, 'How are you feeling?'

Lottie's vulnerability peeked through. 'A bit tender, but the show must go on.' She put on a brave face to mask her discomfort.

Tauchert's concern deepened. 'Not at the expense of your health,' he warned, a note of caution underlying his words.

A hint of playful banter punctuated their exchange, 'Now you're sounding like Raymond,' she chided with affectionate jest. 'We can't stop now. We're so close.'

Their quiet conversation came to an end as Raymond's call to action broke through, 'Lottie, Arthur. Ready?'

Tauchert nodded, eager to proceed. With a subtle glance towards the leading lady, he and Raymond checked in with Lottie. Her nod offered reassurance, a clear signal to begin. Attuned to Lottie's unspoken commands, the crew and cast took their cue from her.

'Positions,' called Higgins.

'Quiet on set,' Victor instructed, an easy-going reminder of the solemnity of the impending scene.

'Rolling camera.' Higgins's directive set the wheels in motion, ready for Raymond's final command.

Raymond took charge, calling to everyone on set, 'Let's see if we can get this in one take. Action!'

In the emotional scene, thinking Doreen was truly ill, Bill went for the doctor. Tauchert's performance was nothing short of captivating. His portrayal of Bill's concern for Doreen's well-being was conveyed in every gesture and expression. Perhaps his genuine concern for Lottie's well-being inspired the emotional depths on display in the scene.

Encouraged by their momentum, Raymond wasted no time laying the groundwork for the next sequence. 'Okay, Arthur, for the next set up, you're back with the nurse.'

Feeling like he was on a roll, Tauchert led the actress playing the nurse to Doreen's bedside. Bill anxiously remained outside the door, waiting for the doctor's arrival. Yet, Bill's hopes were dashed when the doctor arrived because he strode past Bill into the bedroom, and Bill was shut out. Distressed and on edge, Bill frantically paced and paced.

The nurse emerged from the bedroom, her joyous proclamation breaking through the tension like a ray of sunlight. 'It's a boy!' she happily announced causing a sense of elation to ripple throughout the set.

At this poignant emotional release, Bill dramatically dropped into the nearby chair, a wave of relief washing over him like a waveless tide. When the doctor departed, the nurse extended a silent invitation for Bill, who followed her into the room to see Doreen with the baby cradled in her arms. As he drew near, Bill gently cuddled up close to Doreen and the child on the bed. In that fleeting instant, they were a family. The emotions of the captured scene settled over them like a comforting embrace.

The baby howled, its cries piercing the air. The nurse swiftly ushered a reluctant Bill out of the bedroom.

Raymond's pleased declaration, 'Cut!' signalled the end of the heartfelt scene and the return to reality.

With bountiful reverence, the small crew huddled around Lottie as she tenderly settled the baby.

The actress who played the nurse observed Lottie and the infant with admiration and empathy. 'You're a natural.'

Despite the poignant beauty of the occasion, Lottie smiled to conceal her sorrow—the stark reality was that she wouldn't have the experience of bringing a child of her own into the world. It was another unspoken ache of a future she wouldn't realise, a reminder of dreams that would be unfulfilled.

Meanwhile, Victor, not having been around any babies in his eighteen years, was in awe of the tiny human before him. 'It's hard to believe we start out that small.'

Raymond adoringly looked on at Lottie with the baby, his heart swelling with a mixture of tenderness and longing. He was quickly cast back in time to when Victor was a newborn, a tiny bundle of promise nestled in his arms. He was so proud and joyful back then. What he would give now to encounter that life-changing event full of promise and optimism again, this time with the woman he truly loved. For a short time, Raymond was lost in a pleasant thought where this scene, this family, was his reality.

Lottie motioned for Victor to join her on the bed, her movement graceful and reassuring. With gentle guidance, she placed the baby in a nervous Victor's arms. She adjusted his arms into position so both he and the infant were comfortable and at ease.

As Victor tentatively cradled the newborn, Raymond's heart swelled with pride.

'One of my proudest moments was having you, son.' Raymond burst with emotion as he shared this touching confession with his only child.

Following that emotion-filled statement, father and son shared an instant of profound connection. Victor shone with Raymond's disclosure. The others gathered around, cooing with delight and admiration over the cherubic babe in Victor's arms. They shared a sense of joy and wonder, and an appreciation of the enduring power of love and family.

Lottie excused herself to change clothes for the next scene, slipping behind a nearby decorative divider screen. His heart heavy with unspoken longing, Raymond was drawn to her as she deftly navigated the intricacies of her costume change. His voice expressed a fusion of concern and yearning as he broke the silence to check in with her. 'You okay?'

Caught off guard by Raymond's question, Lottie's focus remained on the task at hand. She reached for the next ensemble, a fashionable mid-calf length dress featuring long sleeves, a drop waist, and a V-shaped neckline with sailor collar and contrasting decorative bow. She awkwardly drops the dress over her head. 'Sure,' her reply was firm and composed, not betraying any of the tumultuous emotions swirling beneath the surface.

Raymond looked longingly at Lottie, his manner soft as he struggled to articulate his feelings. 'Seeing you with the baby—'

Lottie knew where the conversation was headed and quickly intercepted his train of thought. 'Raymond, you know that isn't an option.' She didn't want to hurt his feelings, but bringing the subject up at that time... well, indulging in fantasies of a life they could not share would only lead to heartache.

Raymond refrained from letting her cutting assessment ruin his joyful reverie, suspended between reality and desire. A man could dream. He held his longing gaze, hoping that she would feel the way he did.

Lottie's inner turmoil threatened to engulf her. The unspoken emotions pressed firmly against her fragile façade of composure. Lottie closed her eyes for an instant, garnering all her strength to corral her emotions. She knew the idyllic scene was not one she would ever experience. Especially since she was headed to America without Raymond.

She slowly opened her eyes and locked her gaze with Raymond's in a silent plea for understanding. She had hoped that he would see things from her point of view, but to her dismay, Raymond was still looking at her intently, with that look of mistaken wishful thinking. It was a cruel reminder of what would never be. She felt a pang of regret for the experiences that had brought them to this impasse. As doubt threatened to overwhelm her, she knew they could not go there. The bitter sting of reality was too much. It was simply not fair to ruminate on what could never be reality. Resolute, Lottie stared defiantly back at him.

Before the strain between them could escalate further, Higgins unintentionally broke the tension by issuing instructions to the team. 'Okay, folks, light's disappearing, and I need the cast required for Ma's death scene.'

Everyone hustled to prepare for the next scene. In the flurry of activity, a telegram boy appeared and handed Raymond a telegram. Raymond's heart sank with each word as he read the contents.

'Oh, hell,' Raymond said.

With a heavy sigh, he resigned himself to the harsh reality of their predicament.

Turning to Lottie with a blend of anguish and resignation etched upon his features, Raymond said, 'Pugliese lost.'

Pugliese's defeat in this second case was a bitter pillow to swallow. Fatigue overcame him as he contemplated the dire implications for their shattered investor relationship.

With shaking hands, Raymond folded the telegram and spiralled into the depths of his own despair. 'That's two strikes for *The Church and the Woman*. Maybe we should cut our losses and file for bankruptcy?' Raymond said in a passionate expression of his sorrow.

Lottie took the letter in hand and read it, her jaw set in a defiant line as she absorbed the contents. She was disappointed by the outcome because, while it was a strike against Pugliese and Raymond, it directly affected her and the business they shared. The spectre of bankruptcy loomed, one of the harsh realities of the fledgling motion picture industry.

But Lottie was made of sterner stuff and resisted surrendering to despair. She was not about to let the ship go down if she could help it. She would find a workable solution.

She took Raymond to task, confronting him with her fierce will. 'Your career is my career, and we're not going to let this beat us. And we are definitely not letting this affect this picture,' she reiterated her commitment to the shared enterprise. 'Besides, Pugliese says here that he will appeal the other case too.'

As the echoes of her impassioned declaration faded into the ether, Raymond was filled with a renewed sense of purpose. They would find the strength to weather the storm together, their bond stronger than ever before.

'Places,' Higgins' authoritative command called the film crew to order.

Raymond and Lottie were instantly distracted from the emotional stress of their own concerns and compelled to refocus their attention on the sombre scene at hand where Doreen's mother, Ma, lay near death on her bed. It was an emotional scene for the film, so everyone focused on delivering their part.

Stepping out of the frame, Raymond commanded the crew, 'Rolling camera. Quiet. Action.'

The actors found their footing within the confines of their respective roles and hit their stride. The older woman playing Ma delivered a performance of quiet poignancy and died a dignified death. A short time later, Doreen moved with great haste to reach her onscreen mother, only to find she was too late as she rushed past the doctor who was speaking with Bill.

Doreen, Bill, and Ma's neighbours and friends surrounded the deathbed. Doreen cried for the loss of her mother, and Bill comforted her.

Satisfied with the performance, Raymond called, 'Cut!'

The tension that gripped the room dissipated like smoke in the wind and was replaced by a sense of collective relief that the mournful scene was captured in the first take. The crew and the actors relaxed and took a break.

However, the sadness lingered for Lottie. She expertly hid her emotions behind a smile while vaudeville actor, Arthur Tauchert, the consummate showman, attempted to lighten the mood amongst the small cast and crew with his irreverent humour. He hammed it up as he helps Ma out of bed.

'It's a miracle, Ma rises from the dead. More lives than a cat, this one.'

Chapter 25

At the end of the long day of filming, Lottie, her emotions still raw from the intense earlier scene with her screen mother's death, sought solace in the comforting presence of her natural mother. Lottie crawled into bed beside Charlotte. With a tenderness born of unconditional love, Lottie held her mother close in an extra-long hug.

Charlotte, attuned to her daughter's needs, sensed Lottie's fatigue. She was touched by Lottie's loving nature and responded in kind, offering her own embrace as a source of strength and comfort.

Like a child seeking refuge from a storm, Lottie snuggled closer still. She loved her mother with all her heart. In Charlotte, she found not just a mother but a confidante, a protector and a friend.

The day's filming had reminded Lottie of the precious mother-daughter relationship she shared with Charlotte. She didn't know how she would cope if her mother passed away. It was hard enough when her father died. His absence still loomed large in her heart. One never truly got over the grief of losing a parent and the pain of saying goodbye.

Her father had loved all his girls. He was a wonderful father, husband and human being, well-respected by all he encountered. He was a pillar of strength, a beacon of love, and a guiding light to their family.

Then death came again with Rita's passing. So final and emotional in a different way. With her older sister's passing, she lost her best friend. Rita's absence left a profound emptiness in Lottie's life—a void that no amount of time could ever hope to heal.

As she lay beside her mother, these memories weighed heavily on her heart. Lottie gingerly broached the subject of impending loss with her mother, her voice barely above a whisper as she asked, 'How did you cope with losing Father and Rita?'

Not expecting the question, Charlotte was somewhat thrown off balance. She gained her composure before replying, 'Oh, my darling girl, I had you and Lynda. I could've collapsed in a heap. Blamed the world. But like most, they got consumption by chance,' her words were filled with sorrow and resilience.

In the quiet intimacy of their conversation, Lottie hung onto her every word. It was a conversational direction they'd seldom taken. Lottie, consumed by her own grief in the aftermath of her father's passing, had never paused to consider how her mother may have felt.

Not one to shy away from expressing her perspective or sugar-coating things for her children, Charlotte continued her explanation with candid honesty. 'Your father had to work, after all. We had three girls to feed. Collecting rents from the poor exposed him. You can't fault him for doing what he thought was best for us.'

For what seemed like an eternity, Charlotte was lost in treasured memories of her beloved husband. Her gaze softened with a bittersweet longing. 'Oh, I loved him. Still do,' she confessed. 'And yet, in his pursuit of providing for us, he unwittingly brought this tragedy upon our family... for which he paid the ultimate price.'

In the safe confines of their shared confessions, Lottie found the courage to express her deepest fear. In almost a whisper, she confided in her mother, 'Some days, I do wonder when my time will come.'

Charlotte wrapped her arm tighter around Lottie, sending out a fervent wish for more time with her daughter. God only knew when it would be Lottie's time. Hopefully, they would have many more shared experiences.

For Charlotte, the distress of past sorrows bore down upon her with an unrelenting force. The pain of burying her dear husband and cherished eldest daughter still lingered. With her dear child firmly in her embrace, she couldn't help but wonder what lay ahead. The thought of losing Lottie filled her with profound sadness. She couldn't imagine what Lottie's departure from life would entail, although she hoped that when the time came, Lottie would face it with the same enduring courage and presence she had carried with her into all her other experiences.

'No one knows,' Charlotte murmured. 'We've all worked so hard to keep it a secret. There will come a time when the truth can no longer be concealed.'

For Lottie, the reality of her mortality loomed large, casting a shadow over her thoughts and fears. The younger woman was frightened. She had witnessed the devastating effects of consumption first-hand—the merciless progression of the disease as it robbed her sister of her vitality and strength. Rita's decline was a cruel spectacle. Her rosy complexion was replaced with a pallor so extreme that she looked like a ghost. Her cough worsened over time, until the mucus eventually contained more and more blood. As the liquid filled her already compromised lungs, she struggled to get the necessary oxygen required to do the most basic things. Bedridden, Rita swiftly lost her vital spark. Her spirit was depleted to the point that she lay in her bed wheezing, every breath a painful effort. It was awful to watch her die in that way. The only saving grace for Rita was that the disease claimed her within two months.

Lottie continued to struggle with the haunting memories of her father's demise, which was longer and more drawn out. Her strong, fit father experienced a myriad of symptoms in a slow, agonising descent into the depths of the disease. The first sign of his illness was a very high fever followed by sheer exhaustion. He went from energetic to listless and feeling very tired all the time. Then he lost his healthy appetite, which made his body mass diminish, shrinking his frame and his spirit to the point where he was a mere shadow of his former self and barely recognisable.

The nights were the worst. The punishing cycle of sweating alternated with chills tormented him mercilessly. He was scarcely able to sleep through the night. In the end, he groaned with pain at any little movement. And through it all, Charlotte remained honourable by his side, lovingly caring for him. She vowed to keep him at home and shield him from the sterile confines of the consumption ward where so many met their end.

Her mother kept her promise that the love of her life would die a dignified death at home, surrounded by his loving family. Only the highest quality of care until the very end for her father. Charlotte, in her unfaltering love and devotion, made sure Lottie's father was granted the dignity he deserved in his final days. And then he was gone.

'I don't want to end up in the consumption asylum.' Lottie unburdened herself to Charlotte.

'I will never let that happen,' vowed Charlotte. She would ensure that Lottie received care and comfort to the best of her ability, just as she did for her husband and eldest daughter.

Lottie was engulfed in a cloud of despondency. Her usual positivity and joie de vivre had deserted her. Her mind swirled incessantly with negative thoughts, casting shadows over her vibrant spirit. The doubt crept in. 'Maybe our family is cursed?'

Her daughter's distress and departure from her usual buoyant attitude was shocking. Charlotte was so alarmed by Lottie's behaviour and sentiments that she sat upright and coaxed Lottie to sit too. Charlotte took Lottie's face in her hands. Locking eyes, Charlotte refused to entertain the notion of defeat. 'I won't accept that talk from you.'

Tears cascaded involuntarily from Lottie's sorrowful eyes. 'I'm sorry. It's just that sometimes it's all too much.'

Charlotte's heart ached at the sight of her daughter's suffering. She hated seeing her Lottie in this state of despair. 'I'm sorry for burdening you as the breadwinner,' her apology was imbued with regret. 'Maybe that was your father's and my fault, encouraging your theatre dreams over what's expected of young women.'

Lottie snuggled close, seeking solace in her mother's embrace.

Yet, beneath Charlotte's remorse lay an immovable commitment to nurturing Lottie's dreams, a defiance against the societal constraints imposed upon young women. How could she and her husband deny Lottie's innate calling? How could they refuse Lottie? From her earliest days, she had radiated a magnetic energy. She had an affinity for performing and bringing people joy with her seemingly limitless talents. She took to professional acting like a fish to water. She was such a natural talent that all who saw her then, like now, were captivated by her energy and flair. Her magnetism was undeniable, her talent a force of nature.

Charlotte and her husband recognised Lottie's potential from the outset, yet never dared to imagine the breadth of her future infinite possibilities. It was only with the arrival of Raymond that Lottie's destiny, career-wise at least, opened to them. A symbiotic partnership emerged. They made a formidable team, blending Lottie's artistic prowess with Raymond's entrepreneurial acumen. Together, they formed an indomitable alliance, channelling their collective talents into a flourishing enterprise. The money flowed into the family's account.

Lottie was an effervescent young girl, thriving and developing personally and professionally into a young woman with limitless opportunities. Through meticulous planning and strategic foresight, Lottie's career trajectory had soared to new heights. This enriched her life and brought many advantages to their family. As Lottie's star ascended, so too did the spirits of audiences far and wide as she brought much joy and entertainment all over the country.

In a doting instance of maternal guidance, Charlotte coached Lottie, reminding her daughter of the transformative power with which she enthralled others. 'You may not realise it now, but you are making a difference to people. You're here for a purpose. Use what time you have wisely.'

Lottie's conversation with her mother from the previous night was all but forgotten as the cast and crew prepared for the wedding feast scene.

In the middle of the commotion, Lottie and Raymond were locked in a heated exchange. With eyes ablaze, Lottie argued, 'They're sabotaging our livelihood!' She unleashed her displeasure at their precarious financial situation on Raymond. 'We'll be ruined financially and lose everything.'

Lottie was incensed. The stakes could not be higher. It was life and death; their very existence hung in the balance.

Raymond watched her with admiration and concern. He was impressed by her impassioned stand and clarity around their plight. 'I won't let it come to that,' vowed Raymond. Or at least he hoped he wouldn't. Uncertainty gnawed at his conscience. Yet, he chose to shield Lottie from the burden of his own apprehension, to save her from any further burdens, given the intense emotional state she was already in.

Lottie, her mind racing with possibilities, was already devising workable solutions. 'I could return to the theatre.' She paced with purposeful strides before stopping and turning back towards Raymond. 'But I know in my heart, this is the future.'

Lottie just knew that moving pictures were the future of entertainment. The allure of the silver screen was irresistible. Its promise of innovation and boundless potential beckoned her forward with an irresistible pull. Though she acknowledged the enduring charm of traditional forms of entertainment—vaudeville, theatre, opera and the like—she felt that the future belonged to the moving picture. And she wanted to be part of that trajectory. She wanted to seize the opportunity to be at the front of the wave that was fast making an impact on entertaining the masses in Australia and around the world.

Raymond reassured her, 'Making pictures is our future. Let it—'

'I haven't got time to patiently wait like a good girl for these men to decide my fate,' Lottie bluntly told it like it was. She didn't have time, literally. She needed to make a difference before it was too late.

Raymond sensed Lottie's rising agitation. He was concerned that she was fast working herself up into a moment of female hysteria. Mindful of Charlotte's stern admonition to shield Lottie from undue stress, he offered a gentle entreaty. 'Slow down.'

But Lottie, her mettle constant, had a strong aversion to heed his counsel. With a fiery strength of will, Lottie countered Raymond's caution with defiance, warning him, 'Don't tell me to slow down.'

Conscious he needed a different approach, Raymond changed tack and adopted a softer intonation, distracting Lottie with an offering to keep the peace, 'Look, we can talk about your official credits.'

Lottie knew she needed to choose her battles to win the war. She considered Raymond's attempt to calm her anger at the situation in the male-dominated motion picture industry. For Lottie, the set of circumstances was one of tension and quiet resistance, especially for women creatives and talent. Lottie was visible yet ephemeral, easily overshadowed by Raymond's imposing presence.

Despite all her efforts and dedication that shaped the essence of their productions, it was the men who stood in the limelight. Lottie had played along but began to push against the constraints imposed by other sectors of society. Her battle was fought in the editing room, behind the camera and in the delicate yet determined negotiations for credits on their productions.

Raymond, her protective partner, sensed the undercurrents of Lottie's struggle. She had shared her feelings about the complexities of asserting her creative influence and being recognised for her efforts. His own efforts to shield her from the industry's harsh realities were tinged with an awareness of his own privileged position.

Lottie's talent was undeniable. However, each day on a production was a test of endurance for receiving the recognition she deserved. Though Raymond lauded her work privately, advocating for her behind closed doors, he was one of the privileged few. Society expected men to lead and bask in the glory and accolades while women remained in the shadows. Her existence was a challenge to the status quo. Her's was a path fraught with obstacles because even their financiers and distributors didn't see her as equal to Raymond. Her ideas and contributions were often overlooked or outright dismissed. In their eyes, Raymond was the visionary. The men held the director's chair, managed the production, and controlled the finances. Women, despite their talents and indispensable roles, were relegated to supporting positions. The societal norms of the era dictated that women were not to outshine men. Her ideas were often presented through Raymond to gain acceptance, a frustrating but necessary strategy. The struggle for recognition was a delicate dance.

'It should be more than that,' Lottie finally said.

Raymond knew that her creative genius was instrumental to their success, though he also knew how the motion picture business worked.

'I know that, but for the here and now, the financiers, the industry, need to see me in charge.'

Lottie's anger over the injustice of the situation simmered beneath the surface. She was furious and lashed out at him as the face of those who were trying to deny her. 'At the expense of giving deserved recognition... We're meant to be a team.'

Raymond next words were a futile attempt to bridge the growing chasm between them. 'We're making pictures, just like you wanted.'

Lottie's exasperation reached breaking point. In a flash of unguarded candour, she brusquely snapped at Raymond. 'That is exactly what those men would say. You're so focused on what you think everyone wants, Raymond, instead of what they need,' her retort was a potent blend of resentment and disappointment.

Stung by the accusation, Raymond's pride bristled and his stubbornness kicked in. He defiantly declared, 'I won't apologise for who I am. That's what men do.'

Equally stubborn and unwilling to concede ground, Lottie dug her heels in. 'Yes, but it doesn't mean I have to put up with it!'

She coughed then but couldn't catch her breath.

Watching her gasp for breath raised fear in Raymond. His concern for Lottie's well-being was visible for all to see.

'You'll kill yourself at this pace,' his words carried a note of genuine fear. Lottie disregarded his desperate plea for her to heed the warning signs of her illness.

Undeterred by her physical distress, Lottie straightened and said, 'At least it will be on my terms and won't be the white plague.' The peril of tuberculosis haunted their lives and continued to cast a long shadow over their hopes and aspirations.

Raymond's anxiety mounted as he fussed over Lottie, his gestures betraying the depth of his concern. 'Keep working like this, and that's exactly what will happen.' Frustration and fear filled him with dread. God, he couldn't stand it when she was like this. The thought of losing her terrified him beyond measure and was a prospect he could not bear to contemplate.

Lottie collected herself and relented, her strength of will tempered by a begrudging acknowledgment of the graveness of their situation. 'Alright. Fine.'

He needed Lottie to realise the severity of her disease and their professional predicament. In a rare display of vulnerability, Raymond laid bare his heartache. 'Everyone needs you, well... I need you.'

Raymond's declaration was a tender balm to Lottie's frayed emotions. As his words settled, Lottie felt her resolve begin to soften. The frustration that had clenched her heart eased, replaced by a warmth that spread through her chest. She looked at Raymond, seeing past the moments of exasperation to the man she loved dearly. His earnest eyes and the sincerity in his voice melted her defences, despite everything.

'Lottie, Raymond, ready when you are,' Higgins unwittingly interrupted.

Raymond consulted his fob-watch, where the seconds ticked away with an unfaltering cadence that mirrored the racing beat of his heart.

While Raymond stared at the steadily ticking hands of his fob-watch, the excited female cast members swarmed around Lottie, their joy genuine as they fussed over her. Their chatter about the latest wedding trends filled the air like a symphony of anticipation.

'Have you given any thought to what Doreen would have for good luck? Something old, something new, something borrowed, something blue?' asked the actress playing Ma, Doreen's mother.

Not to be outdone, Arthur Tauchert joined in the spirited banter, gently teasing Raymond, 'When are you going to make an honest woman of Lottie?'

Raymond had had enough. Frustrated by the mounting chaos and eager to regain control of the situation, Raymond cut through the din with a decisive command, yelling, 'Okay, let's get back to work.' His words brought an abrupt end to the lively commotion.

Lottie, feeling for those excited to be part of Bill and Doreen's nuptials, tentatively approached Raymond. She sensed that he was struggling. Her eyes met his, filled with understanding. She attempted to explain the situation, 'They're excited. Weddings do that to people.'

'It should be our wedding,' he stated bluntly. It pained him to see Lottie dressed in the wedding costume, looking radiant. It should be their wedding celebration.

Lottie took a deep breath as Raymond grasped her shoulders, his touch loving yet emphatic as he implored her to answer his longing and unfulfilled dreams, 'What do you want?'

Caught off guard by the directness of Raymond's question, Lottie hesitated, blinking, her thoughts scattered like leaves in the wind. 'Doreen would be like—'

Raymond shook his head. She had missed his point. 'No, what would you like?' he repeated. 'That's what we'll see on screen.'

It took Lottie a second to register what Raymond was asking her. Lottie was silent. Her gaze fixed on Raymond in a jumble of uncertainty and apprehension. She knew that to answer his question honestly would mean confronting her deepest fears and desires, which terrified and tantalised her in equal measure.

She was not sure she wanted the conversation to go to that place. Lottie chose to deflect with a light, non-committal, whispered plea, 'Don't be silly.'

'I'm serious. It guts me that I can't show my love for you. Let's treat this scene like the wedding we can't have,' he pleaded, trying his hardest to convince Lottie to see his perspective. It could be their secret. A visual aside shared only by Lottie and him. Only they would be privy to the inside scoop.

Lottie was not convinced. 'I don't know. I'm at peace with what we have. In a way, it's art imitating life.'

Not expecting that response, Raymond was confused, struggling to make sense of her words. He sensed a deeper meaning hidden beneath the surface, a truth that eluded him.

She saw that he had not followed her reference. By way of an explanation, Lottie started to outline her train of thought. '*The Woman Suffers*. The negative, destructive force of divorce results in little compassion for women left by their husbands. You left Melena and Victor to—'

'That isn't fair. I've supported them both,' challenged Raymond, quick to defend himself. His words were a reflexive response, born out of a deep-seated need to protect himself from the sting of her accusations. He knew that another confrontation could easily spiral into a bitter exchange of words and was hell-bent on avoiding such an outcome at all costs. Raymond softened, his pause a silent plea for understanding and forgiveness. 'I want to make an honest woman of you.'

The spell was broken. Lottie was not so easily swayed. The mention of marriage ignited a fire within her. And honest! Really? 'This whole notion that marriage makes a woman honest is ridiculous. Honest in whose eyes?'

Lottie spurned the need to be defined by society's narrow expectations of womanhood. She bristled at the implication that she needed a man to validate her honesty. She didn't need Raymond to marry her to make her honest. She was as honest as they came.

Oh, how her blood boiled, especially coming from the man who was supposed to love her and be her equal in their partnership. By living together as they had for years, she had learnt that they didn't need marriage to experience the deep bond that they shared. What they had transcended the confines of traditional marriage. They had built a life together based on mutual respect and understanding, and she rebuffed society's outdated norms that dictated the terms of their relationship.

Though, how would she ever convince the man who was so intent on doing the right thing by her in everyone else's eyes to see her point of view?

He was so intent on doing what he believed to be the right thing, so single-minded about fulfilling his obligations as a partner and a provider. Not wanting to hurt Raymond's feelings or start another argument, Lottie chose her next words carefully. 'Despite society frowning upon what we have, all that matters is that I'm honest in the eyes of God. I am with the man that I love, doing what I love.'

Raymond's rebuttal came swiftly. 'But—'

'No, you have to let go of what we can't be,' she asserted gently, 'and enjoy what we have right now.' Even though it pained Lottie to see his hurt and confusion, she had to stand strong in her principles to have him fully understand once and for all that they, given the current circumstances, would never be husband and wife in the acceptable way that society expected. If they were to remain partners, they must come to terms with this, for their love transcended the limitations of societal norms and expectations.

Raymond saw that she was adamant. He found solace in the simple truth of their connection, reaffirming their commitment to each other and the life they had built together. With that, he called an end to the day's filming, 'Okay, everyone, we'll pick up tomorrow for the wedding vow scene.'

Chapter 26

Early that evening, a sense of foreboding permeated the silent look exchanged between father and son as Victor let Raymond into Melena's house.

As they headed towards the living room, Raymond whispered, 'And you have no idea what your mother wants to talk about?'

Victor was full of dread, his own fears mirrored in his father's words. He did not know what had set his mother off.

'No idea. But whatever it is, she's not happy,' Victor's hushed undertone was a prelude to the storm that awaited them in the living room.

Melena waited for them in icy silence. Her presence was a study in controlled anger. Personifying the proverb, no one is angrier than a woman who has been rejected in love, her face was frozen in an expression of contempt. It sent a shiver down Raymond's spine. The men shared a look.

With a dismissive gesture, Melena said, 'That will be all, Victor.'

Victor glanced at his father, who nodded his assurance. Victor took his leave, leaving Raymond alone to face the brewing tempest. However, curiosity piqued, he hid by the door to eavesdrop on his parents' conversation.

Melena turned on Raymond and cut straight to the chase. 'I ran into the jeweller today at the bank.' Her words were laden with accusation and disappointment.

Raymond, caught off guard by her directness, tensed. This was not what he was expecting. It sent a chill down his spine.

'Imagine my surprise to hear that you're spending money you supposedly don't have for me and your son on your mistress,' Melena fired her first shot with restrained contempt.

From the hallway, Victor listened carefully.

Each syllable was uttered as a calculated strike aimed at her husband's heart. Melena relished the discomfort in Raymond's eyes as she spoke. However, watching her husband wrestle emotionally with her accusation was nothing compared to the range of emotions she had experienced that afternoon.

Raymond recognised the signs of Melena's fury simmering beneath her barely controlled surface. He needed to be careful, however, as his own anger had risen with Melena's disrespectful remark about Lottie. He couldn't let the exchange get out of hand. He tried hard to keep his composure. 'What exactly did he tell you?'

'Your face has told me everything I need to know,' Melena spat with indignant contempt.

'Trust me, you have no idea what you're talking about,' Raymond kept his words even, not wanting to fuel her anger. Regardless of the turmoil roiling within him, he swept aside the words aimed at provoking him into an emotionally driven reaction.

Melena's words were delivered with a scornful laugh. 'No, Raymond, it's you who has no idea. It's always about you. Self-absorbed and chasing your dream,' her words were a bitter reminder of the rift that had widened between them. 'It's not enough that you abandoned me and you've been an absent father to Victor, but your obsession with Lottie Lyell has gone too far this time.' She watched for Raymond's response to her aggrievement at being unfairly treated.

Melena's accusations cut Raymond deeply, reopening wounds of being accused of abandonment and absenteeism he thought had long since healed. With silent resignation, he bore his own feelings of resentment at being unfairly accused by Melena when he had tried his hardest to support her financially and be a loving father to Victor. It was a savage blow to his character as he was once again forced to come to terms with his feelings of guilt and inadequacy. Even after all his efforts to make Melena see reason, he was at a loss.

Melena pressed again. 'Why do I get *this* Raymond? Traitorous. Absent, Neglectful. Why can't I have the *romantic* Raymond? The *loving* Raymond?' Each probing question was like a one-two punch to his gut.

In the tense silence that followed, Raymond was visibly affected but didn't react to her taunt. He knew he must maintain his composure and refuse to be drawn into the emotional fray. Engaging in her verbal sparring would only escalate the conflict further.

He chose to remain silent.

She took his silence as his acceptance without protest. She softened, pleading with him, 'Come home.'

His heart ached at the sound of her tender-hearted plea for reconciliation. It is a painful reminder of the love they once shared and the distance that separated them.

When she spoke of coming home, something snapped within him. The notion of returning to a place that no longer felt like home and where deep wounds had been inflicted upon their marriage was too much. 'This isn't my home.'

Melena's softness soured, 'You've made that abundantly clear, not to mention brought deep shame.'

Raymond's patience withered. 'You could fix that,' he challenged Melena to take responsibility for her own actions and take the necessary steps to mend what had been broken. Their future hung in the balance, and he was unwilling to bear the burden of their fractured relationship alone.

'So, it's me who gives up everything, and you two get each other. Who do I have?'

Raymond could not shake the feeling of guilt that burdened his conscience, a reminder of the pain he had caused and the wounds that may never fully heal. He pleaded, 'How many times do I have to tell you—'

'What? That you regret marrying me. You don't have to. Your actions speak loud and clear.'

Another cursed jab at his character. Raymond's quiet exasperation surpassed annoyance. His honourable comportment was fast disintegrating. All his usual noble civility had slipped away, replaced by a simmering rage that threatened to consume him whole. He returned fire. 'You trapped me.'

In the deafening aftermath of Raymond's damning revelation, Melena stood before him, stunned into silence by the brutal honesty of his confession. Time seemed to stand still as the magnitude of his admission sank in.

Raymond, too, was reeling from the impact of his own words, his chest tight with regret and remorse. In the heated exchange, he lost his composure and lashed out, driven by a primal urge to defend himself against Melena's punishing and stony-hearted onslaught. Though now, faced with the fallout of his impulsive outburst, he could only watch helplessly as the damage he had wrought unfolded before him.

Melena's expression was a mask of disbelief, her eyes wide with shock and betrayal. She had never expected Raymond to be so callous, so cruel in his assessment of their marriage. His devasting revelation cut deep, slicing through the fragile threads of trust and affection that once bound them together.

Even though she knew that their marriage was beyond repair, she was still reeling from his cruel blow. His three words were like a red flag to a bull. The chasm between them was now too vast to bridge. Melena abstained from accommodating his pleas for her help any more. Her anger burns bright and ferocious, 'Trapped you? It takes two to make a baby.'

Raymond, too, was consumed by rage, his temper flaring uncontrollably without hesitation or warning. He lashed out with a ferocity born of desperation. 'I needed freedom.' His words were a weapon aimed to hurt her as deeply as she had hurt him. As the words left his lips, he regretted them. His victory was hollow.

'No, you wanted escape,' her supposition was shrill and loud, confronting the harsh reality of their shattered marriage. Her vengeful words of retaliation landed hard. Melena had struck dead centre at his gentlemanly pride. She took solace in her ability to hurt him to his core. Her look was one of total disdain for him.

Raymond's ire rose to meet hers, quickly escalating to the point where he lost control. 'And you wonder why I never loved you!' His words were a scorching indictment. Bullseye! She wanted a battle. He just won the war!

There, he'd said it. He couldn't take it back. His breath was quick and shallow. He now saw the aftermath of expressing his truth. It was an empty victory. He saw the devastation his declaration had on Melena. The pain was etched into every line of her face.

She reeled from Raymond's crushing revelation. All her defences stripped away. She was raw and exposed.

They said the truth hurts.

Hurt was too lenient for that type of impact. It was more like unremitting devastation. Close to tears and with little left in her arsenal, Melena could not help but make a declaration of her own. 'Tragically, I still love you.' Her words were a desperate plea for acknowledgment and validation. 'Where's my escape from that?' She stared at Raymond, awaiting his response. Seeing no glimmer of hope, she spitefully fired off at Raymond with the only other thing she held dear. 'We share a son. Or don't you care about him?'

Tears traced silent paths down Victor's face as he entered the room. Caught in the crossfire of their bitter exchange, he looked from his father to his mother and back again, searching for a sign that they loved him and wanted him more than just as a manipulated pawn in their game of life. He was not sure if he wanted to know.

Yet he yearned to know.

He trembled as he posed the question that deeply saddened his heart. 'Is it true?'

Raymond's own heart broke at the sight of his son's anguish. He was devastated that Victor had been drawn into his marital strife with Melena. A father and mother should not concern their children in such matters. Victor did not deserve to be ensnared in his and Melena's tangled web. He needed to convey to his son that their argument was not about him. Their issues were between husband and wife and about their marriage, not about Victor.

'About your mother, yes,' his explanation laced with sorrow.

'And me? Do you care about me?' his voice quivered with uncertainty. Desperate for reassurance, Victor studied Raymond's face for the truth.

Raymond met his son's gaze, 'Always!' he unhesitatingly declared his constant and steady devotion to his only son. 'I was changed after the war. But I never abandoned you,' he affirmed. 'I've always supported you and your mother,' Raymond was adamant. He needed Victor to understand his position and that he never abandoned his responsibilities.

Melena rolled her eyes and snorted with contempt. 'Demonstrated by taking up with your leading lady?'

It was a king hit, and Raymond had no rebuttal. Only then did he realise the true extent of the damage their conflict had wrought upon his family.

Chapter 27

That evening in the study, Lottie was surrounded by film offcuts and reels, absorbed and in full swing editing the film. Working by lamplight, she was intensely focused on her work and hunched over the desk. With painstaking care, she delicately cut the film negative by hand. She added frames of white text on black caption card and taped the two pieces of film together. The work was a delicate dance of skill and precision. It took all of Lottie's concentration as one mistaken cut could spell disaster and result in needing a reprint, which would cost time and money they didn't have.

As she worked, lost in the rhythm of her editing, E J Carroll popped his head through the doorway. He witnessed Lottie's dedication. It was inspiring to see her engrossed in the edit. Her tireless work ethic was perfectly suited to independent filmmaking. He softly tapped his knuckles on the open door to avoid scaring her.

Bathed in the warm glow of the lamplight, Lottie looked up and was pleased to see him. She lit up as Carroll entered, presenting a welcome distraction from her solitary practice. With a cordial smile, she beckoned him inside.

She stood stiffly and came around the desk to shake hands with him. Carroll was eager for an update.

'How's it coming together?' he asked, his curiosity charged with anticipation.

Lottie's response was reflective. 'It's getting there.' It was the truth. The edit assembly was taking a lot longer than she hoped, but it had improved with every tweak she had made. She was proud of the progress so far and quietly excited by how it had come together.

Carroll recognised her measured enthusiasm. 'Trust me, Lottie, re-editing the picture and rewriting the intertitles in plainer English will help. In fact, it's a must for the American audience,' his insight was infused with selfless encouragement and wisdom of experience.

There was a constant tension between her artistic convictions and the pragmatic demands of the film industry. Deep down, Lottie knew Carroll was right. Though, it didn't mean she had to like it. She trusted Carroll enough to open her heart to him about her creative frustrations. 'When will Australians realise that we have sufficient romance in this country to entertain ourselves and the world. I just feel all this takes away from the essential Australian culture... what C J Dennis envisioned with the poem.'

Carroll listened with empathy. While he sympathised with Lottie and appreciated her allegiance to C J Dennis and his original work, she must balance the artistic sentiment with commercial reality. As distributor and the person ultimately responsible for selling *The Sentimental Bloke*, Carroll tried to temporarily allay her artistic frustrations by advising, 'All in good time. We've got to think of the current audience.' He offered his perspective in a gentle yet pragmatic tone. His number one priority was to get the picture finished and delivered.

Lottie's fleeting despair was countered by her business smarts. She fully understood what *The Sentimental Bloke* meant to all involved. 'I understand it's a global market.'

Distribution was a numbers game. With a population of only five million, the Australian market was miniscule compared to the one hundred million-plus people in the United States of America. Carroll didn't need to spell out that America represented a giant opportunity for the movie and their production company, not to mention his distribution business.

They all wanted to find an Australian movie that was universal enough to transcend borders and resonate with audiences around the world. If they completed it and got it right, *The Sentimental Bloke* could achieve that very thing. At long last, they would have the distributor's holy grail.

Noting her disenchantment, Carroll reminded her, 'And let's not forget the money. We have to do right by the investors.'

It was alright to want to remain true to C J Dennis and his underlying work in the movie. However, it had been a point of contention between them. As investable producers, they needed to be vigilant in balancing out the art and business aspects to ensure the business's survival and keep the investors happy.

Their success hinged not just on the creative merits of their film but also on its ability to generate returns for those who had placed their trust—and capital—in their hands. Without their investor's approval and commitment, they wouldn't have the money to continue making movies. Securing international commercial success of *The Sentimental Bloke* could be the saviour for all of them: the investors, the distributor and the filmmakers. It could be the making of their filmmaking company, setting them up for many years to come.

The abrupt interruption of loud, urgent knocking distracted them.

Lottie stood, and her signature enthusiasm returned. 'Excuse me, E J.'

Observing Lottie's purposeful stride, Carroll was relieved to see Lottie's ever-present exuberance. In her, he saw not just a talented filmmaker but an inspirational force to be reckoned with—a woman of immense intelligence and charming wit.

If he didn't see a feisty woman standing before him, he would say she thought like a man.

Melena rapped on the front door of Lottie's Moncur Street home. Her jaw was set rigidly and she mentally prepared herself.

After a brief time, a sickly Lynda opened the door. It had been a while since she had the energy or will to greet and welcome anyone into their home.

She was surprised to see Raymond's wife standing before her. The unexpected visit sent a ripple of unease through Lynda. What on earth was Mrs Langford doing here? Her presence could only spell trouble. Curious and fiercely protective of Lottie, Lynda immediately became defensive, narrowing her eyes and stiffening her posture, ready to shield Lottie from whatever confrontation lay ahead.

Lynda's surprise was echoed in Melena's astonishment. She struggled to maintain her composure. She had mentally prepared herself to deliver her speech to Lottie. She had even rehearsed the speech countless times in her mind. Being greeted by Lottie's diseased sister was not part of the plan.

Eyes wide, Melena pulled her handkerchief over her nose and mouth without delay. She stepped back. 'I must speak with Lottie.'

Expecting this response, Lynda was neither offended nor caught off guard by Melena's behaviour. But she was protective of her sister. She knew Melena's disdain for Lottie all too well. She was both curious and wary, and sensed Melena's underlying concern. It took effort to call out to her sister, 'Lottie, Mrs Langford is here to see you.'

With a mix of amusement and sympathy, Lynda watched a graceless Melena squirm with discomfort.

From inside the house, Lottie called, 'Ask her to wait in the front room.'

'I think she'd prefer to wait outside,' Lynda replied flatly. With a curt nod, Lynda retreated inside and closed the door on Melena.

A flummoxed Melena was left standing on the porch. She looked out to the street, conscious of who might have seen this exchange.

After what seemed like an eternity, Lottie emerged from the house.

Melena wasted no time and promptly turned on Lottie. 'We made a deal.'

'Which I intend to uphold. I'm booked to go to America as soon as the filming is finished,' Lottie replied, her voice devoid of emotion. She would not be drawn into Melena's drama.

'Not soon enough,' Melena sniped back.

Intrigued by Melena's sudden appearance and cryptic words, Lottie's curiosity about the true nature of her visit rose, and she asked, 'What's this really about?'

Melena straightened before delivering what she thought would be a destructive blow to the starlet. 'I will not grant Raymond that divorce. Stop pressuring him to ask me.' She watched Lottie closely for her reaction.

Lottie experienced a surge of empathy and compassion for Melena. She could only imagine the depth of Melena's distress. While she sympathised with Melena's plight and was sorry they were caught up in the emotionally charged incident together, she did not want to be embroiled further in the complicated dispute between husband and aggrieved wife.

She had never intended for Raymond to fall in love with her, or she with him. She had tried in vain to put an end to their relationship. Working together and then living under the same roof, it was inevitable that the chemistry she shared with Raymond would prevail. But that was before. As much as she didn't want to, she could see both sides. The reason for Raymond's unhappiness in his marriage was obvious from the few encounters she'd had with Melena. At that moment, while face-to-face with Melena, she saw the anguish and hurt caused by Raymond's perceived betrayal.

Even though Lottie knew how hard Raymond had tried to make things easier for Melena, it was clear to Lottie that he would never make Melena happy, even if he'd stayed in the marriage. Their marriage was irrevocably broken.

And yet, Raymond persisted in asking Melena for a divorce, even after Lottie had called an end to their intimate relationship. Lottie saw that Melena would never grant Raymond a divorce. Lottie and Raymond's relationship was doomed from the start. Couldn't Raymond see that he was torturing both women with his repeated requests of Melena?

With her own pressing obligations, including supporting her mother and sister and all she must do before leaving for America, Lottie recognised the imperative of maintaining her distance from the toxic entanglement of Raymond and Melena's crumbling marriage. She wouldn't be drawn further into Raymond and Melena's cycle of conflict and heartache.

She calmly explained, 'I don't need to tell you that I can't make him do anything. And I certainly don't encourage him to make you feel like this by continually asking you. I can only imagine how that must make you feel.'

Melena was the woman scorned, suffering untold hurt and pain. Being rejected in love was painful enough without the added burden of societal rejection that would follow a divorce. Melena feared she would never recover from her husband being unfaithful. Full of resentment and despair, Melena took a verbal swipe at Lottie. 'You make one film about this type of thing and you're the expert. You'll never understand because you're the precious star.'

At this juncture, Charlotte stepped outside. She was gracious yet showed staunch firmness and strength of character when she said, 'I would appreciate it if you'd leave... Now.'

Melena was at first stunned and offended by Charlotte's assertiveness. She looked to the street before refocusing on the women. Melena hesitated before issuing a low warning, 'This is not over, Lottie. Mark my words, you'd better keep your side of the bargain.'

With that, Melena departed.

Equally stunned and troubled by Melena's parting threat, Lottie and Charlotte watched her leave and disappear down the street.

Charlotte was concerned. 'What deal?' she inquired as she closed the front door, retreating into the sanctuary of their home.

Safely inside their home, Lottie was visibly shaken. Her façade crumbled, and she looked exhausted from the exchange. So many emotions surged through her that she was conflicted and deeply hurt.

Charlotte was very worried about the deterioration of Lottie's health and her precarious mental state. She was dealing with the demise of her relationship with Raymond, compounded by the unrelenting assault of her tuberculosis. It was too much for even the strongest soul to bear.

Lottie collected her thoughts. She attempted to articulate the whirlpool of thoughts and emotions that swirled within her mind as much for her benefit as for Charlotte. 'She sees herself as the victim in all this. And who can blame her?' Lottie mused with sorrow and empathy. 'For years now, she's lived with the threat of becoming the woman left by her husband... and becoming a societal outcast. She is, like so many others, at her husband's mercy. I can't help her change that either.'

Charlotte looked Lottie in the eye with unswerving empathy and advised, 'You can't help everyone. The system is flawed.' It was a poignant acknowledgment of the harsh realities women faced in a world where justice and compassion were often elusive commodities.

Lottie considered her mother's sage counsel. Charlotte's wisdom was sound, but it didn't mean Lottie felt okay about any unresolved turmoil. She tried to relieve Charlotte's concern and shake off the heaviness of this last exchange with Melena with her signature optimism. 'I keep telling myself that I'm almost done. I just have to make it through the wedding ceremony and feast scenarios so we can end on a high note.'

Attuned to the complexities of her daughter's exuberant spirit, Charlotte saw through Lottie's bravado. She saw the hurt and exhaustion that lingered within Lottie's weary frame. With affectionate insistence, Charlotte gently urged her daughter, 'Go rest.'

Done with fighting for the day, Lottie conceded to her weariness. 'I will after I finish with E J. God knows what he heard.'

After Charlotte watched Lottie disappear into the study, she went to the living room to check on Lynda, who she found lying on the sofa.

Lynda was quick to express her opinion with the sharp clarity of youthful perspective. 'I can see why Raymond wants a divorce. Melena's not a nice person.'

With a mother's loving touch, Charlotte felt Lynda's fevered brow. 'Remember compassion, Lynda.' She counselled. 'You girls have been raised to accept people for who they are, without judgment. Of course, I'm your mother, so perhaps I'm biased, but no good can come of the festering hatred that woman has for Raymond and, by association, our Lottie.'

Chapter 28

The energy was high and excitable on location in the hallowed confines of the church antechamber where the actress playing Ma and two other vaudevillian actresses, embodying the spirit of joy and mirth, helped Doreen transform into the radiant bride in the wedding scenario.

Raymond and his assistant directors watched the rehearsal. Satisfied, Raymond nodded in approval before instructing, 'Everyone, take five.'

Raymond pensively approached Lottie, who was a vision as Doreen in her wedding dress. Raymond's expression softened, showing a rare vulnerability. 'I, ah, wanted to make this day special for you.'

Lottie's heart swelled with affection for the man who stood before her. His sincerity was endearing. She appreciated this side of Raymond. He could come across as gruff and business-like to others, yet there was a softer, more emotional side to the man she adored and treasured above all else. Lottie smiled.

Full of nervous tension, Raymond presented a surprised Lottie with a jewellery box. 'I wanted to give you something that only we knew the true meaning of.'

She gave Raymond a curious look before taking the jewellery box in her hands. Her eyes searched his for clues as to what was within the box. He watched her with bated breath, his heart pounding in his chest as he eagerly awaited her reaction. He didn't have to wait long.

Lottie opened the satin-lined jewellery case to find a most exquisite string of pearls. Her expressive face was overcome with emotion. She looked from the lustrous white pearls to Raymond's eyes, wide with anticipation, and back to the ivory gems. The pearls were strung together with silk thread. A perfect knot between each ivory gem protected their delicate surfaces from being damaged by rubbing together.

A symbol of prestige, Raymond felt the lure of this string of pearls would surely be a stunning inclusion for the wedding scenes being filmed. However, they were also an impassioned token of his true-hearted love for Lottie. A gift she could take pleasure from long after the filming concluded.

Lottie felt the raw emotion of Raymond's impassioned gaze. Instantly, she was swept away by the depth of the love that coursed between them. The pearls nestled within the delicate confines of the jewellery box were a sign of his affection but represented so much more. The pearls were symbolic of his devotion to her. Lottie felt a surge of gratitude within her that threatened to spill over in a cascade of tears.

'They're beautiful,' she murmured, her eyes shining as she caressed the pearls with trembling fingers. Yet in the wake of this swell of emotion, a nagging question rose at the back of her mind. 'But how did you afford these?'

Before Raymond could respond, Higgins's familiar voice broke the spell of their emotive interlude. 'Ready when you are, Raymond.'

Jolted back to the reality of their surroundings, Raymond habitually reached for his fob-watch. It was not there. He checked his wrist-watch, sending a ripple of unease between the couple.

'What have you done?' asked Lottie, apprehensive. She searched Raymond's face, eyes widening in disbelief as she waited for his explanation.

In an occurrence of uncharacteristic defencelessness, Raymond confessed his unconventional act of devotion, 'I may seem crazy, but I needed something obvious to everyone to show how much I love... For the love of my life,' he declared, his voice low and thick with emotion as he met Lottie's gaze.

Lottie's initial joy was tainted with a hue of sorrow as the realisation of Raymond's sacrifice sank in. 'You sold the gift I gave you. You loved that fob. We can't afford this,' she protested. Lottie struggled to find a logical reason for what he had done.

'It's done.' It was his solemn confirmation of the depths of his devotion. 'I've used my fob-watch as security until the picture is released.'

Lottie was lost for words. The revelation shocked her to the core. This was a monumental gesture on Raymond's part. He loved that fob-watch. She remembered gifting him that timepiece. He had been almost reduced to tears when he opened the box. His fingers had fondly caressed the engraving on the back, a personal love note from Lottie. How could he have parted with such a treasured keepsake?

Raymond studied her face, his gaze brimming with hope and uncertainty as he awaited her response. Eager for her approval, he pleaded, 'Until then, can't we share in this moment?'

The cast and crew appeared, injecting a sense of joviality with their preparations for the wedding scenario, distracting Lottie from answering. Ma and the other actresses fawned over the necklace. They helped Lottie position the string of pearls just right, lifting her veil to ensure the gems circled her neck and elegantly cascaded down over her bosom. Happy with their styling, they stepped back to admire the silk-threaded strand that perfectly completed the wedding outfit in a mesmerising display of elegance.

Even Arthur Tauchert looked impressed, offering Lottie a rare compliment. 'You look alright, girlie.'

Lottie blushed as she shook her head. Even in the face of the patronising term, she was too overcome with a rush of warmth to take Tauchert to task. She glowed in their adoration, her spirits lifted.

Tauchert's eyebrows rose as he whispered an aside to Raymond, 'Nice touch, Longford. Set you back a pretty penny, to be sure.'

Raymond ignored the veiled jibe. He knew exactly what it had cost. And Lottie was worth every pound and more. Although he was not about to disclose that to Tauchert, or anyone else. It would all be in vain if he didn't deliver the movie to the Carroll brothers soon.

Back to business, he rallied the cast and crew. 'Alright, alright... We have some wedding vows to exchange. Places!'

The cast and crew stood before the ornate church altar, rehearsing the wedding vow scenario. A soft glow of sunlight streamed through the beautiful stained-glass windows that framed the raised platform. The chancel held large bouquets of flowers on the altar table, surrounded by religious artifacts, crosses and candles. It added an ethereal quality and authenticity to the spiritual atmosphere required for the wedding day scene.

The cast were dressed in their finest clothes, as were the extras playing the couple's friends and family. The women's outfits were offset by their hats and gloves. The men, too, were all fashionably styled in their best suits, ties and hats.

Lottie, resplendent in her role as Doreen, wore the wedding dress and string of pearls from Raymond. Her joy was real. She was a vision of loveliness in her in-vogue wedding dress and shoes. Small flowerets held her simply designed chiffon veil in place at her temples. Her gorgeous bridal bouquet completed the picture of timeless elegance. Looking every part the happy bride, she appeared happy and well, genuinely enjoying the energy and excitement the other performers brought to the scene.

In addition to directing the cast for this rehearsal, Raymond stood in for Tauchert, showing the cast and crew exactly what he wanted for the scene. Tauchert stood nearby, devoting his attention to Raymond, ensuring he could re-enact every movement flawlessly. He meticulously watched Raymond go through the paces, keeping track of what the director pointed out was needed for his character.

The parson led them in reciting the vows for the scene. At the point of the exchange of rings, Lottie and Raymond were lost in the emotion of the scene. They shared a silent exchange. Each of them privately wondered if that was what taking their wedding vows would be like if it were for real. They locked eyes, conveying a depth of emotion that transcended words.

Oblivious, Tauchert said, 'Okay, I think I've got it.'

With that, the enchanting affair's spell was broken, and the rehearsal concluded.

Conscious of maintaining professionalism, Raymond and Lottie shared a subtle, coy smile. The others were none the wiser of the silent communication between the two lovers.

And just like in the finished film, upbeat music of the era played over the silent images that replicated the wedding day scene. Raymond seamlessly transitioned back into directing and continued to issue his instructions to the cast. 'Now, Ginger Mick, you help Bill add the finishing touches to his suit.'

'And Lottie, we see Doreen in her wedding dress.' Lottie appeared as a vision wearing the wedding dress and elegant string of pearls. 'Okay, places everyone,' he added, setting the stage for the pivotal exchange of wedding vows.

The cast assumed their places: the parson, Uncle Jim, Ma, Ginger Mick, Bill, flower girls, family and friends. Raymond positioned himself behind Tauchert out of the camera shot. He continued to call the shots, 'Parson, you'll say a few words. Then Bill, you're all nervous, and Ginger Mick needs to give you a quiet nudge.'

Raymond looked lovingly at Lottie as Doreen, who stood facing Bill before the parson. Lottie looked past Tauchert to return Raymond's loving gaze.

The parson, Bill and Ginger Mick all follow Raymond's directions. When it was a nervous Bill's turn to answer, Ginger Mick gave him a quiet nudge.

'Back to you, Parson, to prompt Doreen for her vows. Lottie, you have no hesitation,' Raymond directed. Parson prompted Doreen and she did as instructed, but Lottie looked directly at Raymond when she replied.

'Now for the rings. Parson, you announce them husband and wife,' instructed Raymond, his authoritative directions echoing through the parish church.

With the exchange of rings, the symbolic union of Bill and Dorren was sealed. The happy on-screen couple were now husband and wife.

'And now all their friends and family congratulate the happy couple and casually follow them out of the church.'

Higgins, entrusted with immortalising the celebratory event, captured the genuine warmth and camaraderie as the on-screen friends and family congratulated the couple and followed them out of the church.

'You getting all that, Arthur?' Raymond asked.

'Got it, Boss,' Higgins confirmed.

'And cut! Brilliant everyone. Bloody brilliant!' Raymond was overjoyed with the day's filming. His cast and crew went above and beyond, delivering exactly what he envisioned for this high point of the movie.

The mood amongst the cast and crew was celebratory. They basked in the satisfaction of a job well done, united in their shared triumph and the knowledge that they had created something truly extraordinary.

Chapter 29

The air was electric with anticipation as the cast and crew's festive mood continued in the living room location for filming the happy occasion of the wedding feast scenario.

'Cameras rolling,' Higgins said, signalling the commencement of another pivotal story beat in the film's narrative.

'Quiet on set,' Marsh's command ensured that the stage was ready.

'Action. Okay, like we rehearsed. Parson, you'll say a few words...' Raymond directed the parson who stood at the head of the dining table.

The parson stood to address the bridal party gathered around the fine dining table laden with food, the finest crockery, and the piece de resistance—a tiered wedding cake as the centrepiece. Bill and Doreen exchanged smiles, and their on-screen family and friends clapped. At the conclusion of his heartfelt speech, the parson took his seat between Doreen and Ma. A jubilant love and happiness filled the room.

The next shot set up was a purposefully emotional scene in the movie as Higgins captured Doreen's mother wiping away tears of joy with her handkerchief.

Raymond directed, 'Now you, Ginger Mick...'

On cue, Ginger Mick stood and delivered a fitting tribute to the newlyweds with a few best-man words basically saying Bill was fortunate to have found Doreen, for she was the pick! Ginger Mick's full speech would be included as white text on black caption cards.

Bill and Doreen basked in the glow of their happiness as they enjoyed their meal and wedding celebration.

With a final directive, Raymond orchestrated the closing of the scene, 'And now, Doreen and Bill, you leave with Ma.' The actress playing Ma led Lottie out of the shot.

'Now the rest of you lot continue to celebrate,' Raymond commanded.

Given the jovial mood, it did not take much encouragement for the cast to oblige. Everyone was into it, enthusiastically swept up in the jubilant mood of the ensemble. Lottie and Arthur retreated to stand behind the camera with Raymond, all smiles, revelling in the joyous atmosphere.

'And cut! Thank you everybody. That officially finishes the filming.' The triumphant Raymond beamed. He was proud to have finished, feeling positive about what they had captured. He was also relieved to finally bring a close to filming. Those last scenes were all that was needed to complete the edit so they could deliver the movie for distribution.

The cast and crew applauded each other, appreciating the bonds of camaraderie that had propelled them through the production.

Arthur was right into the festive mood, too, his infectious enthusiasm igniting the spirit of revelry, 'Time to enjoy the spread.'

With a flourish, Tauchert sat back down at the table, joining the other cast members in savouring the culinary delights laid out before them. With laughter and cheerful chatter filling the air, they partook in the communal joy of shared triumph.

E J Carroll, Dan Carroll and Sir David Gordon, figures of authority and influence, were present, too. Each was welcomed into the fold with a glass of wine, their presence adding a touch of gravitas to the proceedings.

'Attention, everyone,' Raymond called, then waited for everyone to focus on him. 'On behalf of Sir David Gordon, our financier, the Carroll Brothers, our distributors, and Lottie, I want to say thank you for your part in making *The Sentimental Bloke*. I have a very good feeling about this picture.'

The cast and crew exchanged heartfelt applause.

Lottie gracefully stepped up next to Raymond. Her appreciation resonated with warmth and gratitude as she paid tribute to the assembled cast and crew. 'Yes, we've created something very special.' Her words were steeped in appreciation for their efforts. 'So enjoy our little celebration. You all deserve it.'

As her heartfelt sentiments washed over those present, the room erupted in cheers and applause, glasses raised in reverent toasts for Lottie, Raymond, *The Sentimental Bloke* and their collective effort. There was joy and laughter all around.

Tauchert called out to Lottie, 'Come celebrate with us, Lottie.'

The jovial invitation for Lottie to join the celebration was met with a bittersweet smile.

In a subtle yet significant gesture, Tauchert had dropped *girlie*. Lottie found solace in him dropping the now-familiar epithet. It was a time of conflicting emotions for her.

'I'll bid you farewell,' she said with a touch of melancholy. 'I must rest up before heading off to America.'

Tauchert was having none of it, taking her to task with a playful interrogation. 'America. America. What's so great about America?' All eyes turned to Lottie, awaiting her response to his jovial taunt.

Feeling everyone's eyes on her, Lottie maintained her poise, offering her best reassuring smile as she replied, 'Don't worry, Arthur. I'll be back for the premiere.' Even in the spotlight of scrutiny, Lottie's manner remained composed as she deflected Tauchert's probing question.

Satisfied with her answer, everyone crowded around Lottie, offering well-wishes and farewells.

Raymond, however, was crestfallen. His heart sank like a stone in his chest. The heavy sorrow he felt at Lottie's departure bore down on him with a crushing force as Lottie hugged everyone goodbye.

Not one to miss an opportunity to share his commentary, Tauchert needled Raymond. 'You just going to let her leave like that?'

Raymond's attitude shifted from one of joy and celebration to regret and remorse because he knew he couldn't stop Lottie from leaving. Without a divorce from Melena, neither could he offer Lottie what he so wanted to give her to make her stay... with him. His inability to prevent Lottie's departure was a bitter pill to swallow.

Victor, a silent observer of the unfolding drama, watched Raymond hold Lottie's gaze for a second before she was gone.

Raymond was instantaneously lost.

Victor offered his father some counsel of rare insight and clarity for one his age. 'I understand that you don't love Mother. If you love Lottie as much as I think you do, don't let her go.'

Yet Raymond, consumed with his inner turmoil, brushed off Victor's well-intentioned counsel with a brusqueness born of regret and frustration. 'Stay out of it, son. You understand nothing. She's made her decision.'

Raymond was oblivious to the hurt and pain he had inflicted upon his son.

Victor took off.

'You're burning bridges left, right and centre today,' observed Tauchert in his usual light-hearted way. 'Come on, I hear an ale calling your name.'

In the dimly lit ambience of the pub, Raymond was drowning in a sea of remorse and regret. He sat at the bar, quite drunk and feeling sorry for himself. He recounted his own missteps and failures as he struggled to deal with the harsh reality of his current circumstances.

It was his fault that this had happened. He understood the lifetime value of investors like Sir David Gordon and Humbert Pugliese. He knew all too well the importance of maintaining the trust and support of investors, yet he allowed his own pride to cloud his judgment. If only he had heeded Lottie's warnings. Oh, why didn't he listen to her? They could have avoided the whole mess and catastrophic failure for Pugliese.

Without any other possible investors, it was paramount that Raymond delivered a hit with *The Sentimental Bloke* for Sir David Gordon and his consortium of investors. The success of *The Sentimental Bloke* was no longer just a matter of personal pride. It was a matter of survival. Without the backing of Sir David's consortium, Raymond wouldn't have a business.

No money meant no more films.

Without the financial means to produce more films, he stood to lose not only his livelihood but also any chance of winning back Lottie's affections. What a mess!

In his state of despair, Raymond found fleeting companionship in the form of Arthur Tauchert and Gilbert Emery, who attempted to cheer him up to no effect other than getting quite drunk in the process.

The once confident and driven filmmaker was now adrift in a sea of disappointment, his dreams shattered and spirit broken. 'I've messed everything up. Lottie, Victor, Pugliese... I'm washed up. Without Puglise's finance... I'm done,' laments Raymond, presenting a pitiful sight of melancholic desperation.

Arthur Tauchert's previous endeavours at levity, though valiant, had fallen flat. He changed tack and sang an Irish ditty, accompanying the tune with comical clown moves. Even though Tauchert's good-humoured antics raised smiles and laughter from other patrons, Raymond did not react. The unpleasantness of his own self-condemnation enveloped him in a suffocating shroud.

Tauchert did not give up. Undeterred by Raymond's solemn school of thought, he nudged Emery, who caught on, imparting what he felt was a glimmer of hope in the darkness that threatened to consume them all. 'Everything changes, mate. Ain't that right, Arthur?'

'Too right. Everything's changed for us.' Tauchert said with steadfast pluck.

'Look at what's happened to vaudeville,' said Emery, recognising the shifting tides of fortune that shaped their lives.

Tauchert grabbed the train of thought, reflecting on the evolution of vaudeville, a once vibrant and flourishing industry that was now fading. 'This isn't a eulogy for a time that's gone. All it does is show how impermanent theatre is, but you're capturing that with pictures. I see that now.'

Tauchert's rambling discourse unveiled a profound truth. In the ebb and flow of life, nothing remained constant. Though, in this transient world, the art of filmmaking offered a glimpse of immortality, a means of capturing the fleeting matters of life for eternity.

In a haze of alcohol and camaraderie, Tauchert's words provided a beacon of inspiration. Raymond's head swivelled back and forth as he followed his companions' spirited exchange like a spectator at a tennis match. As Tauchert and Emery returned philosophical volleys, their words struck a chord deep within Raymond's soul.

Buoyed by their newfound sense of purpose, Emery was on a roll, emboldened by the warmth of companionship and intoxicating effect of alcohol. 'Lottie and you have a vision. Pictures is art.'

Touched by Emery's poetic phrasing, Raymond nodded in silent agreement. A glimmer of hope stirred within him. Perhaps all was not lost.

Feeling his heart resonate with the truth of Emery's words, Tauchert interjected with a drunken proclamation. 'If you ask me, she needs you as much as she needs you.'

'What?' Raymond asked.

With an amiable touch of wit, Emery unravelled the mystery, offering insight into Tauchert's ramblings. 'What I think my good, intoxicated friend here is trying to say is, she needs you as much as you need her.'

Tauchert nodded, on a roll, like a terrier with a bone. 'And what about Lottie? Best thing that ever happened to you, and you let her walk away... to America of—'

That was it! Raymond couldn't take any more talk about Lottie or America. Arthur delving into the wounds of Raymond's heart unearthed deep-buried pain and regret. It stirred a tempest of emotions long held at bay.

In a moment of unchecked fury, Raymond snapped. Unable to bear another mention of Lottie or the distant promise of America, he lashed out, taking a swipe at Tauchert.

Drunk or not, Tauchert would have none of it. It didn't take much for him to get riled up, igniting a furious battle between the two men, fuelled by alcohol and unaddressed grievances. Raymond's single violent gesture of one punch gave way to another and quickly escalated into an all-out fistfight. Sensing a catastrophe with each new blow exchanged, Emery tried to break up the warring couple. But his efforts were in vain, as he was hit too, drawing him into the fray.

The publican's desperate call to end the fight punctuated the clamour to no avail. Raymond and Arthur continued to clobber each other. The melee attracted a small, enthusiastic crowd, who cheered on the three men. The publican ran to the front entrance, summoning the authorities to intervene before the events of the evening spiralled out of control.

Two police officers arrived on the scene and cautiously approached the commotion. The small crowd's cheers turned to murmurs of disappointment, their enthusiasm dampened by the abrupt end to the spectacle that had gripped the pub.

The officers moved in to restore order, breaking the fight up permanently by taking Raymond, Arthur, and Emery away.

As the dust settled, the pub fell silent once more.

The show was over.

Chapter 30

Charlotte led E J Carroll into the quiet confines of Lottie's study. Lottie's eyes lit up with a mixture of curiosity and hope. She was pleased to see him. With a gracious nod, Charlotte excused herself, leaving the two to their conversation.

Carroll was buoyant. 'I dropped by hoping to catch both of you with the good news.'

Eager to know Carroll's good news, Lottie's ears pricked and her heart quickened. She explains Raymond's absence. 'I'm not sure where Raymond is. We're meant to be editing the last scenarios.' She hoped wholeheartedly that his absence would not delay her hearing Carroll's news.

Unable to contain his excitement, Carroll settled into the seat opposite Lottie's. His excitement bubbled to the surface. Eager to share the latest update, he said, 'Well, I guess I can share it with you. We got distribution!' Thus unveiling the long-awaited and much-needed news that *The Sentimental Bloke* would have a national release.

In the wake of Carroll's revelation, Lottie was over-the-moon elated. It was an unadulterated triumph, a culmination of unceasing dedication and non-stop perseverance. 'That is wonderful, such a relief!' And she meant it.

Her heart swelled with gratitude, for without distribution, there would be no showing at picture theatres, which meant no audiences paying for tickets. No ticket sales meant no money to pay back their investors or any backend to live off for Raymond and herself.

Without distribution, their labour of love would remain confined to the film can, forever denied the opportunity to grace the silver screen and capture the hearts of audiences far and wide. This was brilliant!

Carroll, ever the ideas man, was on a roll. His manner brimmed with excitement as he outlined how they could leverage this win. 'Now I was thinking we should look at doing a Ginger Mick sequel to *The Sentimental Bloke.*' Without taking a breath, he continued his pitch, 'We can use C J Dennis's *Moods of Ginger Mick* verses for inspiration.'

Lottie laughed at Carroll's infectious enthusiasm, heartened by his endless eagerness. He was the consummate salesperson. His lively and animated excitement was wonderful to see. However, she couldn't help but offer a friendly reminder. 'Can we get this one done first?'

Carroll stopped for a moment before voicing his real intentions. 'I'm thinking ahead, that's all,' he ventured. 'It'd be great to have a reason for you to return to Australia.' Working with Lottie had been wondrous, and success seemed inevitable. Anything she touched resonated, with audiences. People couldn't get enough of her. And, based on what he had seen of *The Sentimental Bloke*, the next picture could be a license to print money. But only if Lottie returned.

'Ah. Did Raymond put you up to this?' The light and energy she felt to this point dampened. She recognised the subtle machinations at play. She would give it to Raymond. He should receive an A for effort.

Carroll's momentum faltered, and confusion washed over his face as he considered her question. But then, like a phoenix rising from the ashes, he resumed his pitch with renewed zeal. 'I haven't flagged this at all with Raymond yet, so I don't know how he feels. But I do know the picture needs you, Lottie.' His words were fuelled by an enduring belief in the transformative power of Lottie's talent.

Lottie's assessment was matter-of-fact. 'The film needs Doreen.'

Carroll earnestly pleaded with Lottie. 'You are Doreen,' he said with a sense of conviction that bordered on desperation. He had never been so sure about anything before in his life. To him, Lottie embodied the very spirit of the character. Audiences were going to go mad for Lottie's portrayal of Doreen. She brought a naturalness to her performance that everyone would relate to when they saw *The Sentimental Bloke*.

Lottie, though hesitant, acknowledged the truth in Carroll's words. Against her reservations, she nodded half-heartedly, not wanting to close the door on the opportunity. She appreciated how Carroll could make someone see the potential in themselves.

Smiling excitedly with his efforts, Carroll looked hopeful. In her performance, he saw the potential to elevate *The Sentimental Bloke* to unprecedented heights of success.

An authoritative knock at the door jolted Lottie and Carroll back to reality. 'What now?'

It was an unexpected interruption given the late hour.

After a moment, Charlotte directed two police officers into the room. The arrival of law enforcement officers brought a sense of unease over Lottie and Carroll.

The police officers delivered an embarrassed Raymond, Tauchert and Emery into the room. All three looked the worse for wear. Their dishevelled appearances were a stark contrast to the composed façades they usually presented.

Lottie was not impressed, as evidenced by the stern set of her features. Her brow furrowed in frustration at the disruption and the timing. Her patience wore thin in the face of yet another surprise turn of events.

Carroll was alarmed by the sudden intrusion and embarrassed on Raymond's behalf. While curious, he felt an urgent need to depart.

Whatever happened or was about to happen did not fall under his responsibilities as the distributor. The film was finished, Lottie said so herself.

Eager to distance himself, he politely excused himself, leaving the room with Charlotte.

It had been a long night for the warring trio, and the events of the evening had taken their toll. Arthur and Emery's expressions were apologetic. Raymond was moody and quiet. The trio projected a sense of deep regret.

The younger police officer was starstruck, and his voice quivered nervously when he spoke. 'Sorry to disturb you, Miss Lyell. I believe these three belong to you.'

She tried to contain her shock and embarrassment in front of the police officers and managed to keep her voice cool and collected. 'Before I claim them, may I ask what happened?'

The other police officer was also starstruck but seized the opportunity to explain. 'Drunk and disorderly, Miss Lyell.' Keen to impress her, he added, with a hint of pride, 'As a favour to you, we won't be charging them this time.'

Despite the officer's attempt at generosity, Lottie's disappointment was evident. The usually unflappable Lottie was less than impressed. She had so many pressing matters demanding her attention before she left, without having to deal with this lot of men behaving badly.

Drunkenness at the local pub was one thing, but drunkenness and brawling was sinking to a whole new level. What were these grown men thinking? Perhaps they weren't thinking at all. As cranky as she was about having to come to the aid of her colleagues, she couldn't simply turn her back on them in their time of need.

Tauchert and Emery stood before Lottie. They were apologetic with red-faced, sheepish looks and awkward body language. It had not been a good night, and they were keenly aware of the disappointment they had caused. They were beyond ashamed.

For Tauchert, having the girlie bail them out added salt to the wound. He couldn't look her in the eye.

Raymond, on the other hand, was down in the mouth and withdrawn. His sullenness reflected his feelings of profound shame and humiliation. This was not the way he wanted things to go with Lottie.

He couldn't believe it had come to this. He had hoped for a different outcome, a chance to prove himself to Lottie. Instead, he was mired in regret. This was not the way to win her heart and persuade her to remain in Australia.

After quickly assessing the trio, Lottie turned her attention back to the police officers, who, for the most part, were awed by her very presence.

Lottie directed her next words equally to the officers and Raymond, Tauchert and Emery. 'Thank you so much, officers, for dropping the charges. You won't see them again.' With those words, she asserted her authority and offered a final assurance that the matter had been settled.

A wave of relief flashed across the faces of Raymond, Tauchert and Emery. Their tense features softened at the prospect of escaping without formal repercussions.

It was not every day that a person of Lottie Lyell's esteemed stature featured in their night shift, and the senior officer, keen to impress the star and chastise the men, gave a bullish response. 'Let's hope not,' he asserted firmly. 'And don't let it be known that these three got off with a warning because of you. We can't have the public thinking we're soft on this type of behaviour.'

'You have my word,' Lottie assured him. 'And tickets for *The Sentimental Bloke* film premiere,' confirmed Lottie, even though that would be money they would lose off the bottom line.

Those tickets would be worth every cent, though, to keep this incident under wraps and preserve Raymond's reputation. The picture's release would also be safeguarded: they could not afford for it to be tarnished by negative publicity. Lottie had no choice but to do what she did to keep Raymond's name out of the papers and him out of court.

There was simply too much at stake for that.

At the news of tickets to the picture—the premiere, no doubt—the officer's moods became electric. It was a remarkable twist of fate, transforming what would have been a routine night into an unexpected encounter with stardom. Who would have thought that arresting three drunks would lead to meeting Lottie Lyell and receiving tickets to the premiere of *The Sentimental Bloke*? The senior police officer and his colleague were swept up in the thrill of it all and fell even more in love with Lottie.

Thanks to Lottie, the three men were free and clear of any official wrongdoing. They looked at her with respect and gratitude. Thank God she possessed a remarkable ability to navigate even the most challenging situations with grace and poise. She had effortlessly defused the tension of the scenario, earning her even more admiration from the trio.

With a perfectly executed farewell, Lottie bid adieu to the elated police officers, leaving them with a lasting impression of her kindness and star quality.

Raymond, Tauchert and Emery remained silent, their thoughts a vortex of emotions. They were keenly aware of the debt of gratitude they owed Lottie, as her intervention spared them from the consequences of their senseless actions.

Lottie's command carried the power of authority as she issued curt instructions to the trio, 'Arthur, Gilbert, go get cleaned up. Raymond, we need to talk.'

A despondent Raymond remained rooted to the spot while Tauchert and Emery made a quick exit. Raymond followed Lottie deeper into the study, where she sat and returned to work.

'I am sorry,' Raymond was full of remorse.

His apology, though sincere, was met with a stern rebuke from Lottie. She wasted no time addressing the issue head-on. She turned on him, looking him in the eye, demanding accountability for his actions. 'Good, because you getting arrested could've ruined everything. E J came by to say we got distribution.'

Lottie's words of warning barely sank in, as Raymond focussed on the news of distribution. 'Really?'

Even as she admonished him, Lottie could not help but be swayed by the flicker of excitement in Raymond's eyes at the mention of the news of distribution. Even with all that had transpired that evening, she could not deny the significance of this development. It had the potential to alter the course of their future endeavours.

'Yes, so now we have a date for the premiere,' stated Lottie.

Raymond's mind became a whirlwind of excitement and anticipation. In the wake of the distribution news, he was over the moon with enthusiasm and eagerness. There were so many things for him and Lottie to do. The picture would be successful if all went well with distribution.

Lottie would be needed at home for press duties and movie promotion to make that dream a reality.

Hope blossomed within him as he dared to entertain the notion that perhaps—just perhaps—he wouldn't lose her after all. He could be with her and care for her. His heart jumped with joy at the thought. His eagerness spilled over, and his words tumbled out in a rush of earnestness and longing. 'So, you won't need to go to America?'

'I'm still going,' she replied in an unemotional, practical manner.

Her response was a cold splash of reality for Raymond, leaving him stunned and disbelieving, his hopes dashed. 'But...'

Sensing his inner turmoil, Lottie stopped what she was doing, and fixed him with a steady gaze. 'But what?'

Raymond's hangdog expression betrayed his inner turmoil. He stood exposed before her, ashamed that she read his intentions so easily. He knew there was no hiding from her penetrating scrutiny.

In this instance of raw honesty, she revealed her motivations. She, too, laid bare the complexities of her heart.

'Going to America allows me space from you and the consumption,' revealed Lottie, exposing a lifetime's worth of struggles and aspirations.

She needed a clean break from the disease and all the drama with Raymond and Melena. She hoped that America would give her the freedom and fulfilment she so desperately desired.

Lottie needed Raymond to understand her without judgment. For Lottie, America represented more than just a physical journey—it was a chance for a rebirth, a clean break from the shadows of the past. It was an opportunity to seize control of her destiny and carve out a life on her own terms, unencumbered by the tribulations of disease and tangled web of relationships that bound her.

Beneath her vibrant exterior lay a vulnerability, a yearning for understanding and acceptance.

'When you're faced with your own mortality, it motivates you to do more... to seize every opportunity, here and now. There is still so much I want to achieve, but not like this. Having consumption doesn't mean that I should miss out. America offers me a chance at the life I want—an equal relationship, professional work, material comfort and the freedom to be whoever I want to be,' explained Lottie.

She wanted it all, and had earned the career opportunity.

Raymond pleaded with Lottie to reconsider, 'You can stay here and get that.' Raymond watched her process his words and formulate her response.

She carefully chose her words and quietly voiced her doubts so Raymond would not judge them as more female hysteria. 'I'm not convinced I can. There's little or no encouragement for my efforts. Not to mention the constraining attitude to women in this country. It's hard to believe we women have had the vote here since 1902. It seems that the only ideology is either wife or mother. I can't be either.'

Raymond countered, citing the limitations that awaited her in the United States, 'What makes you think America will be any different? Women still can't vote there.'

She knew that the struggle for equality transcended borders, and that the fight for recognition and respect was not only occurring in Australia. Lottie closed her eyes for a moment to gather her thoughts. She wanted to offer a glimpse into the depths of her being. Finally, she found an explanation that justified her feelings. 'This is bigger than you and me. I won't be ignored. I won't.'

There, she had said it. For better or worse, she had put it out there. It was her rallying cry for empowerment and agency. Raymond glimpsed the fire that burned within her, the enduring spirit that propelled her forward against all odds. And, though he did not fully grasp the magnitude of her aspirations, he could not deny the fierce bravery that defined her.

Raymond reached out a hand and grasped hers in an aching plea for connection. But Lottie withdrew. Her shying away from him was evidence of the chasm that lay between them. His heart sank at the rejection. He was gutted. He earnestly asked, 'Where does that leave you and me?'

Lottie's response was a matter of fact as it was inevitable. 'There is no possibility of us. Melena will never grant you a divorce. And we don't know how long I have.' Her truth was a dagger to Raymond's already wounded heart.

Raymond was hurting. His look was one of excruciating pain, a window to the turmoil that raged within him. Deep down, he knew that she spoke the truth, that their love was doomed to wither in the face of such insurmountable odds. And he was at a loss, because there was nothing he could do about it.

Lottie continued to lay bare her thoughts. 'It's too much. I think I need a break from you and from the struggles we've had with the picture,' she confessed wearily. 'Perhaps just acting in pictures for a while will mean less stress and be better for my health. That's why—'

'I'll come with you,' Raymond interrupted in a last-ditch effort to salvage what remained of their shattered dreams. Yes, that could work. That way they could still be together. He watched for any sign of Lottie's affirmation.

If he thought he would get the reconciliation for which his heart ached, he was sadly mistaken. Lottie was forthright in her assessment of Raymond's suggestion, 'It's like you're listening, but you're not hearing me,' her frustration was now evident. 'Perhaps me being a woman, I am illogical. No, I need some time to work out what I want. I sail tomorrow.'

With that she returned to her editing, leaving him to stand there stewing in his own dissatisfaction. Without further discussion, Lottie dismissed Raymond, 'You should get cleaned up.'

Raymond seethed, angry at her ungracious rejection of his offer. He turned and stormed from the room. The echo of the slamming door reverberated through the house.

Lottie's hands trembled as she handled the film, her nerves frayed by her spirited defence in standing up to Raymond. It was the first time she had taken that approach. It was a bold move and a huge risk. Although the sense of liberation it brought was undeniable. She had come out the other side, relieved. Or perhaps she felt more reassurance after releasing the distress of everything threatening to consume her.

A wave of exhaustion washed over her, and she coughed into her handkerchief. Short of breath, she recoiled as she caught the sight of a multitude of large bright red drops of blood. With a gasp, she collapsed.

Charlotte cautiously opened the door. 'What's going on?'

Charlotte rushed to the unconscious Lottie. Then she saw the blood. 'What has he done to you?' her accusatory inquiry was embedded with fear.

Charlotte swiftly checked that Lottie was still breathing. She held Lottie close and sobbed. With tears of future grief and a silent prayer on her lips, she desperately wished Lottie would not share the same untimely death as that of her darling husband and beloved eldest daughter.

A fiercely unrelenting Raymond strode into the jewellery store. The jeweller, recognising one of his best customers, greeted him with practised charm, 'Good day, Mr Longford. Are you here to settle the remaining balance for the pearls?'

Raymond shook his head, his response unequivocal. 'No, I'd like cash for the balance. You can keep the fob-watch.'

Taken aback by the unexpected request, the jeweller hesitated. 'Are you sure?'

'Never been more sure,' Raymond asserted. 'I have to catch a boat to America,' stated Raymond fearlessly.

Chapter 31

Raymond stepped out onto Woollahra's main street. He walked with a spring in his step and was bathed in the warmth of the sunshine. He had never felt so self-possessed. He strode down the bustling street with an air of newfound self-assurance. Elated with himself, he was propelled by a sense of purpose and rushed to complete his other tasks.

He unexpectedly encountered Lottie's family doctor. Doctor Wilson greeted him enthusiastically. 'Hello, Raymond.'

Lost in his mental checklist, a second or more passed before Raymond registered the doctor's salutation. 'Oh, hello, doc.'

Intrigued by Raymond's apparent haste, the doctor inquired, 'Why in such a hurry?'

'I'm off to America to follow Lottie,' Raymond proclaimed, his declaration fuelled by love. The doctor seemed confused. Raymond didn't care if he appeared impulsive following a woman to another country. He was in love for God's sake.

'Don't you mean the Blue Mountains?' The doctor corrected Raymond.

Now Raymond was confused.

'I thought she sailed for America?' Raymond's running mind came to a screeching halt. The doctor must have Lottie confused with another one of his patients.

'No. She collapsed and was too sick to travel,' advised Doctor Wilson. 'Charlotte took Lottie and Lynda to the sanatorium in the Blue Mountains to recover,' he continued, his tone laced with regret. 'I don't think she'll ever be well enough to travel to America.' The finality of his statement evident in his furrowed brows.

Shocked by the news and bewildered by the lack of communication, Raymond's mind raced with a constant stream of emotions and thoughts. *Lottie collapsed! What the hell happened after I left her last night? Is she alright? Why didn't anyone inform me? How could Lottie, or Charlotte for that matter, not send news about this?*

A million thoughts ran through his mind before he realised she must be okay. Then, just as quickly, relief set in that Lottie was still in Australia. Raymond got his strong feelings under control. He forced a smile and managed to compose himself, 'This is welcome news, doc!'

Though the circumstances were far from ideal, Lottie's illness meant she would remain in Australia. Raymond felt a bittersweet relief, knowing her stay granted him another chance. The weight of this latest episode with her disease pressed against his heart. He resolved to seize the opportunity to express his feelings to her, for it could be the last time he would be able to do so. An ecstatic Raymond abruptly changed course and raced off in the opposite direction, leaving the bewildered family doctor wondering what had just happened.

An exhausted and rumpled Raymond presented himself at the reception desk of the Blue Mountains Sanitorium. It was late evening, and the man behind the desk cast a bewildered glance at the dishevelled man. He was surprised that anyone would arrive with no luggage and even more surprised that Raymond was in such a haggard state.

Raymond had no time for the man's silent judgment. He was consumed by a singular purpose, and God help any person who stood in his way.

In a serendipitous twist of fate, Lottie, Charlotte and Lynda emerged from the dining room at that precise second. Eyes wide in astonishment at the unexpected sight, Lynda was first to spot

Raymond. Her immediate response was one of surprise, followed immediately by delight. However, Charlotte's initial surprise quickly gave way to a disapproving glare.

Raymond was unaffected by their reactions to his presence, for he only had eyes for Lottie. Without hesitation, he rushed to meet an exhausted-looking Lottie.

'Please, hear me out,' his immediate plea to Lottie trembled with earnest sincerity.

It was a heartfelt reunion between Lottie and Raymond. They drank each other in. Undeterred by the circumstances, they were equally relieved to see the other.

Not taking his eyes from hers, Raymond emphatically declared, 'I promise to try harder,' each syllable laden with a promise of redemption and renewal.

Lottie searched his eyes, 'Raymond—'

Raymond cut her off, his plea cutting the air with raw intensity. 'Lottie... please. I want us to spend the rest of our lives together.'

'Despite the risks?' she inquired, her voice a soft echo in the stillness.

With a feeling of gentle affection born of his love for her, Raymond took her hand and kissed it. 'For as long as we have left,' Raymond reassured her, his words a solemn vow of commitment.

Refusing to shy away from their relationship's complexities, Lottie did not hold back. She could not afford to hesitate, as she must address the elephant in the room. 'And Melena?'

'I wish I could make Melena grant a divorce. But I can't,' confessed Raymond. He knew that now. He accepted the insurmountable barriers of Melena's refusal. If that was the way it must be, then so be it. He didn't want Melena to come between him and the woman he truly loved. In a loving gesture, he took her other hand and kissed it, too.

Ever mindful of her own mortality, Lottie was loath to ignore the looming spectre of her condition. 'And my health?' she pressed, equally firm on this issue. She could no longer pretend the disease would not affect her life. It had proven to be a constant reminder that life was short. Nothing and no one should be taken for granted.

Near tears with the anguish of uncertainty surrounding Lottie's fragile life, Raymond was absolute in his reply, 'Worth every risk to my health to be with you.' His words choked with emotion as he bestowed another gentle kiss upon each of her hands.

Undeterred, Lottie ventured further, her gaze piercing with daring. 'And the patriarchy?' she challenged. She might as well shoot for the moon while she was on a roll. It was her simple plea for equality in a world fraught with inequality.

His eyebrows knit in contemplation. With a solemn nod, he acknowledged the magnitude of that task. A smile broke out, crinkling the skin around Raymond's eyes. A soft exhalation escaped his lips. 'Now that's a tough one. I can't promise that will change any time soon, but I can be a better partner to you in work and life.'

He hoped his serious manner was enough to convince Lottie that he was earnestly seeking her forgiveness.

Raymond gently cupped Lottie's face, his touch tender and lingering, as if memorising every contour of her face. His fingers traced a path from her temple to her jawline, and with that soft caress, he drew Lottie close. Their eyes locked, a silent conversation passing between them, his lips meeting hers in an expression of his adoration. 'I love you. I need you... All three of you,' he murmured. A gentle, passionate kiss followed, conveying the sincerity of his heart

Breaking the kiss, he leaned his forehead against hers, his breath warm on her skin. In each other's embrace, Lottie and Raymond found solace and strength. It was like the rest of the world didn't exist for the star-crossed lovers. Their love transcended the barriers set down by her tuberculosis, Melena, societal norms and even the patriarchy. The world faded away, leaving only enduring devotion between two souls bound by fate and love.

He reluctantly released her enough to meet her eyes with a mixture of longing and apprehension. 'Though I'm not the only one who loves Miss Lottie Lyell. We need you for the premiere.'

Lottie's expression softened, her eyes reflecting myriad emotions as she absorbed his words. In the face of the tumultuous journey they had traversed, Raymond's plea struck a chord within her, reminding her of the significance of their shared endeavour.

Chapter 32

Urgent banging on the door echoed throughout the Moncur Street residence. Charlotte hurried to open the front door. She was surprised to find Victor standing on the threshold in a frantic state. Victor entered, breathless.

'Hello, Mrs Cox. I need to speak with Lottie and Dad. It's urgent,' he blurted. He appeared beside himself with anguish, his features etched with distress.

A sense of foreboding settled over the household. Charlotte and Victor turned as the very-much-in-love Lottie and Raymond exited the study. Their expressions shifted from curiosity to alarm at Victor's agitated manner. Attracted by the commotion, Lynda rushed in from the living room, her concern mirroring that of her family. All were alarmed by Victor's panicked conduct, each bracing themselves for Victor's news.

'Mother's on the warpath!' he breathed, his speech trembling with nervous tension.

Raymond did not pick up on Victor's elevated stress and responded with a casualness that did not fit the seriousness of the situation. 'What now?'

But Victor, his anguish unrelenting, shook his head vehemently. 'We were talking about the premiere and Lottie coming back for it. Mother thought you'd gone to America, not to the Blue Mountains with Dad.'

Lottie's mind raced as she interpreted the fear in Victor's eyes and heard the urgency in the young man's words.

She recalled her conversation with Melena at the café where she pledged not to take Raymond or Victor to America with her. Technically, she hadn't broken that promise. But she also hadn't travelled overseas. How would Melena perceive her decision not to go? And how would she react to her and Raymond's upcoming promotional work for the picture? The graveness of those questions bore down on Lottie, stirring a deep sense of unease within her.

She couldn't help but be concerned.

Raymond's ire was quickly ignited, and he demanded, 'Who told her about—'

'That was me... I'm sorry,' Victor interrupted to explain, but was unable to meet his father's gaze.

Raymond caught himself. His anger instantly reduced to a simmer as he realised the unfairness of the matter, recognising the strain he and Melena's constant battling had placed on his son. He and Lottie should be able to converse and go about their business without Melena losing her mind. He moved to reassure his son, swallowing his own frustration.

'No, it's me who's sorry, son. I realise it's been unfair to put you in the middle between your mother and me.'

Victor was relieved to have his father's support, yet he was burdened by guilt. He felt responsible for the situation and acknowledged his mistake once more. 'You were right. I knew nothing and should've kept out of it.'

Raymond empathised with his son and took the blame upon himself. 'I wanted to keep all this from you,' he admitted to Victor, an acknowledgement of his own role in all the drama. Their silent exchange of understanding revealed much about their growth and demonstrated just how much their father-son relationship had strengthened.

Even with the tension, Victor's love for his father and Lottie shone through. He could see they loved each other and understood that what his parents shared was not even close to Lottie and Raymond's deep affection for each other. He wanted to fix it. He needed to warn them of his mother's rage. Intent on protecting them, he issued a solemn warning, 'Doesn't matter. She thinks I lied for both of you. I've never seen her like this. You both need to be careful.'

Victor's cautionary words sent a shiver of apprehension through them all, underscoring the danger of the occasion.

'Just what we don't need for the premiere,' lamented Lottie, her voice heavy with uneasiness.

PART 4 – CUT!

Chapter 33

In a bustling print media newsroom, Melena exuded an air of frenzy. She was a woman possessed in speech and manner.

'Have I got a story for you? Lottie Lyell is a liar, a harlot and is living in sin!' she spat with venom.

Her audience of one, the *Picture Show* magazine journalist, Mr Carhall, sat across a typical cluttered newsroom desk from Melena, listening intently. She had the journalist's attention. How could she not? Her scandalous claims were about his favourite actress of the stage and screen. He was a seasoned journalist and sensed that there was more to this woman's frantic state than met the eye.

'I know Miss Lyell, and I wouldn't describe her in that way at all. What's this really about?' His question hung in the air between them.

Wound tighter than a coiled spring, it didn't take much for Melena's emotions to burst forth unrestrained. She unleashed a torrent of accusations, sparing no discretion. 'Lottie Lyell not only has the white plague, but is also living in sin with a married man—my husband, Raymond Longford.'

Mr Carhall digested the breathtaking accusations, his expression a mask of professional composure. Sensing there was more of Melena's story to uncover, he selected his words carefully, merely acknowledging her initial disclosure. 'I see.'

Melena was not one to tolerate games of interrogation. She was quick to take him to task. 'No, I don't think you do, Mr Carhall. I will no longer be silenced. The world deserves to know the truth about Miss Lyell.'

Her impassioned plea was not lost on the veteran journalist. She was a woman obsessed with exposing what she perceived as deceit, the ultimate betrayal. And yet, he remained unmoved. He had seen it all in his time, all the worst of humankind, in his role reporting on the entertainment business.

Faithful in his principles, he vowed early on not to discredit himself with the shadowy side of celebrity. He declined to be swayed by personal vendettas or sensationalism. He greatly disliked it when people felt it was their right to extort those in the spotlight for their own vengeance.

Despite the allure of the salacious story, he valued integrity above all else. True as the love affair may be, it was not his story to write. Regardless of the allegations swirling around her, Lottie had always conducted herself with grace and professionalism. Besides, Lottie Lyell had been nothing but gracious to him and the *Picture Show* magazine.

In his characteristically direct manner, Carhall made his sentiments known. He addressed Melena head-on, unflinchingly expressing his perspective. 'Truth is we've all known about their love affair.' The journalist was forthright in his assessment, candidly acknowledging the widely whispered secret. Undeterred by the scandalous nature of the revelation, he continued with a blunt honesty, 'Consumption no, but who cares. Kinda makes their love even more real if Raymond's willing to risk his life to be with her.' He couldn't be more straightforward than that. His was a sentiment born of observation and a certain pragmatism.

Melena's fury simmered beneath the surface as she absorbed his plainly spoken words. She did not expect his forthright response and was beyond incensed. In a fit of indignation, she lashed out, 'Well, if you won't print it, I'll find another reporter who will!' Her threat buckled under the strain of her desperation.

Mr Carhall remained uncompromising in his journalistic principles, unmoved by her ultimatum. 'This magazine won't print a word of it, and I suspect no other respectable reporter will either. The story's dead, love.'

With that stark reality, the woman scorned was summarily dismissed. As the harsh reality of her experience settled in, it became clear to Melena that she would get no sympathy from this stalwart representative of the press nor, indeed, from any other quarter. In the face of such seemingly endless indifference, Melena's simmering resentment towards Lottie boiled over.

'Dear God! Another man who is in love with Lottie.'

Chapter 34

All the glamour and power were present as Sydney society's exquisitely attired movers and shakers gathered in the opulence of the Town Hall for *The Sentimental Bloke* film premiere. Packed to capacity, the ornate foyer teemed with excitement. There was an energy and excitement surrounding the city's elite—people of influence and power, resplendent in their finery—as they mingled.

Exuding an aura of confidence and poise, Lottie and Raymond cut striking figures. Lottie wore the very latest in fashion and her beautiful string of pearls, and Raymond was dressed in formal attire. They were the perfect couple for this significant occasion. If they were nervous at all, they did not show it.

Meanwhile, E J Carroll was visibly nervous as he reviewed his last-minute speech inclusions. Beside him, J D Williams valiantly attempted to distract E J Carroll from his nerves.

At the core of the gala event, Charlotte and Lynda engaged in lively conversation with Victor and the policemen who were the fortunate recipients of Lottie's generosity. They all enjoyed the festivities. Laughter and camaraderie filled the air.

Victor's joyous expression quickly faded when he spotted his mother making a beeline for Sir David Gordon. Victor swiftly cut through the crowd, unsuccessfully attempting to intercept her. His desperate bid to intervene was in vain.

On the warpath, Melena barrelled up to the financier. Emboldened by her rage, she threw her question out, not caring who heard her.

'Do you know your star has the white plague and your director is an imposter?'

In the elite company and opulent surroundings of the gala event, Sir David found himself unexpectedly thrust into the spotlight of scandal and intrigue. Bewilderment clouded his features. Caught off guard, Sir David Gordon was horrified by the spiteful accusations hurled his way.

Confusion set in as he tried to place this woman. Who was this woman, and what motivated her to tarnish the evening's grandeur with such malevolence? Her presence cast a dark shadow on the evening's celebratory proceedings.

Like many others, Lottie and Raymond's eyes were drawn to the woman screeching before Sir David. Lottie and Raymond shared a silent but urgent panicked communication when they realised Melena was causing the fracas across the room.

All eyes were on the unfolding drama. In a flash, Raymond and Lottie arrived to hear Melena spitefully attacking Sir David. Their hearts sank as Melena injected an unwelcome dose of chaos into the splendour of the evening.

'How can the mighty Sir Gordon support a man who abandoned his wife and child to live in sin with a woman with the white plague. You are unchristian!'

Melena's words hung heavy in the air, a scathing indictment of their personal lives laid bare for all to witness. The accusation reverberated through the room, shaking the foundations of their carefully constructed façade.

Victor blushed the brightest red, his face flushed with embarrassment, ashamed of his mother's unbridled fury. He struggled to reconcile the woman before him with the mother he once knew. He was torn between sympathy and revulsion, for she was reduced to a spectacle of resentment and scorn. Seeing her lose her composure in this very public display, attacking Sir David Gordon and airing the family's laundry, was more than he could handle.

He was mortified, yet also felt sorry that it had come to this for his mother. What little love and respect he had for her had been extinguished with this latest tirade. He longed to shield her from the public spectacle she had become. 'Mother, please.'

Raymond attempts to intervene. 'Melena—'

'You betrayed me, Raymond, taking up with this starlet.' Melena turned her attack on Raymond, then Lottie. 'You only got the roles because you're Raymond's lover.' Her spiteful words landed with maximum impact. Their private lives were laid bare for all to see, each accusation striking like a dagger to the heart.

In the hushed tension of the grand hall, every eye was fixated on the unfolding spectacle. Fully invested in the unfolding drama, the crowd collectively gasped, then held their breaths in suspended anticipation. The air crackled with the tension of each uttered word as if the very essence of the evening was suspended in a precarious balance.

Lottie, her graceful poise instantaneously shattered, couldn't believe what she had heard. How dare Melena cast aspersions on her life's work in such a brazen assault. Lottie would not stand for Melena's disparaging remarks. 'How dare you!'

Melena revelled in her role as the orchestrator of chaos. She enjoyed upstaging the perfect Miss Lottie Lyell. When she made her next showstopping comment, her words cut through the air like poisoned arrows, each barb aimed with lethal precision. 'You may be his muse now, but what happens when the next starlet with no morals comes on the scene?

Now it was Raymond's turn to lose his temper with Melena's loaded accusations. She couldn't just cast doubt upon Lottie's integrity in this way. 'Melena, that's enough!' His usually booming theatrical timbre was low and strained. He was undone by the venomous tirade of his estranged wife and trembled with a quiet fury.

Enjoying her powerful dominance and emboldened by the crowd's rapt attention, Melena showed no sign of relenting. Her eyes burned with a fire fuelled by vindication. In pursuit of retribution, she issued another threat, 'I will not be silenced! People need to know.'

Lottie opened her mouth to speak but stopped for several breaths. Her sustained silence, a calculated pause, was intentional. She needed to be careful, as she didn't know how Melena would respond. Though, with so many people starting to tune into the unfolding drama, Lottie needed to act quickly to end whatever Melena had planned. For every word she uttered would shape the course of events to come. She also recognised the danger of giving in to the impulse of the fracas. Caught between the urge to defend her honour and the wisdom of restraint, Lottie stood up to Melena. 'You're right, they need to know.'

Alarmed, Raymond searched Lottie's face. She didn't need to engage in Melena's underhanded public display. Melena was smug, pleased her missile made a direct hit. Raymond reassured Lottie that she needn't respond to Melena's taunts. 'Lottie, you don't have to do this,' he encouraged, offering her a lifeline of support in the face of Melena's onslaught.

Made braver by the unmissable drama she had wrought, Melena remained undeterred in her pursuit of wreaking havoc on the glamourous affair. Her smirk, a twisted echo of triumph, betrayed the satisfaction she derived from her calculated incursion on Lottie's dignity.

Guided by an inner strength, Lottie stood her ground before Melena. Refusing to be cowed by Melena's theatrics, Lottie spoke in a low, dignified timbre, 'Melena, this has nothing to do with Sir Gordon. This is about you, Raymond and me,' she stated firmly. 'You talk about morals. And yet it is you who has broken our agreement and publicly announced the status of my health. I feel it only right to set a few facts straight.' Lottie's quiet tenacity shone bright, ready to confront whatever challenges lay ahead.

Equally horrified, Raymond checked in with Lottie because he, for one, was livid with Melena for bringing their personal life into what should be a joyous event for *The Sentimental Bloke* team, family and friends. This was the last thing he expected to happen on what should have been a festive occasion.

Raymond's protective instincts flared to life as he witnessed Melena's audacious intrusion into their private affairs. He was concerned about the stress this was putting on his beloved Lottie. He was committed to shielding her from further distress because he didn't want her to suffer the level of exhaustion that had recently sent her to the sanitorium.

Seeking solace in their unspoken connection, Raymond turned to Lottie, his eyes ablaze with concern. With her unfaltering strength of character, Lottie silently nodded to him and continued, 'The white plague, as you incorrectly called consumption or tuberculosis, is not a death sentence. I'm proof of that.' Undaunted by the spotlight thrust upon her, she made a transformative decision to challenge the misconceptions that had shrouded her illness in secrecy and shame.

For an instant, the crowd was stunned into silence. They collectively gasped at the humble and heartfelt admission. A ripple of shock and disbelief swept the room as more and more attendees turned their attention to Lottie's frank disclosure, acknowledging the truth about what had previously been her very private health condition. A wave of empathy washed over the room, and Lottie's humanity emerged, transcending fame and fortune. Her resilience and candid admission forged a powerful emotive connection between the performer and the audience.

Lottie knew there was no shoving the genie back in its bottle. Without hesitation, she decided to own her situation as a beacon of resilience. She would not have another person, least of all Melena, determine her narrative. Delivered with a quiet strength, Lottie made it very clear to her growing audience, 'It's not dirty. It isn't the plague.

I contracted the disease through no fault of my own. Many of you only see the public me or the characters I play. My real life isn't that glamorous or perfect. Now you know. While I didn't ask for any of this, I thank God for every day I have left.'

The crowd, captivated by Lottie's courage and grace under fire, hung on every word of her impassioned plea for understanding and acceptance. Another collective intake of breath from the now-invested crowd seemed to suck the air out of the room. All eyes were on Melena to see how she would counter Lottie. They were not disappointed.

Melena remained unrepentant as she doubled down on her efforts to tarnish Lottie's reputation. Her vindictive self-righteousness knew no bounds. 'You thank God and call yourself religious!' spat Melena. With a sense of growing interest from the mass of people who thrust forward for a fly-on-the-wall account of the drama first-hand, she was more obsessive than ever to make sure people know the truth about their precious Lottie Lyell.

As the tension mounted to fever pitch, the air crackled with anticipation, the stage set for a showdown between two women locked in a battle for control of their own destinies. The true test of strength and toughness began with Lottie refusing to buy into the increasing tension. Lottie responded with respect and grace. She told it like it was for her without shame or fear. She admitted, 'Spiritual, yes. Not that it's any of your business. If you must know, I did question God's existence.'

Lottie's revelation struck a chord of raw emotion in the charged atmosphere, resulting in another audible gasp from the wide-eyed onlookers. For some, in laying bare the depths of her anguish, Lottie had taken the Lord's name in vain. *How could she speak sacrilegiously about God?* A hush befell the crowd as they, initially taken aback by her candid confession, were now drawn deeper into the heartrending drama.

Lottie intuitively softened, voicing her most inner thoughts that had plagued her mind since she was diagnosed, 'I obsessed over why me? I got angry. Then I grieved. Oh, boy, did I grieve. Where's the fairness?'

Her words, infused with vulnerability and pain, resonated with many who had faced their own struggles and hardships. And for that reason, they did not look away. They were hooked on the spectacle playing out before them between the two warring women.

Charlotte and Lynda, their faces damp with tears, stood as silent witnesses to Lottie's inner turmoil. Their hearts broke with the heaviness of her suffering. It pained them to hear Lottie's frank admission. They knew all too well the payment that tuberculosis had demanded of their beloved Lottie and how the disease had robbed her of her full potential. It had been a shared struggle every day for the entire family. Their grief mirrored hers.

And yet, even as Lottie confronted the harsh realities of her condition, she would not be defined by it. Lottie held Melena's gaze. 'I was reminded recently that I have a choice. I can lay down and die, or I can do something with what's left of my life.' Lottie shared a heartfelt glance with Charlotte before addressing Melena once more. 'Melena, I'm sorry if our love doesn't seem fair to you. For a long time, I felt guilty about that. I truly feel for you. But I love Raymond... and Victor.'

Melena was incensed. She bristled, deeply offended by Lottie's assertion. 'I am his mother!' The audience watched with bated breath, unsure of what would unfold next.

Lottie empathised with Melena, 'You will always be his mother.' All she pleaded for in return was compassion and understanding, 'Something I will never get to experience thanks to what I have.' Lottie remained firm. 'But like it or not, Victor is like a son to me.' In Lottie's eyes, Victor was more than just Melena's son. He was a cherished member of her own family, a beloved son in all but name.

For Victor, Lottie's words were a balm to his wounded soul, a validation of the love and acceptance he had found within their familial relationship. In a world marked by betrayal and disappointment, Lottie had been a constant source of comfort and support. A guiding light in his darkest hours.

This loving declaration was too much for Victor, who openly cried. Victor had grown up with Lottie, who had been nothing but amazing to him. She had seen him for who he was and accepted him into her family when his own was disintegrating. Even with her growing fame and the shadow of tuberculosis hanging over her, she had remained true and loyal. Over the years, she has been like a sister, a friend... and a more caring, loving mother than his own. For that, he was most grateful.

Seeing his openly sensitive, tearful response, Lottie added, 'I am exceedingly proud of Victor and very glad he is with us, unlike so many young men who never returned from war or those who returned broken men.'

Lottie's inspirational words in her heartfelt tribute to Victor had many men and women in tears. The public display that they were all so enthralled by left them feeling appreciation for the preciousness of life.

Lottie's words served as a reminder that love and acceptance could transcend even the deepest divides. Inspired by the transformative power of unconditional love, Raymond pulled Victor into his and Lottie's embrace.

'And for the record, I'm not an imposter. I'm a proud father who loves his son very much, despite the claims made here tonight,' Raymond declared, defending his family against the slings and arrows of Melena's baseless attack and unfounded accusations.

Raymond's declaration of paternal pride echoed through the hall. For him, it was not just a matter of defending his honour; it was about reaffirming the bond that united them as a family. Inspired by his courage, the crowd murmured their approval.

Not unaffected by Lottie and Raymond's loving declarations, Sir David wiped his tears before addressing Melena. 'I respectfully ask that you stand down, Mrs Longford,' his quiet authority commanded reason and compassion.

The invested crowd murmured their agreement. Melena looked about the room and realised she was outnumbered and outmanoeuvred. The once fervent energy that fuelled her attack now waned. She felt the energy overwhelmingly shift against her as the two police officers approached.

While Melena was forced to confront the reality of her choices and consequences of her actions, Sir David added his thoughts. 'Lottie is a testament that there is no shame in her experience of consumption. For me personally, there's no stigma attached to Lottie, nor should there be for anyone suffering from this dreadful disease.'

Lottie was touched by Sir David's public support of her and her disease. It was a source of immense comfort and validation, a reminder that she was not alone in her struggle with consumption.

Standing together, the cast and crew rallied around Lottie and Raymond.

Arthur Tauchert piped up with a light-hearted quip, 'At this rate, with more drama happening off-screen, we won't get to see the picture.' His words injected a sense of levity that lightened the mood.

Sir David took his cue from Tauchert's reminder that they had indeed gathered to see *The Sentimental Bloke*. 'I couldn't agree more. As financier for this picture, I have seen nothing but great professional effort from its writer, producer, editor, designer and not least, star, Miss Lottie Lyell. After tonight's premiere, I have no doubt that everyone will respect Lottie as much as I do.'

Lottie was touched by Sir David's appreciation for her efforts in the many roles she played and his public acknowledgment of his respect for her professionally. That meant a great deal to her, more than anyone would truly understand.

Encouraged by Sir David's words, Raymond stepped up, declaring, 'This here is the woman I love more than life itself.' He meant every word. He had much to be thankful for, and it all had to do with Lottie and their enduring love.

The crowd was enraptured by Raymond's impassioned declaration. Caught up in the emotion of it all, many realised they were involuntarily smiling with pleased, kind or amused expressions. The collective human experience was laid bare, uniting everyone in the universal longing for connection and understanding.

Declarations of love tended to do that.

For Lottie, Raymond's words were a balm to her soul, a reassurance that their love transcended all the trials they faced. Tears of gratitude welled in her eyes as she was overcome with joy. She felt the collective love in the room for her. She was buoyed by the love and support of those around her. Lottie acknowledged the depth of their bond. 'Darling Raymond, you've shown me that life is precious. You love me for who I am in spite of what I have. That's a tremendous sacrifice, making what we share even more special. I don't care who knows that I have consumption or who knows about us.'

As Lottie and Raymond embraced, not caring who saw them, their love radiated outward. This embrace, simple yet profound, became the nucleus of a wave of happiness that descended upon all present. A feeling of hope blossomed, spreading like wildfire through the crowd. Friends and strangers alike felt the surge of newfound optimism. The grand hall was transformed into a sanctuary of collective happiness and hope. Every laugh, every tear of joy, every whispered word of affection contributed to this unforgettable, transcendent experience.

'I don't care who knows about our love affair either,' declared Raymond, daring anyone to challenge the legitimacy of their love. 'We fell in love. That doesn't make us bad people,' he uttered with a mixture of defiance and vulnerability. 'I don't know what else I can do to make you see that, Melena.'

Once again, Raymond pulled Victor into his and Lottie's embrace. It was clear the bond that this trio shared was intense.

Disinclined to yield, Melena would not surrender. She challenged Raymond's assessment. 'Again, you talk of this great love, but all you've inflicted upon me is pain.' In her eyes, Raymond and Lottie's love was a betrayal, a wound that festered, refusing to heal.

Raymond recognised that Melena was hurting. He acknowledged her suffering and apologised. 'That was never my intention. I returned from the war changed, such a waste of life. When I met Lottie, something was awakened within me.' As Raymond spoke, a sense of understanding washed over the room, bridging the divide between past hurts and present forgiveness. In his words, there was redemption, a path forward towards healing the wounds of the past and embracing the love that bound them together.

Lottie was mindful of Melena's feelings. She understood the delicate balance between honesty and discretion. Perhaps this was too much to share publicly. She interjected to caution him, 'Raymond...'

Driven by an inner compulsion to lay bare his soul, he pressed on, undeterred. He was adamant, his words suffused with an urgent raw honesty, 'I need to say this. I resisted those feelings for as long as I could. Believe me, I had no intention of being *that* man.'

'But you did it anyway,' Melena was unremitting. To her, his words were a bitter pill to swallow, evidence of the betrayal she felt in the depths of her being.

Raymond's response was candid, accepting responsibility for his part. 'I'll cop that.' In this experience of vulnerability, it was not about absolution or redemption. He spoke from his heart. 'You have to understand that what I have with Lottie made me realise what I didn't have with you, Melena... What I will never have with you.' He offered Melena a glimpse into the depths of his soul, laying bare the truth of his heart for all to see.

Melena, incredulous, was not so forgiving, 'She was a child.' Her disbelief reverberated like a thunderclap.

Raymond went on the defensive and was quick with his retort. 'She was not a child. There's barely twelve years between us.' He softened, 'But I was her guardian. People trusted me. She trusted me.' His voice was strained, weighed down by the weariness of his past, acknowledging the heavy responsibility of his role in the lives of those who once trusted him.

Charlotte, who had remained quiet through the entire exchange, now spoke, 'We all did... still do, despite everything—'

Inspired by her mother's support of Raymond, Lynda, in a show of enduring faith, quickly added, 'We trust you because of everything.'

Raymond was buoyed by Charlotte and Lynda's public endorsement. He attempted to regain his footing in the face of Melena's contempt, 'Trust me when I—'

'Trust you?' Melena scoffed at Raymond. Her scorn and scepticism were a bitter reminder of the rift that had torn their lives apart.

Refusing to be cowed by her disdain, Raymond responded to her insensitive rebuttal, 'Yes. Trust me when I say that I didn't plan any for any of this. The more I resisted, the more deeply I fell in love.' He gave a frank admission of his struggle between duty and desire.

Raymond looked longingly at Lottie before continuing his public confession. 'I knew I had a wife and a son. But what I felt for Lottie, what I experienced with the *private* Lottie, far outweighed the consequences.' Raymond seemed lost in his thoughts. Then he found the words. 'You could say that either way, I was doomed. Love won out in the end. Even though I've paid for it dearly ever since, I wouldn't trade it.' Raymond enfolded Lottie in his embrace.

Melena was sickened by the further public display of their affection. Her disdain for Raymond and Lottie reached new heights. Her words brought their reality into sharp focus. 'And yet here we are.'

Sensing no truce in this battle of wills, Sir David emerged as a beacon of authority. He summoned the police officers. 'Constables, please escort Mrs Longford from the building.'

The police officers stepped up on either side of Melena, signalling the end of her disruptive behaviour. She was outraged, her expression a combination of fury and deep embarrassment at being manhandled.

Discontent at how Melena was being dismissed and how the drama had not been truly reconciled, Lottie called, 'Wait.' She pleaded for reconciliation, 'This can end here, Melena. Stay and celebrate with us. See what your son has had a hand in creating.'

Melena glared at Lottie. 'I will never forgive either of you.' Stone-faced, Melena strode away, flanked by the police officers.

Not one to miss an opportunity to ham it up, Tauchert played up to the crowd. 'Now, can we please go see the picture?'

This elicited a collective cheer from the crowd, a chorus of relief, a signal that the time for celebration had finally arrived. Tauchert patted Raymond on the back as the rest of the cast and crew closed in around Lottie, Raymond and Victor, demonstrating their tight bond, love and respect for Lottie and Raymond.

Chapter 35

Inside the Town Hall theatre, the dimmed lights and heavy drapes that framed the stage added to the cinematic ambiance. The ensemble musicians were in place, prepared to deliver the Jewel song, with Miss Doris Struble on piano, Miss Hilda Sutton on violin, Miss Nellie Simpson playing cello and flute, and the talented Miss Carrie Lanceley. The performance was a tantalising artistic prelude to the moving picture about to premiere.

As the final notes of the song faded, the crowd's applause and excitement built. They were eagerly anticipating the cinematic spectacle. Their excitement calmed as the lights went down. With a ceremonial flourish, the red velvet curtain parted to reveal the cinema screen in all its grandeur. A collective intake of breath swept through the theatre, and a hushed spell befell the audience.

Excited and perhaps a little nervous, Lottie and Raymond sat with Sir David and *The Songs of the Sentimental Bloke* author, C J Dennis. They would soon experience the response to the culmination of their labour and love.

With heart pounding and breath held in anticipation, E J Carroll, standing at the back of the theatre, succumbed to his rollercoaster of emotions. It was too much; his nerves got the better of him. As the screen flickered to life, he slipped away into the shadows and exited the theatre.

Lottie and Raymond's nerves gave way to exhilaration, from uncertainty to possibility. The stage was set, the players assembled and the journey was about to begin.

As the first flickers of light danced across the screen, the audience was drawn into the captivating world of *The Sentimental Bloke*. The film screen lit up in black and white, and the first intertitle card announced:

THE SOUTHERN CROSS

FEATURE FILM C<u>O</u> L<u>TD</u>

Presents

"THE SENTIMENTAL BLOKE."

C. J. DENNIS.

PICTURISED AND DIRECTED

By

RAYMOND LONGFORD.

Lottie and Raymond shared a look of total devotion. They took each other's hand, gently squeezing so the other felt their excitement. Seeing all their hard work come to fruition was a proud moment. To get to this point was a huge accomplishment.

With each passing scene, the characters of Bill and Doreen came to life on the silver screen. Their trials and triumphs resonated deeply with the mesmerised audience. When they reached the two-up scene, the returned servicemen in the audience cheered their appreciation for the movie's nod to all servicemen.

During the wedding scene, Lottie squeezed Raymond's hand, sharing a heartfelt moment of quiet intimacy. In a bold display of affection, he leaned in to kiss Lottie, not caring who saw. It was a truth that spoke to the essence of their love and their longing.

As the final frames of the sunset scene with Doreen, Bill and the baby faded to black, the theatre erupted into thunderous applause and cheers, a symphony of appreciation for the artistry and emotion. The heartfelt tribute built until the entire audience rose to their feet in a spontaneous standing ovation.

The response from the audience was overwhelming.

Surrounded by the outpouring of admiration, Lottie and Raymond remained seated, their hearts full and their spirits soaring, knowing they were about to share something truly special with the world.

E J Carroll re-entered the theatre wearing a huge smile of sheer delight. His heart overflowed with gratitude and joy. It was clear that *The Sentimental Bloke* had struck a chord with the audience.

They had a hit on their hands!

The crowd mingled in the Town Hall foyer to celebrate the film's success. There was a tangible buzz about the film, and a throng of admirers surrounded the stars of the picture, Lottie Lyell and Arthur Tauchert.

Tauchert, buoyed by the enthusiastic response to the picture, was on a natural high, grinning from ear to ear. Beaming with pride, he revelled in the attention. 'We did alright, gir—' Arthur caught himself mid-sentence and corrected himself. 'We did good, Lottie.'

Lottie met Tauchert's gaze with a warm smile, acknowledging the significance of his self-correction, making right what was wrong. She knew this was a big step for Tauchert and a milestone for their working relationship. 'That we did, Arthur,' she replied, her joyous expression infused with genuine pride and gratitude for their collective achievement.

Equally excited, J D Williams leaned in close to Lottie and spoke in a hushed whisper flavoured with excitement, 'Great performance, Lottie. You'll be a star in America in no time.'

He could not wait to introduce Lottie to his network in America. In his mind, *The Sentimental Bloke* was poised to make her a star, a force to be reckoned with, putting her on par with the international luminaries of stage and screen. He was genuinely excited to be part of the next chapter of her successful career.

'Thank you for your support, J D,' Lottie returned J D's encouragement with gratitude. 'However, I understand now that going to America was more about my obligation to my family. I can make a bigger contribution by making important stories here.'

J D Williams barely had time to adjust to Lottie's news before the journalist Mr Carhall inserted himself into the circle to ask, 'And Mr Dennis, as writer of *The Songs of the Sentimental Bloke* poems, what's your opinion of the picture?'

C J Dennis, the esteemed writer of *The Songs of the Sentimental Bloke,* responded the only way he knew how—with a candid assessment. 'I had solid doubts. I was expecting, at best, a burlesque and at worst, a fiasco. I came away almost believing in miracles. I cannot say how pleased I am at the faithful reproduction of the characters.'

Lottie and Raymond shone in the glory of C J Dennis's commendation. They had the utmost respect for the veteran poet, and receiving this level of praise from him meant a tremendous amount to them. Humbled by the praise, and the validation of their artistic endeavours, their spirits soared to new heights.

The journalist turned to Raymond, and asked, 'So, Raymond, what's next?' Pencil poised, he listened eagerly for Raymond reply, hoping to get the scoop.

Raymond looked to Lottie for reassurance. He found her nodding in encouragement to answer the journalist's inquiry. 'Lottie's film,' he began. 'She's the writer, co-director, editor and producer. It's called *The Blue Mountains Mystery.*'

Lottie's smile was radiant, her heart swelling with gratitude as Raymond publicly paid respect to her multiple roles for their next picture. She was not expecting him to acknowledge her in that way. She was struck by Raymond's growth, and how far he had come in terms of taking on board her feelings and his willingness to openly recognise her contribution, especially to the press.

She was elated with everything and eager for Mr Carhall to record this truth. 'I couldn't do it without our incredible team, my patient and wise mother, and my beautiful soul of a sister,' she proclaimed, her words echoing with sincerity as she looked fondly from happy face to happy face.

The small ensemble of cast and crew were all smiles. They truly loved Lottie, not only as the star but as a remarkable person who operated with dedication, respect and grace.

Charlotte and Lynda looked at Lottie with genuine affection and appreciation.

Lottie directed her attention to Raymond and held his gaze. 'And Raymond, thank you, my love,' she began, expressing her profound gratitude for the pivotal role he had played in her personal and professional life. 'All those years ago, you saw in me something that I didn't fully see in myself. You helped me develop that essence with the roles I played, you helped me curate the *public* me in interviews, and you encouraged me to do what I love. And now, you're so much more than my manager. I couldn't have done any of this without you.'

'And I can't imagine my life without all three of you in it,' attested Raymond. Leaving no room for a skerrick of doubt, Raymond sealed the depth of his feelings with a passionate kiss.

Full of emotion, Tauchert added his unexpected commentary. 'Ain't love grand!'

Caught off guard, everyone looked at Tauchert, not sure whether he was joking or being serious. This prompted uncertain glances from the group.

Sensing the need to clarify, Tauchert insisted, 'I'm being serious! Like Doreen and Bill, you two are destined for each other... for as long as that may be.'

Touched by Tauchert's warm-heartedness, Lottie took a beat to reflect on her tentative life path. 'I'm not sure about destiny,' she mused, 'But every day I'm reminded that life is short. My promise to myself...

to you all, is that I will follow my heart, do what I love, and live today like it's my last.'

Raymond enveloped Lottie in a joyous gesture of profound love and unity. Sensing the significance of shared gratitude, Victor, Charlotte, Lynda, and the cast and crew all gathered around, drawn by the magnetic pull of affection.

Even Sir David Gordon and the Carroll Brothers, usually reserved in their behaviour, were swept up in the tide of pure emotion, joining in the collective embrace with genuine warmth and sincerity.

The bonds of friendship and artistry united them all.

ELLE CROXFORD

FADE TO BLACK

Epilogue

New York, 1973

B ack in the George Eastman Museum archive vault room, there was silence, except for the noise of the loose end of film flapping against the projector. Peggy and Ray were smiling for different reasons.

Ray Edmondson couldn't contain his excitement any longer. 'Do you realise what this is?'

Rising from her seat to switch on the main lights, Peggy responded with a playful jest, 'Clearly not *The Sentimental Blonde*.' Her chuckle danced through the air.

Ray was swept away by a tide of euphoric excitement. He was bursting with enthusiasm about what they had uncovered. 'You have no idea what we've uncovered here?' he asked, his voice filled with joy and sheer astonishment. 'The original negative of *The Sentimental Bloke* has been lost for fifty years. And we've found all eight 35-millimetre reels.'

Caught up in his infectious enthusiasm, the archivist offered her own observation, 'What a difference a word can make.'

His spirit buoyed by the magnitude of their discovery, Ray nodded fervently in agreement. 'Mislabelling or lost in translation. Either way, what a find!'

'Agreed,' Peggy concurred, in awe and admiration of their newfound treasure. 'It made me laugh. It made me cry. It's timeless,' the archivist shared her personal review of the masterpiece for the ages.

'Even after all this time, it still works,' Ray was incredulous at how well the narrative and characters had stood the test of time. It was remarkable how the essence of Bill and Doreen was still captivating after the passage of countless years.

'It must be one of the first feature-length boy-meets-girl romance dramas ever captured on film,' replied Peggy, her joyous energy visible.

To bear witness to this piece of long-lost film history was exhilarating for Ray. 'Maybe. It certainly was Australia's first blockbuster movie. It was huge in its day.'

Her interest was piqued. 'How huge are we talking?'

Her curiosity ignited a spark within Ray, prompting him to expound upon the magnitude of the film's success. 'I mean, *The Sentimental Bloke* was released in 1919 to solid critical and commercial acclaim, playing to Australian audiences in humble suburban picture palaces to grand city theatres,' his heart brimmed with admiration for its enduring legacy.

The archivist shared his delight, echoing his sentiment, 'I can see why.' The joy and brilliance of what they had just seen was contagious. There was a shared buzz related to their recent discovery.

Ray continued highlighting the expansive success of *The Sentimental Bloke*. 'And not only in Australia. That success was repeated a year later in Britain. And again, when it was released in America.' He was talking a mile a minute, animated in his gestures and movement.

Captivated by Ray's sense of wonder and excitement, Peggy was eager to learn more. 'Did the filmmakers go on to make any more films?'

Happy to oblige her interest in the behind-the-scenes tale, Ray replied, drawing from his arsenal of facts about the power couple. 'Raymond and Lottie were a dynamo team. They continued to do what they loved and made eight more films together.'

The archivist's brow furrowed in contemplation. Puzzled, she leaned in, eager to know more. 'But why only eight? Did they separate?'

Ray's feelings of intense exhilaration were dialled back a notch. His solemn response reflected the heaviness of what he was about to unveil. He knew it would not be news she wanted to hear. 'In a way. Not by choice.'

A sense of caution overcame Peggy. She wanted to know more but instinctively braced herself. 'Why do I feel you're going to tell me it wasn't a fairytale ending?'

'It's more of a tragic ending.' His words echoed with sorrow and regret as he prepared to divulge the bittersweet truth.

'I asked you not to tell me that,' she was conflicted. Her emotions oscillated between curiosity and apprehension. She wanted to know what had happened but desperately longed for it to be a story with a joyful outcome. Yet, she got the distinct sense that Lottie and Raymond's love story didn't have the classic Hollywood fairytale ending.

'I can't tell Lottie and Raymond's story without sharing how it ended,' Ray advised, setting the scene for the narrative's trajectory. 'You see, tuberculosis was a leading cause of death in Australia at the time. Lynda Cox, Lottie's younger sister, died from tuberculosis in September 1925.'

A wave of sorrow washed over the archivist's features as she absorbed this latest revelation. 'That's so sad,' she murmured, empathising with the senseless losses endured.

'That's not the worst of it. Lottie died from tuberculosis three months later in December,' recalled Ray, the unwilling bearer of bad news.

Peggy was emotionally challenged by the news. Watching the movie that captured such vibrant talent on screen and then finding out it was underpinned by so much tragedy off-screen was sobering.

'Oh, what a terrible waste.' Her grief was sincere as she contemplated the untimely demise of an extraordinary talent.

Ray was disheartened to share another layer of sorrow. 'The saddest part is that Lottie and Raymond could never be married as Raymond's first wife, Melena, refused to grant him a divorce. She finally did three months after Lottie died.'

Raymond could not fathom the bitterness that must have been felt at the hand of Melena's action. He felt great empathy for Raymond and Lottie who were denied the chance to have marital happiness. Part of him was incensed at Melena's nerve to withhold what Raymond wanted most, a divorce and freedom to make an honest woman of Lottie. Yet, he also understood that Raymond made his choice, which was Lottie, regardless of the obstacles they faced.

'Oh, no!' Peggy composed herself, pressing on with her inquiries as her insatiable thirst for answers longed to be quenched. 'What about Raymond?'

Ray delved deeper into the aftermath of Lottie's untimely death and its impact on Raymond. 'After her passing, Raymond was unable to duplicate what he achieved with Lottie.' Ray cast his mind back to his previous research. 'Years later, he did acknowledge Lottie as his equal as writer, producer, editor and actress. For him, though, it was never the same.' There was something melancholic about the unhappy turn of events where, although Raymond eventually recognised Lottie as his creative equal, the void left by her absence was never filled.

'That's so sad,' the despondent Peggy said as she came to terms with the untimely end of a remarkable partnership.

'Don't be sad,' he urged.

She was taken aback, 'How can you not feel sad about this? Surely you can't ignore the tragedy that befell Lottie and Raymond?'

He was quick to reply. 'I wouldn't be human if I didn't feel sad about what happened personally to Lottie and Raymond.' While his compassion for Lottie and Raymond's tragic fate was deep, he did not want the sadness of Lottie and Raymond's love affair to overshadow what they had uncovered in *The Sentimental Bloke* film cans. Ray reframed the perspective of the conversation to help her understand just how important it was to unearth what was previously thought to be lost forever. 'Rather, think about it this way, what we've rediscovered today is amazing. *The Sentimental Bloke* in its entirety!'

'Always a silver lining,' she replied, in quiet understanding.

'Out of something bad, always comes something good,' he agreed, his optimism evident.

She liked his Aussie positivity. 'That's a good way to think about it.'

'How could anyone not see the positives after watching *The Sentimental Bloke?*' he enthused. For him, it was impossible not to feel uplifted. 'This film represents the greatest romance on and off the screen of Australia's silent era.'

'Lottie and Raymond's love story and film pioneering legacy are truly remarkable,' Peggy got in on the act, sharing her enthusiasm.

'Absolutely!' Ray wholeheartedly agreed. 'Their enduring love and groundbreaking work deserve to be celebrated and remembered for generations to come.'

Author's Note

In 2019, theatres across Australia and film festivals worldwide celebrated the 100-year anniversary of *The Sentimental Bloke*'s public premiere.

It marked a significant milestone in cinematic history by honouring the enduring impact of this timeless masterpiece.

Now that you have delved into the pages of this book, I encourage you to experience the magic of the original film for yourself.

Allow yourself to be transported to a bygone era, where the poetry of C J Dennis and the artistry of Lottie Lyell and Raymond Longford captivated audiences far and wide. Marvel at the brilliance of their pioneering contributions to Australian cinema.

I trust that watching the original movie will enrich your understanding of the characters, their motivations, and the themes explored in this book. And, hopefully, by seeking out this cinematic gem, you will experience a deeper appreciation for the cultural significance of *The Sentimental Bloke* and its enduring legacy.

Let it enchant you, inspire you and remind you of the power of feel-good entertainment that touches the soul and transcends the boundaries of time and place.

You can watch it for free here:

https://www.youtube.com/watch?v=9T8eH3aau4I

THE SENTIMENTAL BLONDE

With Gratitude

They say it takes a village to raise a child. In the case of *The Sentimental Blonde*, the saying is also true. This creative endeavour has been enriched by collaborative efforts in multiple forms. Inspired by Ann Megalla, who brought me to the idea for Lottie and Raymond's story, this book started out as a movie screenplay, which I wrote and then adapted into a theatre playscript (thanks to Brisbane City Council's Lord Mayor's Creative Fellowship).

Not realising that plays can take just as long as movies to get produced, I decided to further adapt the story into novel form, supported by the Queensland Writers Centre's Fishbowl Residency.

Adapting the movie script to a theatre playscript with Queensland Theatre was a wonderful experience. I have Lee Lewis (former Artistic Director) to thank for championing Lottie's story internally there and then coming on board as my creative fellowship mentor. Working with Lee and dramaturg, Steve Pirie, helped deepen my character development and reworked movie scenes for theatre. The Queensland Theatre team were supportive and my sincere thanks go to Peter Sutherland, Pip Boyce, Samantha French, Helen Hillman and Kate Holloway.

Completing the public table read as part of the Creative Fellowship with some of Brisbane's most talented actors in front of a full theatre of people was both nerve-wracking and brilliant. I thank all those who attended and contributed to the Q&A that followed.

The feedback from that evening, rehearsals with the actors and responses from early beta readers (of all the story forms) helped shape the narrative. Heartfelt thanks to my amazing supportive friends (in and out of Elle's Group chat) your love, encouragement, and support means the world to me. Special appreciation to Libby, Alexandra, Lilian and Miranda—thank you for being brave and playing multiple characters at the initial table read over homemade lasagne. That was the first time I had the opportunity to hear my characters come to life.

ELLE CROXFORD

To the team at Queensland Writers Centre lead by CEO, Lori-Jay Ellis, thank you for giving me the opportunity to work there with a dedicated space at the QWC and for my fabulous mentor, Kylie Chan. Many thanks to the QWC team, Anne, Charlie and Cody, for making me feel welcome.

Kylie, your guidance and advice has been amazing. I thank you wholeheartedly for helping me navigate the world of digital publishing.

And thanks also to Katie Lowe for her attention to detail in the editing of this manuscript. I promise to write the next book in past tense from the outset!

What you have now read is the culmination of all that input and feedback for which I am grateful beyond words. I trust you enjoy *The Sentimental Blonde* as much as I have enjoyed writing (and adapting) it in all its forms.

And lastly, a special shout out to my sons, Isaac and Elijah, such gorgeous young men. I am immensely proud to be your mum. You keep me accountable as I strive to make you proud of me. Remember, in a world where you can be anything, be extraordinary.

252

www.ingramcontent.com/pod-product-compliance
Lightning Source LLC
Chambersburg PA
CBHW020358030726
47496CB00007B/2195